VINTAGE MURDER MYSTERIES

With the sign of a human skull upon its
back and a melancholy shriek emitted when
disturbed, the Death's Head Hawkmoth has
for centuries been a bringer of doom and an
omen of death - which is why we chose it as
the emblem for our Vintage Murder Mysteries.

Some say that its appearance in King George III's
bedchamber pushed him into madness.
Others believe that should its wings extinguish
a candle by night, those nearby will be cursed
with blindness. Indeed its very name, *Acherontia
atropos*, delves into the most sinister realms of
Greek mythology: Acheron, the River of Pain in
the underworld, and Atropos, the Fate charged
with severing the thread of life.

The perfect companion, then, for our Vintage
Murder Mysteries sleuths, for whom sinister
occurrences are never far away and murder
is always just around the corner …

GLADYS MITCHELL

Speedy Death

VINTAGE BOOKS
London

Published by Vintage 2014

2 4 6 8 10 9 7 5 3 1

First published in Great Britain by Victor Gollancz in 1929

Vintage

Random House, 20 Vauxhall Bridge Road,
London SW1V 2SA

www.vintage-books.co.uk

Addresses for companies within The Random House Group Limited can
be found at: www.randomhouse.co.uk/offices.htm

The Random House Group Limited Reg. No. 954009

A CIP catalogue record for this book is available from the British Library

ISBN 9780099582267

The Random House Group Limited supports the Forest Stewardship
Council® (FSC®), the leading international forest-certification organisation.
Our books carrying the FSC label are printed on FSC®-certified paper.
FSC is the only forest-certification scheme supported by the leading
environmental organisations, including Greenpeace. Our
paper procurement policy can be found at
www.randomhouse.co.uk/environment

Typeset in Meridien by Replika Press Pvt Ltd, India

Printed and bound in Great Britain by Clays Ltd, St Ives plc

Contents

Chapter One

The Guest Who Had No Dinner

THE two young men had been waiting exactly two hours and three minutes.

'If she isn't on the six-fifteen,' remarked the younger, larger, more utterly-bored-annoyed-and-anxious young man, 'I am damned well going back without her. That's the worst of girls, especially when you're going to marry them! Always think they can turn up late. There's going to be a row over this!'

'Be of good cheer, comrade,' said the other, 'for, behold, the six-fifteen approaches, and she is bound to be on it.'

She was on it.

'And I'm last, I suppose!' she cried, radiant with blushes and laughter, and beautiful beyond all telling (particularly in the eyes of the two young men, who were both in love with her) from the top of her chic new hat to the buckles of her twinkling shoes.

There was more artless satisfaction than resignation, apology, or fearfulness in her voice, but the two young men had been waiting exactly two hours and four minutes, and they hurried her along to the waiting car.

'Get in, Dorothy, for goodness' sake!' urged the big young man aggressively. 'Here, porter! In here! Buck up, man! Here you are!'

Having tipped and dismissed the baggage-bearer, he turned again to the girl.

'Couldn't finish our round in time to meet the four-thirty! And here it is, nearly half-past six! Dinner at seven-thirty, of all ungodly hours! House full of idiotic people, and the old man in a devil of a temper if he's kept waiting for his beastly food, and the road covered with loose flints, so I expect we're bound to pick up a puncture because, like a fool, I've forgotten the spare wheel, and you're a little devil to keep us waiting like this, and the animals went in two by two, and here endeth the first lesson.'

Dorothy laughed as she entered the car, and the speaker, with a vicious scowl, took his seat at the wheel, while the other young man, slight, short, and with black hair and very red cheeks, squeezed in beside her and slammed the door.

'Right away, Captain,' he remarked cheerfully.

'It's very nice to see you again, Bertie,' observed Dorothy, as the car took the road. 'What have you been doing with yourself since I saw you last?'

'Oh, I don't know.' Bertie Philipson knitted his brows. 'I've been out and about, you know.'

She surveyed him quizzically.

'Still the little lounge lizard? Why don't you get something to do?'

'Oh, I don't know. I mean, not much point, is there? Of course, if you—if things had been different—you know what I mean——'

Dorothy's slim fingers found his wrist and pressed it gently.

'I know. And I'm sorry, Bertie. I can't help it. You see, I do like you ever so much, but with Garde—it's different. There's something about him——'

'Yes, there is. His size and his beastly temper,' grinned Bertie, contemplating the wide shoulders which blocked his view of the road. 'You'll have to be a good kid when you're married.'

Dorothy gurgled.

'I know. You can't think how exciting it is to be scared stiff of your future husband. But he's an awful dud, isn't he? Twenty-six and still taking his examinations!'

'Oh, well, it's a stiff proposition,' said Bertie. 'There's one comfort, he won't need to depend upon his patients for his living. Old Bing hates the doctor idea, doesn't he? But it won't make any difference to Garde's share of the family fortunes.'

'It's a nice name—Garde,' said Dorothy.

The young man in front turned his head for the fraction of a second.

'What are you saying about me, woman?' he demanded.

'Darling, nothing. Do be careful. I'm sure the driver ought not to take notice of what people behind are saying. We nearly sent a chicken to heaven then.'

She turned again to her companion and smiled mischievously.

'And now tell me all about everybody who is invited this year,' she commanded him. 'Are they as awful as usual? And am I to be the only love-lorn female, as I was last time, or are some more girls coming?'

Bertie decided to fall in with her mood.

'Let me see,' he said, and ruminated a moment. 'I think everybody but yourself had arrived when we came away. Incidentally—I hesitate to mention it—but when you say you'll come by the four-thirty, why do you turn up on the six-fifteen? Our brother in the front row has been trying to get through to Paddington to find out whether you'd been rendered dead in the buffet through eating one of their ham sandwiches, or something. What happened?'

'Oh, I thought I was on the four-thirty and it was a bit late,' said Dorothy, quite seriously, as she settled herself a little more comfortably against the upholstery. 'I suppose Garde is frightfully cross with me, then? I always notice that when people have been scared they are frightfully cross afterwards. And we shall be late for dinner, and dinner will be spoilt, and Mr Bing will swear, and the cook will give notice, and they will never be able to get another one, and Eleanor will be sweetly charming to me, and I shall be so unhappy that I expect I shall fall into a decline and die. As it is, I think I am going to burst into tears.'

'Do take a deep breath,' pleaded Bertie, grinning.

'Yes, I will, while you describe all the people. Fire away. Is there anyone I know?'

'I don't think so. Let me see. Do you know a fellow called Mountjoy?'

'The explorer? No, but of course I've heard of him. A large, hairy, loud-voiced, primitive sort of creature, with a red tie and black beard.'

'Oh, rot!' laughed Bertie. 'He is a little, slim, cleanshaven, shy sort of fellow, with hardly a word to say.'

'Oh, I'd pictured him so differently. And isn't he even a sheik?'

'Sheik be hanged! The chap seems terrified out of his life if anybody comes up and speaks to him. Just growls out any old answer, and gets away as soon as ever he can. He may get on well with lions and elephants, but I'm hanged if he's any catch as a fellow-guest. He doesn't golf or motor or walk or ride or swim or tennis or anything. And the only person who seems to be able to get two words out of him is—whom do you think?'

'Not Eleanor?' asked Dorothy, chuckling maliciously.

'Eleanor it is,' said Bertie, solemnly nodding his head. 'Who but our good sister Eleanor!'

'Pull yourself together,' said Dorothy severely. 'I have *never* seen anything so—so wildly improbable as Eleanor's behaviour with young, youngish, and middle-aged men. She might as well go straight into a nunnery and have done with it, I think.'

'Well, she seems to think rather well of this mighty hunter, anyhow. You'll see when we arrive. Then there is Mrs Bradley. Know her? Little, old, shrivelled, clever, sarcastic sort of dame. Would have been smelt out as a witch in a less tolerant age. I believe she *is* one. Good little old sport, though. You'll like her, I expect. Then there's a chap named Carstairs, very decent. Scientific sort of bloke, I believe—beetles or something. And that's the lot.'

'And here we are,' added Dorothy, as Garde shaved paint off the gate-post at the lodge. 'What a rotten driver my young man is!'

The occasion was Alastair Bing's birthday. The place, Chayning Court, was a pleasant Queen Anne house which had been bought by Alastair, its present owner, upon his succeeding to a respectable fortune made by his maternal uncle.

Alastair Bing called himself an archaeologist, thought of himself as a scholar and a gentleman, and was, as a matter of fact, a hot-tempered, muddle-headed, self-opinionated, domineering man, quite likeable if you did not see too much of him, extraordinarily insufferable if you did. He had been a widower for seventeen years, during which time his daughter Eleanor had acted as his housekeeper and secretary. Garde, his son, junior to Eleanor by some years, favoured his mother's side of the family, and was tall, strong, virile, and moody. He had elected to take up the study of medicine—this to his father's disgust. Alastair had imagined his son a Cambridge don. It was significant that no one of their acquaintance had doubted which would win the day—the spitfire, vindictive, explosive older man or the gloomy, moody, saturnine younger one. Garde always got his own way, usually by holding stolidly to the course he had set himself, and declining to be drawn into argument. His proposal of marriage to the beautiful and popular Dorothy Clark had been characteristic.

'Look here, Dorothy, what's a decent month for a wedding?'

'Oh, I don't know. June?'

'Right you are. Next June it is! When can you come and choose an engagement ring?'

'But Garde——'

But Garde had gone.

Dinner, on this rather formal occasion, was in the grand manner, but conversation was dull.

The host concluded a not very scholarly exposition of the results of the Egyptian delvings which had lately been concluded.

His son's voice, apparently finishing a more or less disparaging remark about the food, boomed across a great and embarrassing silence.

Eleanor Bing—plump, placid, drab, self-possessed, and much too freezingly well bred to achieve popularity, her unshingled hair rolled into a mid-Victorian modest bun, her evening dress uninspired but expensive, her small, neat feet

well and attractively shod—spoke quietly and very
clearly in reply.

Her brother glowered at her in his boorish way,
and went on with his dinner.

Between his sister and Dorothy Clark sat a quiet-
faced, grey-haired, whimsically smiling man with
a pleasant voice and engagingly diffident manner.
This was Carstairs the naturalist, a friend of Alastair
Bing's early manhood. His easy, quiet conversation,
his well-modulated tones, and his flashes of mild
humour brought him instant attention from the
rest of the table whenever he made a remark.

On the further side of Dorothy Clark there was
an empty chair.

The most out-of-place member of the house-party
was the woman seated on Alastair Bing's right. Her
name was Bradley —Mrs Lestrange Bradley. Nobody
quite knew who knew her or why she had been
invited. There was a rumour that she had worked
Garde out of a foolish scrape on boat-race night,
but why the boy should have 'dug her up again,'
as Alastair disgustedly expressed it, and brought
her down to Chaynings, no one could make out.
Perhaps, Dorothy unkindly suggested, it was an
inherited taste for fossils!

Mrs Bradley was dry without being shrivelled, and
birdlike without being pretty. She reminded Alastair
Bing, who was afraid of her, of the reconstruction
of a pterodactyl he had once seen in a German
museum. There was the same inhuman malignity in
her expression as in that of the defunct bird, and,
like it, she had a cynical smirk about her mouth

even when her face was in repose. She possessed nasty, dry, claw-like hands, and her arms, yellow and curiously repulsive, suggested the plucked wings of a fowl.

'Mountjoy is very late for dinner,' said Carstairs. 'It's a quarter past eight. I wonder what is keeping him? Got an idea for his new book, and has forgotten about food, I expect,' he added, chuckling.

Alastair Bing, his fierce moustaches bristling, his blue eyes gleaming with intense hatred, and his stiff, tufted little white imperial wagging with passionate denunciation, launched a savage attack upon his absent guest. That same afternoon, it appeared, Everard Mountjoy had offered, as his considered and expert opinion, the statement that the mound on Belldon Down was not an ancient British earthwork, but merely the remains of a bunker on what had been the local golf course seven or eight years ago, before its removal nearer the sea.

'The ridiculous fellow!' cried Alastair Bing, trembling with fury. 'The utter clown!'

'I beg your pardon, sir,' said the butler at his elbow.

Alastair stopped short.

'Well?' he snapped, glaring at the meek manservant as though he were the offending scientist. 'What is it?'

'If you please, sir,' the butler said, 'Parsons informs me that Mr Mountjoy went to take his bath upwards of an hour ago, and has not re-appeared.'

Alastair glowered at him.

'Re-appeared? What do you mean? Re-appeared?' he inquired sourly. 'The fellow isn't a disembodied spirit, is he! Don't be idiotic.'

'He went to take his bath, sir,' the butler repeated, unmoved, 'upwards of an hour ago.'

'Well, it's nothing to do with me,' yelled his employer irascibly. 'Go and tell Parsons to knock at the door and inquire whether Mr Mountjoy requires any assistance.'

'Very good, sir,' said the man.

'I hope he has not been taken ill,' remarked Eleanor solicitously. 'You don't think, Father, that you had better go and see if all is well, do you?'

'No, I do not,' returned Alastair Bing shortly. 'I certainly do not. A man who has the audacity—the effrontery—the sheer, downright buffoonery to tell me to my face that I don't know an ancient British earthwork when I see one——'

'But, sir,' began Bertie Philipson mildly. 'I mean,' he continued innocently—but nobody ever knew what he meant, for at that moment the butler again approached his master.

'Sir,' he said, in as urgent a tone as is compatible with perfect butlership.

'Well?' said Alastair Bing, with the dignified coldness of an irritated man who thinks that a vast fuss is being made over nothing. 'What is it now, Mander?'

'Parsons has hammered and hammered at the bathroom door, sir, and has obtained no answer. We, that is, Parsons and myself, sir, fear that the gentleman must have been taken ill.'

'Nonsense, nonsense!' grumbled Alastair, getting up from the table. 'Rubbish, rubbish!'

Followed by the butler, and muttering some remark about clownishness and earthworks, the irritated archaeologist departed.

The guests and family looked at one another, and Mrs Lestrange Bradley spoke. Strange to say, her voice belied her appearance, for, instead of the birdlike twitter one might have expected to hear issuing from those beaked lips, her utterance was slow, mellifluous, and slightly drawled; unctuous, rich, and reminiscent of dark, smooth treacle.

'I remember that a friend of my own fainted in the bath some four years ago,' she said graciously and with quiet relish. 'She was drowned.'

'Oh!' cried Dorothy. 'How terrible!'

'I think I will go and see if there is anything wrong,' said Garde, rising abruptly from the table. 'Might need some help,' he added ungraciously.

The guests shifted uncomfortably in their chairs and looked along the table to where the mistress of the house was seated. She seemed quite composed, however, and, reassured, they resumed their interrupted meal. The conversation became general, and gained in animation and interest.

Ten minutes, a quarter of an hour, twenty minutes passed by. The quiet, efficient servants performed their appointed tasks. The meal drew towards its close. Still the master of the house and his heir did not return.

Carstairs shifted in his seat, and his eyes turned frequently towards the door. Once he seemed to be intently listening. He took out his handkerchief and wiped his brow.

'Do you find the room oppressive, Mr Carstairs?' asked Eleanor, signing for a window to be opened wider.

'No, I thank you,' returned the scientist, 'but I confess to an extraordinarily strong feeling of apprehension. I wonder if you will be so kind as to excuse me? I feel I must go and see whether our friend Mountjoy is ill or well.'

He rose abruptly from the table and passed out of the room.

'He is Scottish on one side of the family—I forget which,' said Eleanor carelessly. 'They do get such curious ideas at times.'

'Some of the Scottish people have the gift of second sight,' remarked Dorothy. 'I remember a friend of my father had it. He knew when people were going to die. It was rather horrible.'

Mrs Bradley smiled to herself in a sinister manner, but offered no contribution to the conversation. Apparently the natural gifts of the Scots people had no particular interest for her.

The talk languished, and presently died. The atmosphere became charged with tension. It was as though all the persons, not only in that room, but in the whole house, were holding their breaths, waiting for something to happen. The silence weighed upon all their spirits, and they sat, an uncomfortably silent group, straining their ears to catch any sound which might indicate what was going on upstairs.

'Sounds quiet enough. I do hope he isn't ill,' said young Philipson, breaking the silence at last, and shifting uneasily in his chair.

Dorothy moved her slim shoulders as though they chafed beneath an unaccustomed burden.

'I expect it is all a false alarm, but I think Father might send to tell us so,' observed Eleanor in her precise voice. 'Oh, dear, what is that banging noise?'

Above stairs, a vigorous hammering on the panels of the bathroom door was eliciting no reply from the occupant.

'May have fainted,' suggested Garde. 'Vote we break in. Heard of people being drowned through fainting in the bath. Silly blighters have weak hearts, and the hot water does them in. I'll get a chair and smash the panels of the door.'

It was as he returned with a stout chair that Carstairs appeared from below. Garde stepped forward and rammed the heavy wooden chair with violence against the bathroom door.

'Half a moment!' cried the scientist. 'We might as well try the lock first.'

He turned the handle, and, to their surprise, the door opened.

'Well, I'm damned!' shouted Garde, who, in his capacity as a student of medicine, had bounded in before the older men. 'It's a woman. I say! She's dead!'

'A doctor! A doctor!' cried his father. 'I'll telephone. Get the poor creature out of there. Put her in Mountjoy's room for now. Oh—and where the devil is Mountjoy then?'

Without staying for an answer, he bounded with considerable swiftness and agility down the stairs to the hall telephone to call up the doctor, whose skill, in this case, would be unavailing, for, to Garde Bing's already practised eye, there was no doubt that the thin, wet body they lifted out of the bath was a dead body.

He and Carstairs made prolonged and gallant attempts at artificial respiration, but their efforts were vain.

'Hopeless,' said Carstairs, straightening himself.

Garde, seated on the edge of the bed in the room where they had taken the dead woman, shook his head gloomily.

'No doubt about it,' he agreed. 'Better go down again, I suppose.'

As the young man turned to follow his father down the staircase, Carstairs laid ahand on his arm.

'Just one moment, my boy,' he said, and paused.

'Feeling seedy?' asked the young man sympathetically. 'Beastly things, corpses. We get used to them, though, up at the hospitals, you know. Let's have a brandy, shall we? Soon put you right. Weird business, though, isn't it? What the devil was she doing, having a bath in our house? And who is she? And how did she get in? And, oh, a devil of a lot of other things.'

'Such as?' prompted Carstairs quickly.

'Oh, such as the bathroom window being wide

open top and bottom, and the door being unlocked. And that chap Mountjoy—couldn't stick that mealy-mouthed blighter, somehow—but where is he?'

'Dead,' replied Carstairs calmly. He pointed to the bedroom in which the dead woman lay.

'In there,' he concluded.

Garde turned white. His knees felt as though they had turned to water. He held on to the banisters for support.

'In—in—what do you say?' he stammered weakly.

Carstairs gripped his arm.

'Hold up, old chap,' he said peremptorily. 'You are too hefty for my strength to support you. I know it's a shock, but there it is, and we have to face it. That's Mountjoy all right, and I shouldn't tell your sister.'

'Tell—my—sister?' said Garde, like a man in a dream. 'But she'll have to know.'

'About the death of Mountjoy, yes,' said Carstairs, puzzled at the sudden collapse of the young man. 'The fact that Mountjoy was a woman, no!'

'I—yes, I get you. Rather bad luck to find out that the chap you are engaged to is a woman, what?'

He began to giggle helplessly.

'Go and pull the plug out of the bath, and stop being a fool,' said Carstairs sharply.

The little group downstairs, mute and becoming more and more uneasy as the time slipped by, were still waiting and waiting as though for something to happen.

It happened. The door swung suddenly and, as

usual in that well-run house, noiselessly open, and Garde walked in. His face was pale. It was damp with cold perspiration.

'He's dead,' he said, in a queer, staccato voice.

'Who?'

It was Mrs Bradley speaking.

'Why, Mountjoy, of course. That's why he didn't come down to dinner. He couldn't. He was—well, he was dead, you see. Drowned. Drowned in the bath.'

At any less serious news Dorothy would have been compelled to laugh. She wanted to laugh now, but it would have been the laughter of hysteria, not of mirth. She knew her fiancé fairly well, and she realized, with a cold feeling round her heart, that this was not the way he would bring tidings of natural death.

'Garde!' Her voice, harsh and uncontrolled because of this terrible hysteria that she was fighting, rose shrilly upon the tense silence. 'Garde! What do you mean? He can't be—dead!'

'I mean what I say,' said the young man, turning his gloomy gaze upon Mrs Bradley. 'And there's been some funny work in this house tonight. Mountjoy was dead before any of us came down to dinner this evening. Got that? Before we came down to dinner.'

'But look here——' began Bertie Philipson feebly.

'Can't stop,' replied Garde, cutting him short with brutal directness. 'Doctor will be here any minute, I hope, and I must take him upstairs. Not that he can do anything. Poor devil's as dead as a door-nail. Yes, he's dead. Drowned, you know.'

As abruptly as he had entered, he took his departure, slamming the door behind him with such force that those at the table involuntarily started from their seats.

Calm as the setting sun which was glorifying the west, Eleanor 'collected eyes'.

'I think we might repair to the drawing-room now,' she remarked quietly.

Even Mrs Bradley looked astonished.

Chapter Two

Accident? Suicide? Murder?

'OF course, it's rotten for the Bing crowd.' It was Bertie Philipson who spoke, as he lounged gracefully against one of the wooden posts of the verandah next morning after breakfast.

Mrs Lestrange Bradley nodded. 'And most annoying for us,' she added succinctly.

Bertie, who had been attempting to close his eyes to this view of the matter, was compelled to agree with her.

'Dashed annoying,' he said. 'Still, what can one do? It is a great pity Carstairs dragged in *that* aspect of the thing at all, especially as it is bound to be incorrect. Of course, the whole thing was the result of an accident.'

'But was it?' asked Mrs Bradley, with grave earnestness. Her eyes sombrely sought his, and, in spite of the young man's obvious discomfort and embarrassment, held them implacably.

'What—what do you mean?' he asked.

'This,' said Mrs Lestrange Bradley. 'Or rather, these. And they want explaining.'

'Just a moment,' said Bertie, at last managing to avert his eyes. 'Here comes Carstairs.'

Carstairs approached them along the gravel path, and mounted the white wooden steps.

'Ah, Philipson,' he said, 'you here? And Mrs Bradley?'

'Good morning, Mr Carstairs.'

Mrs Bradley smiled a Medea-like welcome.

'You are just in time to join in a serious intellectual discussion.'

'Oh?' said Carstairs politely.

'Yes. Mr Philipson thinks that an accident took place in this house last night.'

'Oh?' said Carstairs again, in the same elaborately colourless tone.

'Now I think it was a suicide,' announced Mrs Bradley, with the air of one who indicates that it is a fine morning for a walk.

'Oh?' said Carstairs, for the third time.

'Look here,' broke in Bertie, 'how long shall we be needed here, do you think? I want to get back to Town.'

Carstairs affected to consider the question. Finally, he said with some abruptness, 'I can trust you two people not to act idiotically if I tell you something very unpleasant, I suppose?'

Bertie nodded, and searched the older man's face with his eyes. Mrs Bradley showed her teeth in a mirthless grin, and smoothed the sleeve of a jade-green jumper which shrieked defiance at her yellow skin.

'There was murder committed in this house last evening,' said Carstairs, with quiet authority.

'Ah!' sighed Mrs Bradley, abandoning the jumper to its creases. 'Fancy that!' But whether the ejaculation expressed surprise, apprehension, relief, or merely a serious kind of mental pleasure to think that something had happened at last, neither of her hearers could tell. She plucked a bud from a rose-bush which grew beside the steps and smelled it delicately.

Bertie was obviously very much surprised. A well-bred young man, he had been schooled to refrain from gaping or allowing his jaw to drop, but his expression was eloquent of his amazement.

'What—what do you say?' he bleated feebly.

'I say murder,' replied Carstairs solemnly. 'And, what is more, carefully planned, deliberately executed murder.'

He paused. His hearers neither spoke nor moved. Then Mrs Bradley smelled the rose again.

'Come into the summer-house,' he said abruptly. 'I must talk it over with someone.'

'A member of the family?' suggested Bertie hesitatingly.

Carstairs shook his head.

'In their different ways they are all knocked out by the tragedy,' he said. 'Bing is not young, and he loved this friend very dearly. Garde—well, he's had a shock, like the rest of us, and, besides, I did give him a hint of what I thought last night. Of course, poor Eleanor was engaged to Mountjoy, as I expect you know—although, I remember, the engagement was supposed to be a secret—so I can scarcely consult her.'

'I knew they were engaged,' said Bertie, somewhat inadequately.

'So did I,' Mrs Bradley gravely agreed; and they followed Carstairs across the lawn to the small but pleasantly situated wooden summer-house.

'We can be in private here, I think,' said Carstairs. 'Well, now.'

They settled themselves comfortably, and Bertie, with a lift of the eyebrows towards Mrs Lestrange Bradley, which brought smiling permission from the lady, took out cigarettes. Carstairs waved aside the proffered silver case, and began.

'The first thing I ought to make clear to you both is that you may regard yourselves as absolutely free to leave this house whenever you like. I must repeat, however, what I said last night. Whether this death proves to have been an accident, as you suggest'—he looked at Bertie Philipson— 'or a suicide—Mrs Bradley's opinion, or'—he lowered his voice—'a murder, as I solemnly believe and intend to prove, the fact remains that the whole affair is very mysterious. Think over the points with me, and I think you will see what I mean.'

He checked off the points on his fingers with a solemn earnestness which at any other time would have diverted both his hearers.

'First, there is the queer fact that, although a man, known to the scientists of two continents as

Everard Mountjoy, went into that bathroom, we found drowned in that same bathroom an unknown woman, and no trace of our friend except his dressing-gown.'

If Carstairs' intention had been to startle his hearers, he had certainly achieved his aim.

'A woman!' cried Bertie Philipson amazedly. 'But who on earth was she? And how the deuce did she get drowned in Mountjoy's bath? And—and—I mean, dash it! Where's Mountjoy? He can't have disappeared! I mean, I took it—we all took it that the dead person—Garde said it was Mountjoy!'

'Yes,' said Carstairs, gazing across the lawn at a fine bed of standard roses.

'You mean,' asked Mrs Bradley precisely, 'that Mountjoy went into the bathroom, locked the door, flung off his dressing-gown, and turned into a woman? It seems incredible.'

'It does,' Carstairs admitted, 'but it must be the truth. Besides'—he knitted his brows—'he did *not* lock the door.'

'Didn't lock the door!' cried Bertie. 'Why, man, what do you mean?—didn't lock the door?'

'No,' said Carstairs. 'It is true that they began breaking one of the panels, but then I myself tried the handle, for I hate to see property damaged, and the door opened.'

'Extraordinary!' said Mrs Bradley.

'Yes, rather,' cried Bertie. 'Especially as——' He paused and Carstairs continued for him.

'Exactly. One would have thought that Mountjoy would have been very certain to secure himself against intrusion if he were—as we now think he must have been—a woman masquerading as a man. Then there is another thing.'

Bertie leaned forward, deeply interested in these revelations.

'The bathroom window was wide open at the bottom.'

'Well, but——' Bertie frowned with the unusual effort of concentrated thinking. 'Might not that show that the real Mountjoy—the *man* Mountjoy— left the bathroom by the window, and that the woman—whoever she was—then entered the bathroom the same way, or by the door, which she forgot to lock after herself?'

'And upset the whole household by fainting in the bath, and so getting drowned,' concluded Carstairs, with a faint but kindly smile. 'No, I'm afraid it won't wash, Philipson. I wish it would, but there are too many objections. First, where did the woman leave her clothes? We found none that could not be accounted for by Eleanor, Dorothy, and Mrs Bradley. Secondly, why should Mountjoy take the trouble to climb out of the bathroom window when he could have walked out of the front door far more easily and much less conspicuously? Thirdly, why should a strange woman break into a house and have a bath? It's not usual, to say the least, is it? Fourthly, supposing that the spirit did indeed so move her, would she really have forgotten to lock the door?—in a strange house? And would she have left the window wide open at the bottom? Open at the top, conceivably . . . but pushed right up at the bottom? Why, she couldn't even have stood up in the bath to climb out of it without being seen by any casual person walking in the garden on that side of the house. No, no! Mountjoy was the lady, and the lady was Mountjoy.' He paused. 'But that does not alter the fact that I liked him,' he added, 'and that I intend to avenge his death, for I firmly believe that he—or, rather, she—was foully murdered.'

There was a pregnant silence. Then words issued from Mrs Lestrange Bradley, words practical and sane. 'How do you intend to begin?' she asked. 'Have you any proof?'

'I have a clue, but I cannot locate its present whereabouts,' was Carstairs' cryptic answer. 'As to beginning, with Mr Bing's permission, I have arranged to turn myself into a private enquiry agent, and stay down here longer than I had intended in order to look into things. Later there may be a case for the police. But a policeman wants enough evidence to hang his hat on before he will do anything, and, frankly, I haven't got it. I could no more prove at this moment what I know to be the truth—namely, that Everard Mountjoy was foully and wilfully murdered—than I could reach the moon. But I *shall* prove it. Let us go into the house.'

Half-way across the lawn they encountered the butler, fluttering a telegram.

'For me? Thank you, Mander.' Carstairs took the orange envelope and tore it open.

'No answer,' he said.

The perfect servant departed, while Carstairs, watched by the young man and the reptilian woman, re-read the flimsy form.

'Good! My people have found someone to take over my work for the time being,' he said. 'I must go and tell Bing.'

Left to themselves, Mrs Bradley and Bertie Philipson strolled the whole length of the splendid Chaynings lawn in silence. As they turned to retrace their steps, Mrs Bradley said:

'Have you ever had any desire to commit murder? Don't answer unless you like, of course.'

Bertie laughed.

'As a kid,' he replied, 'I loathed my father. Funny, because he was never really unkind or harsh, you know. In fact, when I grew up a bit, I discovered what a very decent old bird he was, and we became rather pally, especially after my mother died.'

Mrs Bradley nodded her head slowly two or three times.

'Of course, somebody in this house did it,' she observed sadly. 'You realize that fact, don't you?'

Bertie stopped and stared at her.

'You don't mean to say that you really believe all that tosh Carstairs has been talking, do you?' he exclaimed.

Mrs Bradley grimaced.

'I do believe it,' she affirmed, 'and it was not tosh, young man. And I should advise you to think carefully where you were and what you were doing between seven and seven-thirty last night. And, if possible, get hold of someone who can support your alibi. We are all in deadly danger of getting ourselves hanged for last night's work!'

'But, look here,' said Bertie, 'you are not suggesting that I murdered the poor devil, are you?'

'By no means,' Mrs Bradley hastened to assure him. 'But, still, you know, stranger things than that have been true. And you have homicidal tendencies. So have they all—or nearly all. I should except Mr Carstairs. He has none, so far as I am able to judge.'

'Here, I say!' exclaimed Bertie, in mingled amusement and disgust. 'Whom *are* you accusing of being the murderer?'

'I accuse no one,' Mrs Bradley replied coolly. 'I know what I know, and I deduce what I deduce. But accusation—that is not my business. I am a psychologist, not a policewoman. Some are killers, and some are not. But you, young man——'

She paused, and Bertie broke into happy laughter.

Mrs Bradley shook her head at him like a playful alligator.

'All very well to be amused,' she said. 'But you wait and see! Just you wait and see!'

'No, but speaking seriously,' protested Bertie, 'I am not a scrap amused, I can assure you. Now, honestly, do you, as a responsible woman, tell me, as a responsible man, that Mr Carstairs is sane, and is not going about on this beautiful summer morning with a complete buzzing bee in his bonnet? Do you tell me, and expect me to believe, that one of these quite ordinary, well-bred, decent, civilized people committed a beastly and unreasonable and unnecessary and illogical crime last night? It isn't within the bounds of possibility, and I simply cannot believe it.'

'You must,' replied Mrs Bradley sharply. 'You must believe it. You must get it well into your head. You must visualize it and realize it. And then'—she paused dramatically and wagged a yellow finger in his face—'and then you had better prepare for yourself a sound, fool-proof, water-tight, gilt-edged alibi, against the time, young man, when the county police take over the nice conduct of this mysterious affair. For Mr Carstairs won't rest until he gets a noose around somebody's neck. You make up your mind about that!'

Bertie gazed at the old lady in simple wonderment.

'Well, I'm blessed! Anyone might imagine you thought I did it!' he ejaculated at last. 'You don't think that, surely, Mrs Bradley, do you?'

He blinked at her many times in rapid succession.

'I am not concerned a bit with whether you did it or did not do it,' replied she succinctly. 'What I am concerned about is that you do not get hanged for it, young man. Somebody will be hanged, you see. Oh, yes. And it won't be me,' she concluded, with her dreadful chuckle.

Bertie opened his mouth wide to say something, thought a moment, and then closed it.

'Go on,' said Mrs Bradley sympathetically. 'Do say it.'

'No,' replied Bertie. 'It might be used in evidence against me. I don't trust you, you see.'

Mrs Bradley screamed with delighted laughter.

Chapter Three

The Missing Clue

MRS BRADLEY and Bertie Philipson were not the only people who discussed the point of view held by Carstairs. It was true that he had not taken any member of the family into his confidence, but his remarks of the previous evening, coupled with a lively sense of curiosity, caused young Bing to seek out his father and blurt out certain grave suspicions and surmises which he had formed in his own mind.

'You see, Father,' the young man observed, 'it isn't as though anyone would leave the bathroom unlocked, is it? I mean, especially a woman who had hoodwinked us all for years with her pretence of being a man.'

'I do not, and I shall not,' Alastair Bing interrupted, his eyebrows shooting up to an alarming height on his forehead, 'believe that the unfortunate female whose body lies in an upper chamber of this ill-starred house could possibly have been my old friend Everard Mountjoy. No, it cannot be so. For reasons of his own, which may or may not appear in due course, my friend has seen fit to disappear from my house. However, when, if at all, he thinks fit to return to me, he will find his place prepared, his room ready to receive him. More,' concluded Alastair magnificently, 'I cannot say.'

'But look here, Dad——' his son cried out.

Alastair raised his hand.

'No more, I beg you!'

'But, Father, Mr Carstairs as good as said that the woman had been—well, that there was some sort of funny business.'

'I cannot,' said Alastair coldly—'I must insist that I cannot undertake to translate your idiom into reasonable English. What am I to understand by "funny business"?'

'She was—well, there's been foul play,' shouted Garde, and added, under his breath, 'Damned old fool!'

'I take it very ill that Carstairs should suggest that such a thing could occur in my house,' said Alastair grandly. 'Ask him to be so good as to give me a few moments in the library. And, if this disquieting rumour has spread, be kind enough to reassure the ladies, and tell them that I say it is nonsense.'

Garde departed, and encountered Carstairs on his way from the garden to find Alastair.

'Apropos of what I said this morning, Bing,' began Carstairs crisply, upon entering the library, 'I have received a wire from my people to the effect that they can carry on without me for a little while, and so, with your permission, I propose to get to the bottom of this mystery about Mountjoy's death.'

Alastair, having gazed all round the large room in a conspiratorial manner, tiptoed to the door and closed it.

'I was compelled to speak rather abruptly on the matter to my son just now,' he confessed. 'It will never do for all kinds of wild rumours to spread. After all, there are the servants and the tradespeople to consider. But, I must confess, your remarks this morning impressed me more than I cared to admit to Garde, and I feel that we should take steps, decided steps, to prove at any rate, whether the dead body is that of Everard Mountjoy. It is a most incomprehensible thing to me, most incomprehensible, that a woman could have masqueraded so long without being detected, and that is why I have grave doubts as to the identity of the deceased person.'

'There can be no doubt, I am sorry to say,' said Carstairs. 'Did not Mountjoy lose two fingers on the left hand after an accident with a gun on one of his hunting trips?'

'Yes, he did. I have observed the deformity more than once.'

'I noticed the left hand of the corpse when we carried it into the bedroom,' said Carstairs simply. 'The two fingers are missing.'

Alastair Bing groaned.

'There will be an inquest, of course,' he said. 'And now, I suppose, there will be all sorts of scandalous tales bandied about. Eleanor will be most upset. We have always been so quiet here——'

'I don't see that there need be any scandal,' said Carstairs. 'There is no need for anybody to know that the dead woman ever pretended to be a man. None of the village people know anything about her, do they? No, what concerns me is the fact that she was murdered.'

'You have no proof! You have no right to make such a statement!' cried Alastair. 'I cannot imagine what cause you have for saying such a terrible thing. Don't you see—can you not realize that you are virtually accusing someone in this house of having done to death a fellow-creature? It is monstrous to think such a thing, let alone say it. Besides, where is your evidence?'

'If I had any evidence that I could put to the proof, Bing, we should be compelled to call in the police,' replied Carstairs. 'As to the suggestion that the murderer is a person residing here, well, I cannot see that it is necessarily the truth.'

'But I say that if—mind, I am not convinced that the murder *was* committed—but, if so, then the criminal is someone living in this house, and knowing the ways of this house. Look at the time of day, for instance. My dinner-hour is an unusually early one, and yet the criminal, if criminal there was, carried out his unholy act at a time when everybody else was dressing for dinner. That is to say, at a time when everybody, and yet, in a sense, when nobody can fully account for himself or herself. You understand me?'

'Upon my word, Bing,' said Carstairs, 'you are quite right. Nobody can have a hole-proof alibi, and yet everybody has only to assert that he was dressing for dinner and no one can contradict him. This is going to be extremely awkward.'

'Again,' pursued Alastair, checking off the points on his fingers, 'look what knowledge of the house is shown. The bathroom the deceased was using at the time—the fact that the window was open at the top——'

'The fact,' cried Carstairs, almost dancing with excitement, 'that the intruder knew that poor Mountjoy would not even cry out at the sight of him as he clambered in through the window. That point puzzles me horribly. I mean, people don't ordinarily visit other people in the bathroom, do they? And it is quite certain that Mountjoy did *not* cry out, for I made tests this morning, and discovered that even with both taps running I could be heard when I shouted for help. So the murderer could not have been a stranger to Mountjoy. On the contrary——' He paused, as a new and curious thought struck him.

'Go on,' prompted Alastair Bing. 'Although, I must confess,' he added hastily, 'that I think your hypothesis utterly untenable. Mountjoy could not have been murdered. For one thing, how did the murderer get into the bathroom? You are not going to suggest that Mountjoy kindly left the door unlocked to save the killer trouble, are you? And as for the window being open at the top, it may have been, but the murderer did not get in that way.'

'Why didn't he?' asked Carstairs keenly.

'Because it is a physical impossibility,' replied Alastair. 'You seem to forget that the bathroom window is at least forty feet above ground-level, and there is no foothold for climbing. There's not even a porch or an outhouse on that wall. Come outside, and I will show you what I mean.'

'No, there, is no porch or outhouse, I know, but there is a balcony,' replied Carstairs. 'I have been looking at it from below, and also out of the bathroom window, and I am certain that a person possessed of a clear head and average muscular development would find no difficulty in climbing from the iron railing of the small balcony outside the bedroom which is occupied at present by Miss Clark to the window of the bathroom where the crime was committed. If the window was open at the top to let the steam out, the murderer could have opened it at the bottom, for it is just an ordinary type of sash window, and slides up and down extremely readily, I noticed. Once the stepping from the balcony was accomplished and the bottom of the window pushed up, it would be simplicity itself to climb in over the sill.'

'Oh, nonsense!' snorted Alastair Bing, 'it is too hideously dangerous an undertaking for words. No sane person would dream of attempting such a feat.'

'No sane person——' Carstairs blinked, as a new

thought occurred to him. He shrugged his shoulders, and went on more briskly:

'Look here! We can soon settle whether it is a possible or an impossible feat. You go up to the bathroom and look out of the window, and I'll get someone to attempt the climb.'

'I won't have anybody take unnecessary risks,' retorted Alastair, with spirit.

'Very well. I'll do it myself!' And Carstairs made his way to the door and passed out. Alastair Bing, pulling irritably at his bristling moustache, followed him.

'The bathroom! Let us have another look at the bathroom!' he cried.

It was like all other bathrooms—bare, tiled, sunny, and austere.

'The window was open like this,' said Carstairs, pushing the top of it down some four inches.

'As much as that? I don't remember noticing it myself.'

'Oh, yes. Quite as much. And the bottom was right up like this.'

He pushed it up so that an aperture large enough for a well-grown man to obtain admission from without was disclosed.

'Yes, I remember that,' Alastair assented. 'I thought at the time it was odd that anyone should be having a bath with the window wide open like that. One could be seen from the garden and the stables as soon as one stood up, I should imagine.'

'Quite,' Carstairs agreed. 'So the murderer must

have opened the window, I should say; the victim would not have done so.'

'Of course, the great objection to your theory of murder is that no marks of violence or evidence of poison have been discovered on or in the body,' Alastair pointed out.

'Of course they have not!' Carstairs stared in amazement. 'Mountjoy was drowned!'

'Drowned! But, my dear fellow, people don't allow themselves to be drowned as easily as all that.'

'Don't they? Have you ever heard of the "Brides in the Bath" case?'

'I—yes, I suppose so. Yes, of course I have. A dreadful scoundrel, that man.'

'Yes. Look here, Bing, take off your coat and get into the bath. It is quite dry, so you need not be afraid of spoiling your suit. Just a moment, though. One question. Which of us two do you take to be the stronger man?'

'Myself, undoubtedly,' replied Alastair, without hesitation. 'I am both taller and heavier than you are.'

'And you do your exercises regularly, I've no doubt, whilst I meander around after my flora and fauna. Well, that only lends more colour to my argument. Come, get in. This is not a practical joke. It is a serious demonstration.'

Unwillingly Alastair Bing divested himself of his jacket and boots, and, feeling extremely foolish, stepped into the bath.

'Sit down,' commanded Carstairs vigorously.

Protesting against a waste of time, but interested in spite of himself, Alastair obeyed.

'I sit here on the edge of the bath. I am talking to you on a subject very near to my heart. It is a subject which vitally concerns both of us, so much so that I have even climbed through the window in order to interview you in your bathroom, where, presumably, we shall not be disturbed. You may or may not have known that I was coming, but, at any rate, you are not altogether surprised to see me, or, if you are, you do not betray it by calling out. Picture to yourself, my dear Alastair, the scene.'

'Oh, rubbish!' said Alastair irascibly. 'Here, I am tired of this foolery. I'm going to——'

'Mind your head!' cried Carstairs.

Bing looked swiftly round, and at the same instant Carstairs seized his ankles and jerked his feet sharply upwards. Taken at such disadvantage, Alastair clutched wildly at the sides of the bath, but his fingers slipped on the glazed surface of the porcelain, and his body slid ignominiously along the bottom of the bath until his head struck the end. Carstairs released his feet, sprang towards his head, and, in spite of his frenzied struggles, held it down on to the bottom of the bath.

Then he released his hold, dusted the knees of his trousers, allowed his highly incensed host to climb out of the bath and rub a severely bumped head, and then observed nonchalantly:

'Well, that is how the brides are supposed to have been drowned in the bath. What do you think of the method? Fairly simple, I think. Do say that you are convinced.'

Alastair, still ruffled, allowed himself to be assisted into his coat.

'Mere horseplay,' he growled.

'Well, I didn't intend it as such, and I'm sorry I hadn't realized you would bump your head. But, as a demonstration of how Mountjoy probably met her death, I think it was rather successful. Now, scientifically speaking, don't you agree?'

'If you appeal to me as a fellow scientist,' Alastair conceded, 'I see your point. Your theory is that the murderer climbed through there, drowned Everard Mountjoy, and, unlocking the door, walked out. Of course, if you are right, that lends still more colour to my idea that it must have been someone who knew the house, doesn't it? In fact'—he looked at Carstairs straight in the eye—'it might have been any one of us—unless a servant did it.'

Carstairs made no reply, and Alastair walked to the window and looked out.

'Hum! That bedroom balcony does come pretty close here,' he remarked; 'I had forgotten it was built out so far. A man wouldn't need to be very active to step over that railing on to that bit of the water-spout that's flattened and decorated, and so on to this sill. It would be child's play. Scarcely any danger. And the window was open at the top. And he put his arm over and pulled up the bottom half and climbed in on to——' He paused dramatically. 'The bathroom window is a bit high up in the wall, isn't it?' he said. 'What did he put his foot on, I wonder, to assist him down? You see, if he had dropped and chanced it, he'd have shaken the floor like an earthquake, and somebody would certainly have come very hastily along to find out the cause of the disturbance. So where is——'

But Carstairs could not wait for him to finish.

'The bathroom stool!' he cried. 'My clue! I haven't told you yet! That must be it! Don't you see? The bathroom stool!'

'Where?' asked the owner of the house, gazing round the white, tiled room.

'Gone, man, gone!' Carstairs almost shouted the words in his excitement. 'It was under the window, and the murderer stepped down on to it, and his shoes left some mark which would betray him, and so he carried it out with him when he had done his foul work. That must be the explanation.'

'Where *is* the stool?' asked Alastair irritably, for Carstairs' torrent of words had almost overwhelmed him.

'Gone, man! Disappeared off the face of the earth! That's the point, don't you see? The murderer has hidden it. It would incriminate him. Give him away!'

Alastair Bing's face cleared. 'I see your point,' he said, almost happily. 'Find the bathroom stool. Find some shoes which could have marked, stained, mutilated, or in some way damaged the bathroom stool. Find the owner of the shoes. And there's your murderer! Very neat. Too neat. It can't be as easy as that.'

Carstairs grunted.

'We haven't found who took it nor where it is yet,' he observed gloomily.

Alastair nodded, ran his finger along a ledge in search of possible dust, and finally said: 'Let us go on to the terrace.'

The view from the little balcony was a fine one, but they gave it less than a glance.

'I suggest,' said Carstairs more briskly, 'that we try to reconstruct the crime—if crime there was,' he added dutifully. 'Shall I do the climbing, or do you prefer to do it yourself, as it is your house?'

'We could do with an assistant, I think,' said Alastair Bing, entering into the spirit of the thing. 'There goes young Philipson. I will call him up.'

He shouted down to Bertie, who was crossing the lawn, and the young man immediately entered the house and soon joined them.

'See here, Philipson,' said Carstairs, 'we want you to find out if it is possible to clamber from the end of the balcony here up to that smaller window. See where I mean?'

'Perfectly,' said Bertie, directing his eyes intelligently towards the objective. 'I am to hike over the balcony railing, shove my toe on that bit of flattened water-pipe, and heave my other knee on to the bathroom window-sill. It *is* the bathroom, isn't it?'

'It is,' replied Carstairs.

'*The* bathroom?' murmured Bertie, with animation.

'Yes,' Carstairs admitted.

'And—oh, I twig! Do you really think that's how

he got in? Tough young egg!' cried Bertie admiringly. 'The chap, I mean. The murderer.'

'Half a moment,' said Alastair, who began to remember that he was a local magistrate, 'I think one of us ought to go into the bathroom and witness the experiment from that end, don't you, Carstairs?'

'Very well,' Carstairs agreed. 'You go, will you?'

'Right. Wait a moment whilst I close the window at the bottom. I will wave my handkerchief out of the aperture at the top when I am ready.'

'Very well,' agreed Carstairs. 'Now, Philipson,' he went on, turning to Bertie, 'I want you to climb just as you yourself suggested, and you must enter the bathroom as best you can. Understand?'

'Righto,' said Bertie. 'Best way will be to push up the lower sash to about the same height, as it is now, won't it?'

'You'll see,' said Carstairs non-committally. 'Of course, to make a perfectly convincing demonstration, I should not have allowed you to see the window open at the bottom at all.'

A second or two later a handkerchief fluttering from the top of the bathroom window gave the signal that Alastair had taken up his position, and Bertie commenced his feat.

It presented no difficulty. He was soon seen by Carstairs to push up the bathroom window at the bottom and insert one elegantly trousered leg over the sill. There, however, he remained for quite an appreciable period of time—so long, indeed, that at last Carstairs' curiosity impelled him to pass back through the room which opened on to the balcony, and enter the bathroom doorway. As he emerged on to the landing, however, he was just in time to see Eleanor Bing appear from the landing above, carrying a bathroom stool. She approached the bathroom door, and observed her father standing inside the little room. Carstairs drew back from the doorway.

'Here you are, Father,' she observed, handing the stool to her parent, who appeared to be fully absorbed in Bertie's antics on the window-ledge, 'put this down somewhere for me, if you please. I found it this morning, I am glad to say. Although,' she continued, knitting her level brows, 'why the maids should have put two stools in that bathroom and none in this is more than I can explain. Servants are the most extraordinary—really, Mr Carstairs!'

For Carstairs, without apology or explanation, had darted forward, seized the stool, and was subjecting it to a close scrutiny.

To his intense disappointment and chagrin, it bore no mark of any kind, incriminating or otherwise. Its cork top was guiltless of stain or disfigurement; its white-painted legs were immaculate as they could be. In fact, it was a model of what a twentieth-century bathroom stool in the best stages of preservation ought to look like. Anybody would willingly have given Eleanor a testimonial for managing servants on the strength of it.

Carstairs gave vent to a heavy sigh. The one clue of which he had hoped so much had failed him.

Indeed, as Alastair afterwards pointed out, it was no clue at all.

Eleanor, about to take her departure, suddenly stopped, and stood transfixed with astonishment at the unusual spectacle of her brother's friend waving his leg gracefully in at the window and uttering sharp cries of anguish. She paused, and regarded Bertie, from behind her father's shoulder, with well-bred disapproval. She coughed slightly.

'Dear me, Bertie,' said she primly, 'if you wish to do your physical exercises, I do wish you would find somewhere a little less dangerous. Why don't you——'

'Can't get down,' wailed Bertie idiotically, pretending to cry. Alastair and Carstairs went to his assistance.

'You might have jumped, you young idiot,' grinned Carstairs, 'instead of sitting there gibbering.'

'If I had, I insist that I should have gone clean through the floor, and probably would have landed on somebody's nut below, below, below!' chanted Bertie, dusting himself down. 'And, to turn to more important topics, if anybody wants any more Bill Sykes acts performed, he'll jolly well have to dig me up another pair of bags. I've nearly put my knees through these. And just look at the dust!'

Garde, who had joined them, interrupted at this juncture by dealing the dust a hearty slap, which drew a yell of pain and protest from Bertie, and the conversation lapsed in favour of a scuffling free fight.

'Well,' observed Carstairs ruefully, when the

combatants had been checked and dispersed by the prim Eleanor, and she herself had left him and her father together, 'so much for our little experiment.'

'Yes,' said Alastair, 'the way that stool turned up rather puts an end to your theory, Carstairs, I am afraid.'

'You see, nobody could have climbed in through that window without assistance, or something to put his foot on to help him down, unless he risked making a pretty big noise, and even, as Philipson pointed out, damaging the floor. It's an old house, you know.'

'Yes, that is proved about the stool,' said Carstairs, 'but that doesn't prove that Mountjoy met his death in a natural manner.'

'Oh, surely, Carstairs!' objected Alastair. 'If the stool doesn't incriminate some person or persons unknown, as they put it (and it certainly doesn't, does it?)—why, there's nothing else that will.'

'The open window, man! The unlocked door!' cried Carstairs, exasperated by this doubting Thomas.

'Maybe, of course,' the older man admitted. 'But it's no proof, no proof at all. And where's the motive, anyway? No, Carstairs'—and, so saying, he led the way downstairs—'I'm afraid you're deceiving yourself. You've had a shock, you see, over our friend's death, and so, of course, you're a little inclined to be morbid and fanciful, if you'll excuse my saying so.'

'But I tell you again,' said Carstairs, 'that I am

convinced. I'm not an hysterical person, Bing, as you yourself should know. I'm fairly hard-headed, and am not in the least inclined to be fanciful. And when I say that our friend was murdered, well, I mean I'm sure of it. And, with or without help, I'm going to prove it.'

Alastair shrugged his shoulders, and felt for his pipe.

'You've a bee in your bonnet, Carstairs, you know,' he said. 'Give up the idea that my house has harboured a criminal. You are on the wrong track altogether. It was a nasty accident, and I'm confoundedly sorry and fearfully bothered, and it makes me sick to think of the inquest and the poor fellow's—no, I mean lady's relations coming here, and all that sort of thing—it is all damnably unpleasant! But there you are! It's just my luck. I was always unfortunate. And I suppose there will be a scandal set on foot because of the man-woman impersonation side of the business, for it is certain to come out, and of course Eleanor was engaged to the poor creature, which is the very deuce and devil and all, for it will make the poor girl a laughing-stock over the whole county, and me with her, and altogether I could, and do, curse the whole wretched business from beginning to end.'

He paused for breath. Carstairs regarded him with a discerning smile.

'And you'll curse some more when that pipe refuses to draw,' he said, 'which it certainly will refuse to do if you ram that tobacco down very much harder.'

Chapter Four

Interval

THE Bing family, together with Dorothy and Bertie, were gathered together in the morning-room, a cheerful apartment opening by means of French windows on to the garden, and the talk had turned inevitably to the tragedy of two nights before.

'Did you actually take up the body?' asked Eleanor of her brother.

Her dry-eyed calmness was one of the most extraordinary features of the event, and four pairs of eyes, including those of her father, who sat, affecting to read the newspaper, in the far corner of the room, were turned upon her in surprise as she asked the coldly worded question.

Garde, who was seated on the arm of Dorothy's chair, shifted his position slightly, and drawled coolly:

'Madam sister, I did not. All I did was to pull the plug out of the bath and let the water run away. Then I came downstairs and was sick.'

He stroked the cat, which had chosen that particular moment to spring on to Dorothy's knee.

'Damned sick,' he continued appreciatively.

'Don't be nasty, Garde,' Dorothy admonished him, in her proprietary way. 'Be quiet now.'

'As for you,' said the young man, putting two fingers under her chin and tilting her head back against the cushions of the chair, 'if you don't stop jumping out of your skin whenever the cat decides to vault on to your chair, we shall have to take you to the vet. and ask him to put you out of pain. You nearly upset your old grandfather's equilibrium just now. I am most insecurely balanced on this here arm of this here chair, and I don't care to be pushed. My nerves won't stand it. So mind now! I've warned you!'

'It's that wretched accident the night before last,' said Eleanor. 'I'm sure it has upset everyone's nerves. A most unfortunate affair. I can't imagine anything more trying than to have someone staying in the house who is subject to these wretched heart-attacks.'

'Poor devil, though,' observed Bertie, and then fell silent, for over all their minds hung the fact, insisted upon by Alastair Bing, that there was no need to let Eleanor know that her fiancé had turned out to be a member of her own sex.

'It's bad enough for the poor girl as it is,' Alastair had declared to his son, 'without breaking her pride as well as her heart.'

It was a remarkable fact, however, that Eleanor,

so far, had betrayed no signs that her heart was not
in its normal state of well-being. She seemed less
affected, almost, than anyone by the tragedy.

'Although you never know what she really thinks
or feels about anything,' Garde confided to Dorothy.
'Old Sis never did give herself away.'

He himself seemed to have recovered completely
from his breakdown of two nights before, and
looked his usual cheerful, healthy self.

Eleanor presently left the group, on the plea
that she had the orders of the day to attend to,
and that lunch waited for no man.

Her absence from the circle was a palpable relief,
and the talk circulated more freely.

Presently Carstairs appeared, fresh from a
morning walk which he had taken in order to
persuade himself that his overnight fears, doubts,
and suspicions were groundless.

He had returned, however, more convinced than
ever that a good deal of explanation was needed to
cover the facts, if the death of Everard Mountjoy
were to be counted an accident.

'First thing'—so his conclusions ran—'find
out exactly who the man—woman was, and,
communicate with relations, if any. Must see
whether Bing knows anything about Mountjoy's
private life. I'll get busy with that and see where
it leads me.'

So thinking, he entered the morning-room.

'Well, Mr Carstairs!' Garde challenged him.
'Blown away the morning dew of heavy theory
yet?'

Carstairs smiled somewhat grimly.

'I don't want to discuss my theories, light or heavy,' he said.

'Let's play tennis.'

'What—after—oh, I couldn't,' cried Dorothy. 'I think it's horribly callous of you to suggest it.'

'I bow to your superior judgment,' said Carstairs dryly.

'Nasty,' said Dorothy, wrinkling her nose. 'Very nasty. It isn't fair to crush me like that.'

'No, it isn't,' said Bertie, blushing, but heroically taking her side against the quizzically smiling, elderly little man. 'It isn't that we—well, speaking for myself—cared a hang about Mountjoy really, but—somehow——'

'Somehow your ancient British prejudices won't allow you to follow the dictates of your preferences,' concluded Carstairs. 'Somebody is dead—doesn't matter who, how, or why, but we shouldn't play games.'

Bertie grinned, and subsided.

Carstairs turned to Garde.

'Where's Eleanor?' he asked suddenly.

'Ordering the grub and chasing the servants,' her brother replied glibly. 'Why?'

'I—wondered how she was,' said Carstairs slowly.

'Oh, right as rain. Right as rain,' said Garde, waving his hand expressively, and nearly losing his balance on the arm of Dorothy's chair.

'And how are *you*, Miss Clark?' asked Carstairs, turning to look at her.

The light was full on Dorothy's pretty but, this morning, rather pale face. She gave a little shudder.

'I'm—frightened,' she confessed.

Alastair Bing folded the paper noisily and flung it on to the small table. Then he rose abruptly and stalked out into the garden.

'Thank goodness!' said Garde half-audibly.

'Mr Carstairs,' cried Dorothy, leaning forward, 'it—wasn't—what was—oh, I mean—it *was* an accident, wasn't it?'

'What was?' asked Carstairs levelly.

Dorothy threw herself back in her chair and looked at him reproachfully.

'You do know what I mean,' she told him, pouting a little. 'That—that—accident in the—in the bathroom—it *was* an accident, wasn't it? Oh, do say it was! I want you to say it was.'

'My dear young lady——' Carstairs began, with some embarrassment, for in her wailing cry he detected the note of stark fear. But, before he could continue, Eleanor came in, and an awkward silence descended upon the little party, until Carstairs, murmuring something about a microscopic slide, took his departure.

'Where is Mrs Bradley?' asked Bertie, in order to break the uncomfortable silence which Eleanor's coming had imposed upon them.

'So devilishly awkward having to remember that Eleanor doesn't know her young man was a young woman,' as Garde expressed it to Bertie afterwards.

'She is not down yet. She prefers to breakfast in bed,' observed Eleanor in reply to Bertie's question, with just that tinge of disapproval in her voice which breakfasting in bed appeared to her to warrant. Eleanor emphatically was not one of Nature's breakfasters-in-bed.

'Oh, well,' said Garde pacifically, 'I daresay she's getting on a bit in years, you know, and, anyhow, it does keep her out of the way. Although she's a good old sort, is Mrs Bradley,' he added reminiscently.

'I am glad you find her so,' said Eleanor.

It was one of those conclusive remarks of which the daughter of the house appeared to possess quite a store.

Chapter Five

The Inquisitors

INSTEAD of going to his microscope, however, Carstairs searched his pocket for a pipe, tobacco, and matches, and, walking across to the pleasantly situated summer-house, sat down there to think things out.

'I've got mental indigestion already over this business,' he told himself. 'Now, then, let's get down to it.'

But his thoughts were confused and led him nowhere.

'What I really want is an intelligent listener,' he said aloud.

'Will I do?' asked Mrs Lestrange Bradley, appearing with Cheshire-cat-like abruptness from the side of the summer-house, and confronting him.

'You will do very nicely,' replied Carstairs, courteously rising. 'That is, unless you are a murderer.'

'Of course, I might be,' Mrs Bradley confessed,

'but then so might all of us. And the servants, any of them, or all of them, might be thugs in disguise. It is all very, very confusing, not to say muddling, puzzling, amazing, and irritating. I've been in bed thinking it over.'

Carstairs laughed.

'Let us sit here and take it in turns to talk,' went on Mrs Bradley. 'You may have your say first.' She seated herself, folded her hands, and gazed expectantly up at him. Carstairs sat down beside her and stretched out his legs.

'That's right. Now begin,' said Mrs Bradley, peering in bird-like fashion into his face. Carstairs was silent. 'Here!—have my sunshade and poke the gravel with it,' she went on, pushing it into his hands.

Carstairs laughed again, and took it.

'Well,' he began, detaching a little round pebble from the main body of the path and chivvying it to and fro with the ferrule of the parasol, 'I'm sure Mountjoy was murdered, and the fact that Bing chooses to be pigheaded has not altered my opinion one jot.'

'Oh, our host does not agree with you? That's very amusing,' said Mrs Bradley.

'I'm afraid I find it merely exasperating,' replied Carstairs.

'And he is leaving us to the further mercies of the thug or thugs,' Mrs Bradley continued, in her mellifluous voice. 'That is very amusing too.'

'I'd give a good deal to know what motive anybody in this house had for murdering Mountjoy,' went on Carstairs, pursuing his own train of thought.

'For, of course, we shall not be let off with one death, or even two,' murmured Mrs Bradley, pursuing hers.

'What?' said Carstairs, so sharply that Mrs Bradley stared at him in surprise.

'I beg your pardon?' she said.

'And I yours for shouting at you,' laughed Carstairs. 'No, but, speaking seriously, have you any reason for saying that?'

'Saying what? I was thinking aloud, that's all.'

'Yes, I know. But why should you suppose—you don't really suppose that we are again——'

'I do, though.' Mrs Bradley nodded her head very firmly several times. 'I have thought a good deal about this sudden death of an apparently well-liked, inoffensive woman, and I begin to sense something very queer about this house. Don't ask me what I mean. I don't know myself. But there's something peculiar going on, and it perturbs me.'

Carstairs knitted his brows in perplexity. 'Can't you explain at all?' he asked.

'No,' said Mrs Bradley.

'You do think it was murder, then?' was Carstairs' next remark. 'But the police——'

'Are persons of some common sense,' Mrs Bradley interrupted, 'but usually of no imagination or sensitiveness whatsoever. They want facts, whereas you and I are content with feelings.'

'Oh, I want facts too,' said Carstairs, 'and, after all, we've got them, you know. The facts are here all right. They must be all round us, numbers and numbers of little tiny facts, each one of them impotent and useless without all its brothers. And we can't even see them. It is rather annoying, isn't it?'

'Well, we do know some,' said Mrs Bradley. 'Look here, I'll say them to you, and you see how many of them you can put together. Ready?'

Carstairs drew out a small memorandum book. 'I'll jot them down,' he said. 'Then we shall both know exactly where we stand. Yes, I am ready.'

Mrs Bradley leaned forward a little, fixed her unseeing eyes on the middle distance, and began.

'Window open at the bottom. Unlikely deceased would have had it so. Door unlocked. Unlikely that deceased would have forgotten or neglected to lock it, especially as she must have felt it important to continue concealment of her sex. Bathroom stool missing.'

'Oh, that has been found,' interrupted Carstairs disgustedly. 'My best clue gone west.'

'Oh?' Mrs Bradley turned to him swiftly. 'Found? Where?'

'In the bathroom on the next floor of the house,' Carstairs answered. 'Through some oversight, the maids appear to have put the two stools in the upper floor bathroom and none in the lower one.'

'That is exceedingly amusing,' said Mrs Bradley dryly.

Carstairs glanced at her, puzzled by her peculiar tone.

'I'm afraid I don't see,' he began deprecatingly.

'Don't you?' A strange little smile played about her thin lips. 'Mr Carstairs, I'm afraid you and dear Mr Bing were just a tiny bit foolish yesterday morning, weren't you? Just a little bit blind.'

'Were we? I must confess that I can't see how.'

'My dear'—Mrs Bradley laid a claw-like hand upon his arm—'did you question the maids about it? About the stool—the elusive clue?'

'Well, no. It seemed hardly necessary,' Carstairs admitted. 'But, of course, I can, if you think it should be done.'

'It is unnecessary now,' Mrs Bradley informed him. 'I can assure you, out of my housekeeping and servant-managing experience, that no maid ever moves bathroom stools. They won't even dust them unless you insist, and determinedly stand there while they do it. I don't refer to bathroom stools only, of course. I speak generally, and out of a profound and bitter experience.' She cackled harshly. 'And tell me why it should ever occur to a maid to carry a bathroom stool up on to the next landing. And, again, although I grant you girls are fools, even housemaids have eyes in their heads, and bathrooms are not extraordinarily large or particularly overstocked with furniture. They must have noticed that they were putting a second stool up there, mustn't they?'

'You don't mean that Miss Bing told a lie?' said Carstairs slowly.

'Oh, it was Eleanor brought it down, was it?'

asked Mrs Bradley in a non-committal tone. 'What exactly did she say?'

'Oh, merely that she had found the stool on the landing above, and that she couldn't imagine what the maids had been thinking about to put two stools in one bathroom, and none in the other.'

'Oh, if Eleanor said she had found two stools up there, she was probably speaking the truth. But do you mean to tell me that you didn't even go up to the other bathroom and have a look at the other stool?'

Carstairs smote his knee. 'Good heavens!' he said. 'What a fool I've been! You mean that the *other* stool——'

'Exactly,' said Mrs Bradley placidly, with her eyes on the far end of the garden.

Carstairs was on his feet before the word had left her lips. He literally dashed across the lawn, and ran up the terrace steps.

'Too late, my friend, I fear,' observed Mrs Bradley, noticing with quiet amusement that he still held her sunshade clutched in his hand.

In less than ten minutes he returned, with disappointment and chagrin written on his face. 'Not proven,' he said shortly, sitting down by Mrs Bradley's side.

'Wonderful what a little turpentine will do,' said the lady calmly.

'Are you a witch?' demanded Carstairs.

'No. Merely a fairly observant human being,' Mrs Bradley replied, smiling thoughtfully and not looking in his direction.

'Hum! Well, of course you are quite right. As I went up the stairs yesterday I thought I detected the odour of turpentine, and, sure enough, in the second floor bathroom is a stool which obviously has been freshly cleaned. I met one of the maids on the stairs, and in answer to my question she informed me that Miss Bing had noticed a dark mark on the cork top of the stool, and had given orders that it should be cleaned off.'

'Mark of what nature?' enquired Mrs Bradley.

'According to the girl it might have been paint or tar or even a kind of varnish stain. She couldn't say, and I didn't press the point.'

'Seems to me that Eleanor couldn't shield the criminal better if she knew who he was,' observed Mrs Bradley, as though to herself.

Carstairs seized upon her remark.

'You think she knows something?' he demanded.

'I know she does. So does Dorothy Clark. So does Bertie Philipson. So do we all, in fact. The difficulty will be to get our knowledge from us.'

'You seriously suggest that people in this house would deliberately shield a murderer?' asked Carstairs, horrified and incredulous.

'No, not deliberately, perhaps. Have you ever taught children, Mr Carstairs?' she broke off, with apparent irrelevance.

'No,' answered Carstairs, looking a little surprised at the question, for it seemed to have no possible bearing on the matter in hand.

'Well, I have,' Mrs Bradley slowly nodded.

'Children know quite a number of little facts, Mr Carstairs. More than almost any grown-up person would give them credit for.'

'Indeed?' said Carstairs, polite, but bored.

'Yes, indeed,' said Mrs Bradley; 'but probably you can have no idea of the skill that is needed to extract that knowledge from the children in any sort of coherent and comprehensible form.'

Carstairs began to see the drift of these remarks.

'You mean,' he said, 'that these people may have real information to give, but they don't—if I may so express it—they don't know that they possess information of the kind that is required.'

'Exactly,' agreed Mrs Bradley. 'You must question them, slowly and patiently, until you get what we educationists call a point of contact. Then, probably, you will be so overwhelmed with information, that your difficulty will be to know what on earth to start doing with it, and how on earth it all fits in.'

'In the present state of the inquiry, I cannot even remotely imagine such a possibility,' laughed Carstairs, 'but I will certainly take your advice. But supposing these people object to being questioned? After all, I am not a police officer.'

'They will love it,' pronounced Mrs Bradley, with finality. 'People love to tell all they know, especially when it is about themselves. That accounts for the popularity of the confessional. As for the criminal, he or she—or, of course, it—you have read your *Murders in the Rue Morgue* and Bram Stoker's *The*

Squaw?—must pretend to be as enthusiastic as the others, otherwise——'

'Yes, of course,' said Carstairs.

He looked at his watch.

'It still wants an hour to lunch-time,' he said. 'Shall we begin?'

Mrs Bradley laughed, wrinkling up her yellow face into a series of lines and creases which gave her the reverse of a benevolent expression.

'Must be very careful, of course,' Carstairs went on. 'Don't want to put ideas into people's heads.'

'You are, as always, very right,' observed Mrs Bradley, allowing her features to relax and her unprepossessing countenance to resume its normal expression of slightly cynical amusement. 'Come along, then. The morning-room again, I think. Alastair Bing is there, I know, and I am fairly certain that the others are with him. I will begin, and then you can go on. The playful manner will become us best, I think.'

She herself assumed the expression of a playful alligator, and walked into the morning-room by way of the French windows. Carstairs followed her closely.

'Now, children,' she began, smiling mirthlessly round at everybody present including her own reflection in an oval mirror, 'who would like to play a new game? Quite a parlour game. Nothing strenuous, or'—she glanced wickedly at Bertie Philipson, who blushed and protested—'or, I say, unsuitable and enjoyable—like tennis! Oh, I know I was not among those present, but I heard your fine rhetorical effort this morning, Mr Philipson, on the subject of observing the decencies'—and she wagged a yellow claw at him playfully. 'No, this is a very, very suitable game for the occasion. Now, who would like to play?'

'Not if it includes making idiotic noises,' said Carstairs, in order to suggest to the others that he was not in league with Mrs Bradley, for he decided that it would never do to begin with a conspiratorial atmosphere.

'Or kissing people,' said Eleanor firmly.

'Or hide-and-seek in the attics,' said Dorothy, shuddering.

'You are a mouldy lot, you know,' said Garde, with his moody smile. 'I'm on, Mrs Bradley. It's not a man-hunt, I suppose?'

'Well, in a sense, yes,' said Mrs Bradley. 'And I want one helper. Come here, Mr Carstairs. I think 1 will have you. Go over there, all of you, a moment, while I tell him his part in the proceedings.'

She took Carstairs aside, and affected to whisper in his ear.

Carstairs, playing up to her, chuckled and nodded.

'Ready, all of you?' asked Mrs Bradley, after a few seconds of this by-play.

'Fire away,' said Garde, settling himself more comfortably and leaning against the back of Dorothy's chair.

'Before you begin, you know, Carstairs,' said Alastair Bing, 'you should let me look again at the bumps on their heads. I did look a day or two ago, but I've lost my notes.'

'I won't have my head looked at,' said Dorothy firmly. 'I think it's horrid. You told me last time that I couldn't tell the truth and had no reasoning power.'

'Quite right, too, Father,' said Garde, with approval. 'Right on both counts. But can't we take the bumps for granted this time, and let Mr Carstairs get on with his questions? Anything for a change of subject. We've all been indulging our taste for the morbidly sensational in here. Carry on, Mr Carstairs.'

'Just as you like. Just as you like,' said Alastair, nettled.

'Well, I'd like to start with you, Bing, if you don't mind.'

So saying, Carstairs glanced at Mrs Bradley, and then looked round at the others. 'I'm afraid an absolutely necessary part of the game is that you all go outside a minute while Mrs Bradley and I arrange the room. Yes, you also, please, Bing. And come in when you are called. Better have the French windows shut, I think.'

Bertie closed and fastened them, while the others, with many groans and complaints, meandered out into the hall. 'Chair here for me. One here for you. One here for the witness,' said Carstairs, swiftly arranging them.

He then went across to the door and opened it.

'Come in, Bing,' he said.

'Just a moment,' interrupted Mrs Bradley. 'What are you going to ask them? We haven't settled on any questions.' She hissed the last sentence in a conspiratorial manner which was almost too much for Carstairs' gravity.

'The Lord will provide,' said he, with his whimsical smile.

'Come along, then, Mr Bing,' cried Mrs Lestrange Bradley. 'Sit on that chair, please. Mr Carstairs will ask questions and I will write down the answers.'

'Now, are you two serious about this, or not?' demanded Alastair, seating himself as directed. 'I mean, you are going to talk about Mountjoy, I suppose?'

'Yes,' said Carstairs. 'At least,' he added, 'Mrs Bradley is, but I am to start the ball rolling.'

'Fire away,' said Alastair resignedly. 'What do you want to know?'

'First,' said Carstairs, eyeing his host very deliberately, 'tell me why all the people in this house (I except the servants and myself) are so light-heartedly unaffected by what is, after all, an exceedingly tragic affair. They give up their tennis, and they think it indecent to be noisy, but all the same——'

'I—I don't follow you,' stammered Alastair Bing, going rather pale. 'How do you mean, Carstairs?'

Carstairs spoke with even greater seriousness.

'The death of Mountjoy was sudden, and, in a sense, mysterious,' he said. 'But equally mysterious, I think, is the almost incredible effect it has had on nearly everybody here. You almost all seem, somehow, relieved rather than horrified that this unfortunate woman should have met her death. And it is an attitude which requires explanation.'

Alastair Bing had stiffened angrily during Carstairs' speech, and he now eyed his friend with a certain amount of coldness.

'And so do your remarks require explanation, my dear Carstairs,' he said. 'What, exactly, are you attempting to insinuate?'

'Come now, Bing,' said Carstairs, as tactfully as he could. 'You mustn't take it like that. I say it is strange that nobody seems to mourn poor Mountjoy.'

'Do you yourself?' sneered Alastair.

Carstairs said quietly, 'I mean to avenge her death. Aren't you going to help me?'

'If helping you includes answering a number of idiotic and impertinent questions, I most certainly am not!' snapped Alastair. 'I didn't like Mountjoy, and I don't mind who knows it. In fact, I think the knowledge is common property. Of course, his—I should say, *her* death came as a shock to me, a great shock. But we never got on together. That last little piffling dispute we had about the ancient earthwork on the old golf course was nothing, and I bear no malice, of course. But Mountjoy has said things to me—things about archaeology, you know—in a way which has made me long to strike him—her, I mean—to the ground. I have felt—I won't deny it—I have felt passions rise within me which nothing but bloodletting would soothe. And I do not intend to mourn her. I am *not* sorry that she is dead, but the whole thing is a confounded nuisance, especially if it does turn but to be—well, not an accident.'

He paused. The flush died from his face. He smiled in a half-shamed manner at Carstairs and Mrs Bradley.

'Well, how do you like that for a confession?' he said. 'I feel better-tempered already. Poor Mountjoy,' he added.

Carstairs stroked his chin and reflected. At last he said: 'Thanks very much, Bing. Do you mind going out now, and sending in Dorothy Clark?'

'Dorothy?' Alastair began to bristle again. 'Look here, Carstairs, I won't have that child upset. She was in a bad motor smash before she came down here, and her nerves are in a terrible state. She really must not be harassed.'

Carstairs shrugged his shoulders. 'She knows something about Mountjoy's death,' he said significantly.

'What makes you say that?' demanded Alastair fiercely.

Mrs Bradley interposed.

'Let me talk to Dorothy. I won't upset her nerves,' she said in dulcet tones.

'Well, if you think it necessary,' Alastair began.

'I do think so,' interrupted Mrs Bradley.

'Very well. You are a psycho-analyst and ought to understand what you are about,' said Alastair grudgingly. 'Do you want her at once?'

'Yes, please,' Carstairs and Mrs Bradley answered,

both speaking at the same moment. 'Oh, half a minute,' Carstairs went on immediately. 'Bing, what do you know about Mountjoy's people?'

Alastair frowned thoughtfully.

'Carstairs,' he said, 'what is at the bottom of all this? What is the conclusion you have come to about Mountjoy's death? Do you still think it was murder?'

'I don't know what to say, Bing,' Carstairs answered truthfully. 'I am certain it was no accident which caused her death. That is all. I wondered whether we could find anything in her past life which might throw light on the mystery.'

'What evidence have you in support of your conclusions, apart from what we discussed yesterday morning?' asked Alastair.

'Plenty of evidence,' answered Carstairs. 'Enough, at any rate, to satisfy myself that matters cannot be left as they are.'

'Then,' said Alastair Bing determinedly, 'the best thing you can do is to lay your suspicions before the police. It is your duty as a citizen to invoke the aid of the law if you think that suspicious circumstances surround the death of my guest.'

'I am not at all anxious to call in the police,' Carstairs replied mildly. 'And I'll tell you why.'

He held up a protesting hand to stay the flood of words which the choleric Bing seemed about to pour upon his ears, and continued gravely:

'I believe that Mountjoy was murdered. I believe

someone in this house killed her. And, what is more, I believe I know now who the murderer is!'

While Alastair Bing, bereft of speech for once, gazed helplessly at him, Mrs Lestrange Bradley slipped quietly from the room.

Chapter Six

The Key to the Mystery

'INFORM the police, of course, if you think it well to do so,' Carstairs went on. 'I must say that to shift the responsibility of my knowledge on to the shoulders best trained to bear it would relieve me not a little. But be warned by me, and do not call in the police hastily.'

'What do you know?' cried Alastair Bing hoarsely. Carstairs shook his head.

'I prefer not to say. You know as much about this affair as I do, and all that I have deduced, you also may deduce, if you care to do so.'

'Oh, you mean that you don't really know anything,' observed Alastair Bing, looking relieved.

'Bing,' said Carstairs, 'I don't know anything more about this case than you knew about the Roman villa where you found that piece of broken tessellated pavement last summer. Do you remember? And yet, I recollect that you reconstructed that villa very creditably, and wrote a learned and lengthy treatise on the subject, with, I repeat, no more data than those few tiles you found. Am I right?'

Alastair's face brightened.

'I was personally complimented by Bethermeyr himself,' said he triumphantly. 'He was most enthusiastic.'

'And rightly so, I feel sure,' said Carstairs warmly. 'Well, but you see my point, don't you?'

'No,' snapped Bing, in his courteous way.

'It is this. I have found my few tiles also. They are, in this case, the open window; the unlocked door; the disappearing stool; the stool which re-appeared, but in the wrong bathroom; the rightful stool, which had been soiled and was afterwards cleaned with turpentine that its evidence might be rendered void, and last, but not least, the little pot of dark green paint which someone kicked over on the balcony. Didn't you notice the stain when we were up there this morning? Then, of course, there is——'

'The missing watch,' said Mrs Bradley, re-appearing with the suddenness of the Cheshire cat and with much the same sort of grin on her face.

'What?' cried Carstairs, surprised into forgetting the rest of the sentence.

'Missing watch? What missing watch? I didn't know anybody had lost a watch. Why wasn't I told?' said Alastair Bing.

Mrs Bradley's evil grin changed to an expression of innocent gravity.

'Only my little joke,' she informed them calmly.

'Well, Mr Bing, have you said anything exciting or amusing whilst I have been absent?'

'I am going to call in the police,' snapped Alastair. 'That's what I said, and that's what I intend to do. I'll send for them at once. I refuse to have my house turned into a Sherlock Holmes' paradise.'

So saying, he went out, slamming the door behind him.

Immediately he had gone, Mrs Bradley delved into a capacious skirt-pocket, the flap of which was usually concealed by her jumper, and produced a gentleman's silver watch.

'Poor Alastair,' she remarked, laying the watch on the mantelpiece, 'I thought he would go when I came in. I cannot help sympathizing with him over the private detective business. But it was so necessary that he should go, wasn't it? Do you recognize this watch, Mr Carstairs?'

Carstairs opened the back of the watch, and then, after the most cursory glance inside, shut it with a snap and laid it down.

'It's Mountjoy's, of course,' he said. 'What about it?'

Mrs Bradley sat down and composed her skirt before replying. Then she said: 'That watch was not in Mountjoy's bedroom after her death. It could not be found, I know, because I looked for it.'

'I am afraid I don't follow,' said Carstairs apologetically.

'Of course you don't,' said Mrs Bradley conclusively. 'Why should you?'

Carstairs gazed at her until she laughed.

'Oh, I'm not mad. Not the least little bit in the world,' she hastened to assure him. 'But I don't think I had better explain about the watch.'

'It doesn't matter what you explain to me,' Carstairs countered swiftly, but without a smile. 'You see, I think I know.'

Mrs Bradley, who seemed about to commence another remark, checked herself, and avoided his eyes.

'So you know what I know,' said Carstairs gloomily. 'Well, I'm glad, in a way, because perhaps you'll tell me what on earth we are going to do about it now that we *do* know.'

'Nothing,' said Mrs Bradley quietly.

'Nothing! But, my dear lady——'

She nodded rapidly two or three times, looking more like some cruel but sagacious bird than ever. 'Don't trouble to say it,' she observed, in the same tone of almost hypnotic calmness. 'I know all about it. It was murder, and if we did our duty as good citizens we should take steps immediately to ensure that the murderer was apprehended. If we don't perform this perfectly plain and straightforward duty, we are accessories after the fact—that is to say, persons who have given tacit consent to a crime by helping to shield the murderer.'

Carstairs grinned, but the troubled expression did not leave his face.

'Go on, please,' he said.

'I am going to tell you where I found the watch,' said Mrs Bradley confidentially. She glanced to right and left, and then behind her, emitted a hoarse gurgle which might have signified amusement, relief, or indigestion, and finally murmuring, with a kind of solemn rapture in her voice:

'It was at the bottom of the toilet-jug on Mountjoy's washing-stand. I can't understand why Eleanor doesn't introduce some newer fashions in furniture,' she added, as an abrupt and inconsequential afterthought. 'These antiquated toilet sets—abominable!'

She paused, as though she expected Carstairs to make some remark, but he remained silent.

'The jug was three-quarters full of water,' she added.

Carstairs shook himself, as though he and not the silver watch had emerged from the jug, and turned upon his informant a very puzzled gaze.

'Why ever did he—I mean she—keep a watch in the toilet-jug?' he asked solemnly. 'Or didn't you say that? Am I imagining you said it? It seems so utterly idiotic.'

'You're getting warm,' said Mrs Bradley, with her horrid cackling laugh. 'Put another word in place of idiotic, and I think you've hit it.'

'Idiotic?' Carstairs pursed his lips. 'Idiotic—another word for idiotic?'

He smote the table.

'Mad!' he cried. 'Mountjoy was mad, and it wasn't a murder, after all, thank goodness, but a suicide. Oh, I'm so glad you found that watch.'

'Are you?' asked Mrs Bradley, in a peculiar tone. She paused. 'I hate to undeceive you,' she added, at length, 'but it was not a suicide. It was most certainly a murder, and not Mountjoy, but the murderer, was the mad person.'

'Oh?' said Carstairs. 'Well——' He, too, paused.

'Please go on,' said Mrs Bradley. 'Or shall I finish your sentence for you?'

'I don't think even you could manage to do that,' he laughed. 'But go on, if you think you know the rest.'

'Well,' said Mrs Bradley, promptly accepting the challenge, 'you were going to say that, if I am right, then your conclusion as to the murderer's identity must be wrong.'

'Good heavens!' cried Carstairs. 'Is it clairvoyance?'

'Merely applied psychology,' replied Mrs Bradley, grinning. 'So now do tell me who you thought it was, and when you made up your mind about it.'

'I thought it was you,' said Carstairs, without a smile. 'And I came to that conclusion while I was talking to Bing just before you had slipped out of the room. It came upon me like a flash, and hit me clean between the eyes.'

Mrs Bradley cackled with joy. 'Oh, how too gorgeous!' she cried, with unaffected delight. 'And when, pray, did you conclude that you were mistaken?'

'Well, about two seconds ago.' He sighed. 'And I'm glad.'

'But why me? Although I am awfully flattered. It really was rather a neat method of putting out of the way a person one disliked. Only—*I* should not have forgotten that I'd left the bathroom window wide open. Besides'—she measured herself beside Carstairs—'I am not *quite* long enough in the leg for that climb. I tried it this morning before anyone was up, and found I couldn't quite manage it. I'll show you, if you have any lingering doubts.'

Carstairs shook his head.

'A very obvious point which would certainly have occurred to me later, when I had had time to think over my conclusions,' he said gravely. 'But I assure you I am absolutely convinced now that you did not take Mountjoy's life. You see, you are not mad, and you assure me that the murderer was.'

'*My* assurance ought to carry no weight,' said Mrs Bradley, laughing. 'What you really mean is that another aspect of the matter has struck you, and this new aspect leads to a conclusion which could not involve me—at least, not to the extent of my being implicated in the crime.'

'How the deuce do you do it?' asked Carstairs, half in awe, half in amusement.

Mrs Bradley waved her hand non-committally.

'You see,' Carstairs went on, 'whichever way you turn, you come up against this snag: who had a *motive* for killing Mountjoy? I can't see that anybody had—anybody in this house, I mean. And I'm positive it *was* somebody in this house who drowned that poor woman. Nothing will convince me to the contrary.'

'Poor—woman,' said Mrs Bradley. 'Poor—woman.'

She looked at Carstairs expectantly, but he returned her gaze with a blank, inquiring stare.

She grimaced, and shrugged her shoulders.

'A nod or a wink——' she said significantly.

Carstairs laughed.

'Yes, I'm afraid I'm a blind horse indeed, this time,' he said.

There was a sudden sharp knocking.

'Come in,' called Carstairs, and Dorothy put a laughing face round the edge of the door.

'We're all patiently waiting for our turns,' she said. 'And you've made poor Mr Bing quite cross. Oh, and the Chief Constable of the county is coming to dinner, and will probably stay a day or two. Do have us in and question us. I'm dying to have my turn.'

'Come along in, then,' said Mrs Bradley briskly. 'Sit there, facing the light. Take this paper and pencil, and write the exact opposite of every word I say.'

When the little farce had been played out, and Dorothy dismissed, Carstairs raised his eyebrows inquiringly.

'Some clever creature will give the show away at dinner, either accidentally or on purpose,' said Mrs Bradley, in answer to his unspoken question. 'And once the Chief Constable gets wind of our suspicions there will be no peace for anybody, so you and I, my friend, may as well go out of business. I am rather glad.'

'I am not,' said Carstairs decidedly. 'I had set my heart on unravelling the mystery, and, if you are right, and the police decide to conduct an inquiry, I shall not get much more opportunity for finding out things.'

Mrs Bradley held up one finger. 'Listen! There goes the gong for lunch,' she said. 'I would just like to say this: In your opinion, which is the most remarkable feature of the whole case?'

'Well, apart from the murder itself,' replied Carstairs slowly, and appearing to ruminate as he spoke, 'I suppose the fact that Mountjoy turned out to be a woman is the queerest thing about it.'

'Yes, that was queer,' said Mrs Bradley, in a curiously inconclusive tone.

'You don't help me very much,' said Carstairs, whimsically smiling.

'I don't intend to, my friend,' she answered; 'but if the same idea as has occurred to me does not occur to you before tomorrow morning, I shall be very much surprised.'

Carstairs opened the door for her, and stood gazing after her retreating form as she walked to the staircase.

'Hum! And if I weren't convinced that you are *not* the murderer, I should be equally convinced that you *are*, you extraordinary woman,' he said under his breath. 'I wonder whether you are trying to lead me up the garden with your hints and insinuations, or whether you are trying to make me see something which, left to myself, I should overlook. Mountjoy was a man, and the man changed into a woman, and nobody—yes! By jove! Somebody did! Oho! So that's what you meant, Mrs Bradley, did you. Oh my hat! That puts a new construction on the crime with a vengeance!'

Chapter Seven

Investigation

LUNCH was a cheerful meal. Light and even frivolous conversation seemed to be expected from everyone. Carstairs and Mrs Bradley incurred a good deal of chaff from the two young men on the lengthy and boring game they had invented. Dorothy was cross-questioned as to her share in the proceedings, but no one seemed to care about interrogating Alastair Bing, who alone appeared unable to throw off his heavy mood and join in the pleasant badinage.

'Did they put you through it, Dorothy?' inquired Garde solicitously.

'Rather,' replied Dorothy, smiling demurely at Mrs Bradley. 'It was awful. I shouldn't take your turn if I were you. All one's purple past is dragged out into the light of day.'

'We'll send Eleanor in next,' chuckled Eleanor's brother. 'What about it, old bean?'

'I do wish, Garde,' said Eleanor primly, 'that you would not address me in that ridiculous way.

As to playing this rather childish game, I have no objection at all, but I do think that so soon after Mr Mountjoy's death, I should not be expected to seem too light-hearted, although I have no wish to deprive others of their simple pleasures.'

Garde, turning his eyes heavenwards and then winking wickedly at Dorothy, attacked his food with a healthily boyish appetite.

The meal over, Alastair Bing drew Carstairs aside and said: 'I have invited the Chief Constable to stay here for a day or two, and during his visit I shall request him to make a quite informal preliminary investigation. The police doctor will also be present, although not in his official capacity, of course, and I shall get him to examine the body. Does that satisfy you?'

'I suppose I must leave you to proceed as you think best, Bing,' Carstairs replied moodily. 'But I wish you had been advised by me, and had allowed me to conclude my own investigation of the matter before you called in outside assistance.'

'Oh, I can't help your vanity being hurt,' Alastair replied, with unnecessary rudeness. 'If there is a mystery about the woman's death, it must be cleared up by the authorities. There is no sense in your muddling about at it, you know. Besides, the whole thing will be quite informal. I have come to the conclusion that there is nothing in your theories, but the Chief Constable will clear the whole matter up.'

Carstairs laughed good-humouredly.

'Have it your own way,' he said. 'I hope you

won't be sorry; that is all. But I don't imagine that the Chief Constable will be *able* to make an informal investigation. There is such a thing as his duty to be considered.'

Alastair Bing snorted.

In due course, but not until after lunch next day, the Chief Constable and the police doctor, a friend of the family, inspected the body and looked round the bathroom. Then, the doctor having concluded his examination, the men, superintended by Alastair, all descended the stairs, and passed into the library.

'Well, doctor?' said the Chief Constable, 'what's your opinion?'

'Oh, death due to drowning, the same as my colleague pronounced. Incidentally, I should say there was no weakness of the heart.'

'Is that absolutely certain?'

'Well, there is no doubt at all in my mind.'

'Thank you. Now, then, Mr Bing, where is the gentleman with the theories?'

'Mr Carstairs? You'd like to see him?'

'If you please.'

Alastair rang the bell.

'Ask Mr Carstairs please to step this way.'

Carstairs was greeted with the official twinkle; he smiled in return, and seated himself.

'Well, Mr Carstairs,' said the Chief Constable, 'would you mind explaining exactly your reasons for supposing Miss Mountjoy's death to have been anything but an accidental one?'

Carstairs put forth briefly and concisely, as his

scientific training suggested, his reasons, deductions, and conclusions, and the Chief Constable took notes.

'Is this it, Mr Carstairs?' he asked, and read the notes aloud.

'That's it, Sir Joseph.'

'Hum!' the great man glanced at him quizzically. 'Mathematician, Mr Carstairs?'

'A little of one, I suppose,' Carstairs answered.

'Ye-es. Um! Quite so. Who found the body?'

'I did,' answered Alastair Bing. 'An unpleasant, undignified business.'

'Were you alone?'

'No. My son, Carstairs here, and a couple of servants were there too.'

'Just recount the circumstances, will you?'

'Well, we were at dinner——'

'Time?'

'About a quarter-past eight, I should think. Yes, about then.'

'Thank you. Yes, you were at dinner. All of you?'

'Well, of course, Mountjoy was not there, so we began without him—her.'

'That did not strike you as unusual?'

'What did not? Oh, that she was not there? No. She would get a working fit sometimes, and would not come down to meals. We never worried him—her—of course. Just sent up some food on a tray.'

'Oh, she had been staying with you for some time?'

'About six weeks. There was talk of an understanding between the dead person and my daughter. Of course, we all thought that Mountjoy was a man. Incidentally, I am anxious that the truth about Mountjoy's sex be kept from the knowledge of my daughter.'

'A man? Oh, yes, Mr Carstairs indicated that the deceased had masqueraded as a man. Did no one suspect the truth about her sex?'

'I think not. In fact, I am sure nobody did. We had always—I mean it would never have occurred to any of us——'

'No, I suppose not. Quite so. And your daughter? She never suspected either?'

'Oh no. Surely not. She is a very quiet, modest girl. The whole affair must be a very great shock to her.'

'Undoubtedly. Indeed, yes. Well, now, you were all at dinner except Mountjoy. What happened next?'

'The butler came and spoke to me. He said Mountjoy was still in the bathroom. That his man had knocked and could obtain no answer.'

'His man?'

'Well, that is to say, he is my man really, but I lend him to any men guests who don't bring their personal servants.'

'Oh, so he valeted Mountjoy?'

'Well, no. Mountjoy never required much assistance. The man would lay out a clean shirt, perhaps, and place the suit ready for her to dress, and turn bath-taps on, and so forth, but he was never required to render the more personal services. Of course, that is all quite comprehensible now.'

'Yes, yes. The sex business, of course. I should like to see that man a moment, if I may.'

Alastair rang the bell.

'Ask Parsons to step this way a moment.'

Two minutes later the quiet, pale valet stood in the doorway.

'You sent for me, sir?' he asked, addressing Alastair Bing.

'Sit down,' said his employer, pointing to a chair.

The man closed the door noiselessly, and then did as he was asked to.

'Attend to the Chief Constable, Parsons, and answer him as clearly as you can,' said Alastair magisterially.

'Very good, sir.' The man cleared his throat in an embarrassed way.

'Parsons,' began Sir Joseph, consulting his notes, 'you remember turning on the bath-taps for Mr Mountjoy on the evening of his death, don't you?'

'Yes, sir.'

'Did you turn on both taps at once?'

'No, sir.'

'The hot tap?'

'At first, sir. I then tested the temperature of the water with a bath thermometer, and reduced the heat, by means of the cold tap, to the number of degrees specified by Mr Mountjoy, who was very particular in such matters.'

'Ah! Now you wouldn't remember, I suppose, exactly how high up the bath the level of the water was when you had finished your elaborate preparations, would you?'

'Yes, sir.'

'Splendid!' said the Chief Constable, pushing his chair back from the table. 'Well, come up with me and show me, will you?'

'Very good, sir.'

The man looked at Alastair Bing, was reassured by a nod, and, opening the door for the four men, for the doctor came too, he followed them out, and closed the door noiselessly behind him.

'Now, then,' began Sir Joseph, when they reached the fatal bathroom, 'how far up did the water reach?'

Parsons, without moving a muscle of his face, put his finger on a spot about nine inches from the top of the bath.

The Chief Constable took out a folding pocket-ruler, and gravely measured the distance.

'Nine point three inches down,' he observed. 'Do you note that, Brenner?' he went on, turning to the doctor, who nodded in his bored way.

'But look here!' Carstairs was nearly dancing with excitement.

The Chief Constable smiled paternally.

'Just a minute, Mr Carstairs,' he said, and turned again to the man Parsons.

'Parsons,' he continued, 'wouldn't it surprise you very much to hear that Mr Mountjoy was no man, but a woman?'

'No, sir.'

'Oh? Why not?'

'It has been common talk in the servants' hall, sir, since the poor'—he paused for a fraction of a second—'the poor gentleman's death, sir.'

'Hum! All right. That's all I want you for at present.'

'Thank you, sir.'

The man glanced at Alastair Bing, received the usual nod, and slipped unobtrusively away.

'A model witness,' said the Chief Constable gravely. 'Let us go downstairs, gentlemen.'

'Just a moment, though,' cried Carstairs, unable to contain himself any longer.

'Ah, yes, Mr Carstairs. You wanted to say something. I am sorry I interrupted you before, but I thought it better not to say too much in front of Parsons, discreet fellow though I believe him to be.'

'Oh, don't apologize,' said Carstairs, laughing. 'I ought to possess more self-control. But, you know, he was quite wrong about the level of the water.'

'Was he?' The Chief Constable chuckled delightedly.

'Hopelessly out. The water came right up to the overflow pipe. That's at least three inches higher than he said.'

The Chief Constable produced his ruler again, and solemnly measured.

'To the bottom of these holes, five point one inches down,' he declared. 'Got that, Brenner?' The doctor nodded.

'Let us go downstairs,' said Sir Joseph. 'This becomes interesting.'

'Well,' said Alastair Bing, when the four of them were again seated in the library.

'Well, now,' said the Chief Constable, 'these water-levels. Very interesting, as I say, unless one of you two is mistaken, Mr Carstairs.'

'Well, I know I am not mistaken,' declared Carstairs firmly, 'because I distinctly remember thinking when we lifted the body out of the bath, how foolish it was of anyone liable to fainting fits to have the bath so full of water. That was immediately before I had had time to formulate my theory that Mountjoy had been murdered. I was concluding that death was due to sudden heart-failure.'

'Ah, yes. And the displacement of the body? You didn't notice that, I suppose?'

'Not exactly, of course, but it couldn't have been the four point two inches discrepancy between Parsons' estimate and mine, could it? After all, Mountjoy was not more than five feet five inches tall, and she was quite slim; rather thin, in fact.'

'Hum! Of course, you see where this leads us, gentlemen?'

'No,' said Alastair Bing morosely.

Carstairs wrinkled his brow.

'You are assuming that Parsons' information was correct, then?' he said.

'Yes, I am,' replied the Chief Constable. 'All that thermometer business would give him ample opportunity of noticing the height of the water, you see.'

'I see. And you trust my memory?'

'I do, especially considering the circumstantial evidence you yourself can supply in support of it.'

'Well, assuming that we are both right——'

'Exactly,' said the Chief Constable. 'It means that between Parsons' exit from the bathroom and your entry into it, some person or persons unknown turned on the taps and so raised the height of the bath water.'

'The murderer!' cried Carstairs triumphantly.

'Exactly,' said the Chief Constable again. 'At least, I think we are justified in assuming so.'

'Well, I don't,' said Alastair Bing abruptly. 'I think that is a most unwarrantable conclusion to come to. Of course the person who turned on the tap was Mountjoy herself! The water was too hot, or too cold, or something, and she altered the temperature to suit herself. Done it myself, many a time.'

'What, when you have taken the trouble beforehand to supply the valet with a thermometer and have given him special instructions about the temperature of the water?'

'Oh, thermometers! Lot of rubbish,' said Alastair Bing violently.

'I dare say we can settle the matter,' said Sir Joseph soothingly.

'Not on my account,' began Alastair. But the Chief Constable interrupted him.

'Can we have Parsons up again?' he asked.

Alastair Bing rang the bell.

'Now, Parsons,' said Sir Joseph, when the man appeared, 'I want you to think very carefully. What time was it when you heard Mr Mountjoy turn on the taps again?'

The man frowned in thought. Then his face cleared.

'It was at seventeen minutes past seven, sir. I remember the time, because Mr Mountjoy was what you might call one of those quick bathers, sir. In and out and dry and half dressed inside a quarter of an hour, he was. And that's why I was surprised that he took such a long time over his bath that particular evening. Getting quite worried, I was, when I heard the taps turned on. That reassured me.'

'Taps?' said the Chief Constable quickly. 'Both taps?'

'Yes, sir. Both taps at once. It is perfectly easy to tell the difference the noise a single tap makes from that made by the two going together. Besides, I thought I heard water running away down the waste-pipe as well.'

'Of course, one couldn't swear to that,' said the Chief Constable thoughtfully. 'But it is interesting. All right, Parsons. Go on. This sound reassured you.'

'Yes, sir. I was beginning to wonder if anything had happened, you see.'

'What exactly do you mean by that?'

'Oh, nothing sinister, sir. Only a young athletic gentleman I used to be valet to contracted a weak heart, and would faint in his bath reg'lar. I always had to be in there with him. Never dared leave him in the bath a minute alone.'

'I see. And when you heard the taps running, you were relieved about Mr Mountjoy?'

'Well, relieved, yes, sir. But puzzled too.'

'Oh?'

'Yes, sir. It was such an unusual thing for Mr Mountjoy to do. A gentleman as liked his bath got just ready, proper temperature and all, so that he could just pop in and out of it, wasn't very likely to stop in the bath half an hour or more and then start putting in more water, was he, sir, if you take my meaning?'

'Your meaning is most clear,' said the Chief Constable. 'Now, one more question, and I have done. *Who was it that came out of that bathroom directly afterwards, carrying the bathroom stool?*'

'Directly after what, sir?' The man's face was innocence itself, as he turned his mild eyes upon the Chief Constable.

'After you heard the taps turned on, man!'

'Why, nobody, sir. How could they? There was nobody in there except Mr Mountjoy, and he, poor gentleman, couldn't come out, could he?'

The Chief Constable fixed his eyes on the man's impassive face, and asked coldly, 'Can you be certain nobody came out?'

'I sat watching the door from just inside Mr Mountjoy's bedroom, sir, as I always did when he took his bath, so as to be ready for him at once, should he require my services when he was dressing.'

'And you sat there all the time?'

The man made a slight gesture of recollection.

'I did go away for about three minutes, now I think of it, sir,' he said.

'Ah!' Carstairs glanced excitedly at the Chief Constable.

'Oh? Why?' Sir Joseph's tone was impersonal, but his eyes were gleaming hard.

'Miss Eleanor had asked me to speak to Mander about the flowers, sir.'

'An odd request, wasn't it?'

'Yes, sir.'

'What did you think about it?'

'I am not paid to think about my instructions, sir, but merely to act upon them.'

'Very well said,' chuckled the Chief Constable. 'Well, now, Parsons, would it surprise you very much to be arrested for the wilful murder of Mr Mountjoy?'

The man's figure stiffened involuntarily, but his perfect training caused his face to remain impassive, and his voice smooth, as he replied: 'Yes, sir.'

'It would, eh? Now, why?'

'Because I didn't do it, sir.'

Chapter Eight

The Murderer?

'No,' said the Chief Constable, 'I don't think you did, Parsons. But somebody must have done it, and, if it wasn't you, I wonder who the deuce it could have been? About that message, now. When did you receive it?'

'Immediately after lunch, sir.'

'Who from?'

'From Miss Eleanor herself, sir. Her words, I think, were these: "Oh, you might just tell Mander that I've ordered more roses from William for this evening, Parsons." (William being the head gardener, sir.) "He had better see about them at once." Well, I forgot the message altogether, sir, but as I sat there waiting for Mr Mountjoy I recollected it, sir, and thought I might just have time to run downstairs and speak to Mander while Mr Mountjoy was drying himself.'

'I see,' said the Chief Constable musingly. 'Thank you, Parsons. You have been of tremendous assistance.'

'Thank you, sir.' And the mild man closed the door noiselessly behind himself.

'There goes an innocent manservant of impeccable bearing and behaviour, or one of the cleverest criminals unhung,' said the Chief Constable thoughtfully. 'And for the life of me I can't tell which.'

'You don't mean that *you* think Mountjoy was murdered?' gasped Alastair Bing, before anyone else could speak. The Chief Constable gazed at him in surprise.

'I haven't the slightest doubt of it,' he answered quietly. 'And I shall make it my business to see that a correct verdict is returned by the coroner's jury. The whole matter must be very thoroughly investigated, gentlemen.'

'I would stake my life on Parsons' innocence,' declared Carstairs firmly. 'He is no murderer.'

'Murder is a queer crime,' the Chief Constable said musingly. 'I've known cases——' He paused, and allowed his eyes to travel down the page of notes he had been making.

'Crime committed before seven-thirty,' he read. 'Yes, that is your dinner-hour, I think you said, and Mountjoy was the only person who was not accounted for, was she not? At what time did Mountjoy enter the bathroom? Does either of you gentlemen know?'

'Yes,' answered Carstairs. 'It would have been at ten minutes to seven. I asked Parsons that question yesterday, and he was quite certain on the point.'

'Good! Well, now, gentlemen, you see the big difficulty, don't you?'

'Motive,' said Carstairs succinctly.

'Exactly. An adequate motive, in ninety-nine cases out of a hundred, will hang a man. Now, who in this house had such a strong motive for wishing Mountjoy out of the way that he went to the length of murdering her?'

'But just a minute, Sir Joseph!' cried Dr Brenner. 'Aren't you going a little too fast? I can't see that it is established beyond doubt that it was somebody in this house. Might it not equally have been some enemy of the dead woman, who perhaps had tracked her here? I know every person in this house reasonably well, and I assure you that I cannot imagine one of them being capable of committing a horrible crime.'

'I sympathize with your feelings, sir, and with your objections,' said the Chief Constable, 'but consider the facts. If we accept the evidence of that manservant, Parsons, which at present, in order to form a working hypothesis, we are compelled to do, the facts are these: Some person or persons knew the ways of the house sufficiently well, not only to make a beautifully timed entry into the bathroom where the unfortunate woman was (this house contains more than one bathroom, Brenner, you remember, and yet the murderer picked out the one habitually used by the deceased), but also to seize the few minutes that the valet was absent from his post to walk safely out of the said bathroom——'

'Carrying the soiled bathroom stool,' interrupted Carstairs. 'He, she, or they then walked up a flight of stairs, deposited the soiled stool in the next-floor bathroom, and——'

'This is the first I've heard of this,' cried the Chief Constable. 'Are you sure? Just give me the facts again, slowly.'

'I can't prove it,' replied Carstairs, 'but I'm sure it happened.' And he recounted his conversation with Mrs Bradley and his subsequent discovery that one of the bathroom stools had recently been cleaned.

'Hum! Very interesting, that. Miss Bing, you say, restored the stool to the first-floor bathroom?'

'Yes. But, of course, that doesn't necessarily connect her with the crime, does it?'

'Oh, surely not,' laughed the Chief Constable, while Alastair Bing, at the mention of his daughter's name in such a connection, bristled angrily and showed signs of bursting into loud explosions of indignation.

'Of course,' Sir Joseph continued soothingly, 'Miss Bing, as a good housekeeper, would supervise the arrangement of the furnishings, and would see that anything soiled or marked was immediately cleaned. But we need not go into that at present. There are just one or two little points I want cleared up. The first one is to ascertain which persons in the house (including the servants) definitely can be acquitted of suspicion. I'm afraid I must trouble you to have them up one by one for this purpose, Bing. The servants first.'

The examination of the domestic staff and the testing of their several alibis did not take very long. The Chief Constable, firm but tactful, encouraging the timid and keeping the loquacious within the bounds of the inquiry, established without a doubt the fact that between the most extreme points of time in which the crime could have been committed all were engaged in their several duties, and could produce two or more witnesses to prove it. Even the man Parsons was able to find a first ally in Dorothy Clark, who had seen him waiting about for Mountjoy on the threshold of the bedroom, a second one in Mrs Bradley's maid, who had been sent down on to the next floor to see if her mistress had dropped a lace handkerchief on the stairs, and, in addition, the valet's story of his going to the butler to tell him about the flowers received ample confirmation from that functionary, and also from the knife and boot boy, who had (he now confessed with tears) jeered at Parsons as he passed by the pantry on his way to the kitchen.

'So that's that,' said the Chief Constable, slapping his note-book down on the table with an air of finality. 'And now, Bing, for the more delicate operation of interviewing your guests and family.'

Alastair rang the bell, and moodily resumed his seat.

'I'll step outside, shall I?' said Carstairs obligingly.

'If you will be so kind.'

When he had gone, the Chief Constable turned in a businesslike manner to Bing.

'Well, now, Bing,' he said encouragingly. 'Where were you between the hours of six-fifty and seven-twenty-five on the evening of August the thirteenth? I have to ask you as a matter of form, you know.'

Alastair Bing pursed his lips and frowned.

'I suppose I was in my room, dressing for dinner,' he said.

'Do you know anybody who will bear witness to that?'

'Why, no. Of course not,' replied Alastair testily. 'I don't have the whole household in my bedroom to watch me dress for dinner.'

'By heavens, Brenner,' said the Chief Constable, slapping his knee, 'some intelligence has been used here!'

'You're right, Sir Joseph,' replied the doctor, with faint enthusiasm. 'A clever job.'

'You see the point, don't you, Bing?' the Chief Constable went on, turning again to Alastair.

'What?' said Alastair shortly.

'Well,' Sir Joseph good-humouredly explained, 'I expect nearly everybody will be in the same boat as yourself.'

'How do you mean?'

'Everybody was dressing for dinner. Nobody, probably, will be able to produce what I should call a water-tight alibi. See?'

'That's very interesting,' said Alastair Bing heavily.

'And now, can I trouble you to send in Mr Carstairs?' Sir Joseph went on.

Alastair walked out, and Carstairs took his place.

'Of course I haven't an alibi,' he laughed, before the Chief Constable could frame the question. 'Incidentally, we were all a bit late for dinner—all the men, I mean. The ladies managed as usual, of course.'

'You mean?'

'I mean Mountjoy was occupying that bathroom all the time. The rest of us had to make shift as best we could.'

'Ah, yes. Of course. Did none of you knock on the door, or do anything to attract her attention?'

'I couldn't say. I made a dive for the top-floor bathroom when I found the other was still occupied, and was lucky enough to grab it. Oh, Bertie Philipson met me coming out of it, but heaven knows what the time was. I just fell into my clothes and made a dash for it. Philipson was even later down than I was.'

'You mean, you might have had time to commit the murder and *then* go upstairs to the other bathroom?'

'Oh, yes, easily, I should imagine,' replied Carstairs cheerfully. 'But then, so would Philipson,' he added, laughingly.

'I know,' said Sir Joseph gloomily. 'That's just the difficulty. Nobody will have a complete alibi, unless one of the ladies happens to have had her maid with her all the time.'

This proved to be so in the case of Mrs Bradley, who was the very last person to be interviewed.

'Well, I suppose I can cross you off my list of suspects,' said the Chief Constable, smiling at her.

'Oh, don't do that, Sir Joseph!' cried Mrs Bradley kittenishly. 'I shall feel so lonely if you do. Besides, Mr Carstairs picked me out as the murderer.'

The Chief Constable laughed, closed his notebook, and rose.

'Well, I've seen everybody now, I take it,' he said.

Having all been interviewed, the entire houseparty and family were by this time gathered together in the study, and they all laughed and told him there were no more victims.

'Then,' he said, 'I must go, for all sorts of formalities have to be complied with. But don't imagine you've got rid of me altogether. I shall come again.'

He turned to Alastair Bing.

'We shall, of course, apply for an adjournment of the inquest after the formal evidence of identification and so on has been taken,' he said. 'Good-bye, Bing, I am terribly sorry this has happened. I'll make it my business to see that nobody is harassed more than is absolutely necessary, of course, but we must get to the bottom of the beastly business, whatever happens. Good-bye, and cheer up as much as you can.'

With which last friendly injunction, he drove away.

Carstairs joined Mrs Bradley in the garden.

'You haven't forgotten the cliff walk you promised to show me, have you?' she asked him.

Carstairs looked at her quizzically, and she laughed.

'Yes, that's it. You have guessed the guilty secret. I want to talk to you. And we daren't talk here.'

'No. Here comes young Philipson already,' said Carstairs, smiling at the young man as he came towards them over the beautiful, springy turf.

'I say, I feel all of a dither,' said Bertie, joining them. 'These little diversions may be all right for those of strong moral fibre, but my delicate constitution won't stand much more of it.'

'Of what?' asked Mrs Bradley. 'You don't mean that a young healthy male animal is upset because he's had to tell a policeman at what time during the evening of August the thirteenth he put his clean shirt on, and who saw him do it?'

'It's all very well to rot me, Mrs Bradley,' said Bertie, in an affectedly injured tone, 'but it *is* upsetting and unnerving to a sensitive nature like mine.'

'Well, you didn't give yourself away,' said Carstairs, laughing. 'Nobody thinks you did it.'

'I say, though——' Bertie's voice dropped, and he gave a cautious glance towards the verandah, where, sprawled in attitudes of ease, sat Garde and Dorothy. Their attention, however, was entirely engaged, so Bertie withdrew his gaze from the charming picture of their utter absorption in one another's conversation, and continued:

'I'd like to tell you people something, and then perhaps you'll advise me whether to tell that policeman Johnnie, or whether it is unimportant.'

Mrs Bradley and Carstairs looked as interested as they felt.

'Yes?' breathed Mrs Bradley.

'Well, it's only this——' Bertie gave another stealthy glance around him. 'You know what a devil of a time Mountjoy was in that bathroom?'

'Yes,' said Carstairs.

'Well, I waited and waited, you know, thinking every minute that he—she I mean—would emerge, until at last I got so fed up that I went and twisted at the handle of the door to hurry him up a bit.'

'Her,' said Mrs Bradley, under her breath.

'Yes, her. Well, do you know, I swear the door was locked then. The handle turned, but nothing else happened. I only shoved cautiously, of course, in case the place was still occupied, and then somebody inside squeaked out, "Don't come in!" Just like that. High-pitched, you know, and nervous. Well, of course I yelled, "Sorry!" and came away, and it was after that I met you, Mr Carstairs, on the floor above, coming out of the other bathroom.'

'Yes, I remember,' said Carstairs. 'But I don't quite see why you've told us your little yarn. Naturally, if Mountjoy was in the bath, she would shout to you not to enter the room, wouldn't she?'

'It wasn't Mountjoy's voice,' said Bertie quietly.

'What?'

'I'm sure it wasn't. Mountjoy's voice was low-pitched and rather harsh. But this voice was high and rather shrill. An absolute woman's voice, if you understand me. Scared, you know. I've heard women in an air-raid during the war speak like it. Quite unlike a man in a funk.'

'Well,' interpolated Mrs Bradley, 'that is quite comprehensible, I think. You startled Mountjoy badly, I expect, and so, in her terror lest you should enter and discover the secret that she had success-fully kept for so many years, she shrieked at you in her normal instead of in her disguised voice.'

'By Jove!' cried Bertie, 'I never thought of that! That would explain it, of course. Yes, that must be it. Jolly brainy of you to have thought that out, Mrs Bradley.'

'Opinions differ,' said Mrs Bradley dryly.

Some instinct prompted Carstairs to ask a question.

'Philipson,' he said; and then he hesitated, as if uncertain whether to continue or not.

'Yes?' said Bertie.

Thus prompted, Carstairs went on.

'When you heard that voice from the bathroom—a woman's voice, when you were expecting to hear the voice of Mountjoy—did it sound to you like the voice of anyone you know?'

Bertie frowned thoughtfully.

'Under the circumstances, Mr Carstairs, I don't know whether I am justified in answering that question,' he said slowly.

'Then you *have* answered it,' Carstairs pointed out.

'Oh, damn! Oh, I beg your pardon, Mrs Bradley!' the young man exclaimed. 'But so I have. Well, then, having gone so far——'

'Just one moment, Mr Philipson,' interrupted Mrs Bradley. 'Would you mind keeping the rest of that sentence until after tea?'

Carstairs and Bertie Philipson looked at her in mild surprise.

'I have my reasons,' she smiled. 'Do you mind, Mr Philipson?'

'Why, no, of course not. Not a bit,' Bertie hastened to assure her. 'Do you think I ought to tell the police after all, then?'

'Well, if you will be advised by me,' said Mrs Bradley, carefully choosing her words, 'I should say—not yet. It cannot help them, and might possibly even hinder them in the present state of the inquiry.'

'You know best, of course,' said Bertie, with his charming smile. 'I'll keep mum, then.'

'Do,' said Mrs Bradley approvingly. 'Don't mention it to anybody at all at present. You haven't done so, have you?'

'Rather not,' replied Bertie truthfully. 'Righto. Thanks very much.'

Then he left them, and walked towards the house.

'And now for our walk,' said Mrs Bradley, with such peculiar satisfaction in her tones that Carstairs felt compelled to ask:

'Has that young man's information any special bearing on the case?'

Mrs Bradley smiled horribly, and they passed out of the garden into the road.

For a quarter of an hour or so neither spoke. Then Carstairs said: 'Over this stile.'

They surmounted it, walked on over short grass for a hundred yards or so, and then found themselves on the top of cliffs facing the sea.

'Very charming,' said Mrs Bradley, with gracious appreciation of the view. 'Let us descend to the shore.'

A fairly precipitous but perfectly safe path brought them to sea-level, and, the tide being well out, although it had turned, they walked along the level sands.

'Delightful,' said Mrs Bradley, inhaling the fresh sea breezes as she walked by Carstairs' side.

'Very delightful,' he answered. 'But you didn't bring me all this way just to enjoy the sea air, did you? Come, talk to me, for my mind is enveloped in a thick fog. I do wish Alastair had said nothing to Sir Joseph about the wretched business. I am afraid now of what will be discovered.'

'So am I,' said Mrs Bradley, pausing in her stride.

'Queer about that voice young Philipson heard,' said Carstairs thoughtfully. 'I wonder if there is anything in it. Personally, I incline to the opinion that it must have been Mountjoy's own voice, as you first suggested.'

'Impossible,' said Mrs Bradley seriously, as she

dived into her capacious skirt-pocket and produced a tiny loose-leaf note-book. A tug at a silver chain which she wore around her neck brought into view a little silver pencil. 'Impossible,' she repeated, turning away from Carstairs and writing very rapidly on one of the dainty pages. 'He did not hear poor Mountjoy's voice, for the simple reason that she must have been dead by that time.'

'But your own perfectly plausible explanation of the matter!' cried Carstairs, surprised and bewildered.

'Merely given to put young Philipson off the scent,' smiled Mrs Bradley, as she removed the page from her note-book, carefully folded it, and handed it to Carstairs. 'When you began asking that question, I thought the fat was in the fire. You see, whatever happens, the guilty person must never know that anybody suspects anything. It would be fatal. And when I say fatal, I mean it. If my deductions are correct—and, as they are based on pure psychology, I do not suppose they will turn out to be at fault—we have to deal with a person who values life so little that she will stick at nothing——'

'She?' cried Carstairs in amazement. 'But surely this was not a woman's crime?'

'I think so. No, I will not deceive you, my friend. I am sure of it.'

'But the climb from balcony to window——'

'Not at all difficult. Young Philipson has done it; I could do it if I were an inch longer in the leg. You could do it; so could the two girls, who are both a couple to three inches taller than I am; the maids, with the exception of cook, who suffers with rheumatism, and Mary Peters, who is a trifle shorter than I am, could all have managed it.'

'Yes, but the amount of nerve required,' Carstairs began.

'We are thinking about a murderer, remember,' Mrs Bradley reminded him. 'I imagine that a person with nerve enough to commit a murder has nerve enough to climb from a balcony in order to do it.'

'Not always, I fancy,' Carstairs demurred. 'But allowing that your assumption is correct, how do you think the actual murder was committed? I have my own theory, of course,' he added, 'but I can't quite see the murderer as a woman, now that I am convinced you yourself are not——' He laughed and left the sentence unfinished. 'I'm certain now that it was a man's crime,' he concluded lamely.

'Well, I may be mistaken,' Mrs Bradley admitted. 'But I don't think I am. Look here. Who knew that Mountjoy was a woman?'

'Before her death?'

'Yes.'

'Why—no one.'

'Are you sure no one knew?'

Carstairs shrugged his shoulders.

'I don't want to think it out,' he confessed, smiling wryly at Mrs Bradley's triumphantly grinning face. 'But now, supposing it *was* a woman, how exactly did she commit the murder?'

'Quite simply. To begin with, I'll say this: I don't

believe she intended to murder Mountjoy when she climbed in at the bathroom window, although I do believe she regarded him—her with deadly hatred.'

'Hated Mountjoy? But Mountjoy was the most inoffensive person I have ever met,' cried Carstairs. 'I am sure you are following a false trail.'

'Am I?' Mrs Bradley smiled her saurian smile. 'I don't think I am. Surely you can put your finger on the person in the house who hated Mountjoy with the intense, bitter and never-ending hatred of one whose finest feelings, whose noblest emotions had been played with, mocked at, scorned, derided, lacerated?'

Mrs Bradley's voice rose high with excitement until it reached the last word. Then she drew a deep breath, and gazed expectantly at Carstairs. She chuckled ghoulishly as a great light suddenly dawned in his expression.

'Good God!' he almost whispered, in his intense interest and excitement. 'Of course! I see the point, now, of all that you hinted before. Do you know, that had never occurred to me for one single instant until you hinted at it before. And I don't believe it ever would,' he added honestly, 'if it had not been for you.'

'Let us go back to the house,' said Mrs Bradley abruptly.

They turned and retraced their steps in silence until they came within sight of the tall chimneys of Chayning Place.

Carstairs pointed to the beautiful old house.

'And you have been able to live under that roof, knowing what you have known all this time, and have spoken naturally and unaffectedly with everybody, and have sat at the same table with the murderer——'

He paused, and then shook his head. 'I couldn't have done it. I don't know what I shall do or say, as it is, when we encounter them all again in there.'

'You won't have to bear the burden of our knowledge for long,' Mrs Bradley said calmly. 'I think that what we know will soon be perfectly obvious to every member of that household. Poor, poor girl,' she added, with genuine sorrow and pity in her tones.

'Do you really mean that?' asked Carstairs, interested. 'I don't think I could ever sincerely pity a murderer.'

'We are all murderers, my friend,' said Mrs Bradley lugubriously. 'Some in deed and some in thought. That's the only difference, though.'

'Rather a considerable difference,' said Carstairs, putting into his tone a lightness which he was very far from feeling.

'Morally, there is no difference at all,' said Mrs Bradley more briskly. 'Some have the courage of their convictions. Others have not. That's all. This one saw her opportunity and took it. A person occupying that bath normally has his back to the window, his face to the door. The murderer entered by the window, talked softly but quite naturally to Mountjoy, descended on to the floor by means of the bathroom stool, upon which she left some mark from the green paint she had kicked over on the balcony, and which was later cleaned off, went on talking, perhaps in a chiding tone, perhaps not, and then, having lulled the unfortunate Mountjoy into false security, strolled to the end of the bath, turned on the taps full, jerked out the plug, and, before Mountjoy could so much as protest, caught her by the throat or the feet and so pulled her head under the rapidly rising water. Have you ever noticed how slippery the bottom of that bath is?' Mrs Bradley added, with surprising suddenness, turning to Carstairs.

'Yes,' he replied.

'I know it too,' said Mrs Bradley. 'I used it once—before this affair—and I slid along the bottom of it in a most terrifying manner when I went to immerse myself. Anybody taken by surprise from above——'

She left the sentence significantly unfinished, and Carstairs nodded.

'Yes, I demonstrated the same thing to Bing,' he said.

As they turned in at the big gates, Mrs Bradley observed:

'Say nothing to Bertie Philipson this evening when he tells you that name—if he does tell it to you. Perhaps he will not.'

'He will probably forget,' said Carstairs.

'Yes, I think I lulled his suspicions,' said Mrs Bradley. 'A charming boy. Do you want to look at that piece of paper I gave you?'

'There is no need,' said Carstairs moodily. 'I suppose the name of the—her name is on it. I don't want to see it.'

'No, I suppose not,' returned Mrs Bradley, with a little sigh. 'Hallo! Here's Eleanor come to find us. I expect we are late for tea.'

'For once I can sympathize with the ladies who love their cup of tea,' Carstairs confessed, with a rueful smile. 'Why did the murderer pull the plug out?' he added inconsequently. 'Oh, of course! To drown the noise if Mountjoy cried out or struggled,' he went on, answering his own question.

'I'm so sorry I've kept him out late, Eleanor,' said Mrs Bradley, ignoring Carstairs' last remark. 'It was entirely my fault.'

'Tea is served on the balcony, but you can have it inside if you like,' was Eleanor's prim rejoinder.

'Verandah,' said Carstairs under his breath, as he followed her up the wooden steps, but nobody heard him.

Chapter Nine

Signs and Portents

DINNER, by tacit consent, was a cheerful meal. No one appeared preoccupied with the exception of Bertie Philipson, who occasionally glanced to his left with a hunted expression in his eyes, and then hastily turned his attention to the food on his plate, as though he were obsessed by a secret fear, and was afraid someone might notice his obsession.

When the meal was over, Mrs Bradley took him aside immediately the men joined the women in the drawing-room and, under cover of a general and rather noisy discussion which had followed a remark of Carstairs', said to him:

'Tell me about it. It is important that I should know.'

Bertie seemed disinclined at first to confide in her, but she urged him the more.

'You had better tell me, Mr Philipson. Something is worrying you,' she said. 'I may be able to help.

Old women like me can often help young men like you.'

'Yes,' Bertie acknowledged. 'You got old Garde out of a nasty hole with that tobacconist's young woman. He told me about it. But this is—well, it's rather different, you see. I don't think I can tell you about it. Forgive me. And thanks—er—for offering——'

'Oh, rubbish!' interrupted Mrs Bradley briskly. 'Besides'—she looked at him keenly—'is it so very different a case?'

Bertie resorted to a mode of expressing uneasiness which he had not adopted since he was in the fourth form at school. He shuffled his feet and flushed.

Mrs Bradley took his arm. 'Oh, I should love to see them by moonlight,' she cried, in a voice shrill enough to pierce the full flood of discussion which was still being carried on by the others. 'Do, please, Mr Philipson, come outside, and point them out to me!'

She tugged at the young man's arm with such determination, and the others had ceased talking and were now gazing at him with such interest, that he was compelled to comply, and, feeling foolishly yet wretchedly like the unfortunate Filch, allowed this strong-minded little Mistress Peachum to hale him into the garden.

'Come, now,' she said, 'I haven't really brought you out to show me anything, of course, but we can speak freely out here. Eleanor's been making herself a nuisance to you, hasn't she?'

Bertie's mouth opened and shut again. He blinked. Then he gurgled. Finally he ejaculated:

'How on earth do you know?'

'Tell me when it began, and all about it,' commanded Mrs Bradley, altogether disregarding his question.

Bertie kicked an inoffensive early aster and then looked up at the full moon and scowled.

'It began when I stayed here two years ago,' he said. 'I've known Dorothy Clark since we were kids, and they invited her and told her to bring a man as there was a shortage of males, especially dancing ones, in this part of the county, so she froze on to me and dragged me along. Well, I knew old Garde, of course, so that was all right. Well, it wasn't a bad sort of show. Nearer Christmas than this, and we got some skating, I remember, and Eleanor unbent a bit and I taught her the Charleston or something, and Dorothy showed her a new way to do her hair. Well, after a day or two, when I'd got the hang of the house, I used to go into old Bing's study and swot his books—I'm rather keen and he's got some decent stuff, as I expect you know. One morning I found Eleanor in there. Of course, I knew she sort of devils for the old man when he's got a working fit, so I greeted her in the conventional brotherly way and got down to a book. Suddenly she came over and squatted on the arm of my chair and began to be most pally. Asked me all about myself, and my prospects, and my parents, and everything under the sun.

'I didn't take much notice at first, but then I

found she followed me when I went out walking alone, and would catch me up as soon as the road got a bit lonely, and in every possible way she began to suggest that I should, well, fall in love with her I suppose you would call it. Once she asked me outright to marry her. I put her off—I can't remember what I said—I tried to let her down lightly, of course, and she—well, wept a good bit, and hung on my neck and so forth. It was pretty awful and I felt a frightful fool, and somehow a bit of a rotter, although heaven knows I hadn't given her any encouragement to behave as she did.

'Well, she left me alone for a couple of days after that, and then she made a—a suggestion—I can't go into all that. It is enough to say that I let her see how horrified I was, and next morning, of course, I made some excuse to old Bing, and left the place, thinking that I should never go there again and that it was the end of the affair for me, as Eleanor never comes up to Town or visits round about.'

Mrs Bradley said nothing, and, after a short pause, Bertie went on:

'I soon forgot all about it once I had got back to Town. I think at the time it made little impression on me. I just thought the poor girl probably was a bit bored with the quiet country life and wanted a little excitement. Anyhow, I had forgotten all about it, as I say, until I had a letter from Dorothy a week ago, asking me to come down here again, and saying that she was going to marry Garde Bing some day fairly soon, and that if I wanted to see her once more while she was still a spinster, I had better hop along. I wouldn't have come, even for that, though, had it not been for the postscript, which read:

'"And what do you think? Eleanor has gone and got herself engaged to an explorer who is staying here. I expect you have heard of him. Mountjoy is the name. Everard Mountjoy. But don't tell anybody, because it isn't actually announced yet." She went on to say that she had not seen the fellow then, but would arrive at Chaynings the same day as I did. Incidentally, it was the day after.'

'Well, I was keen on seeing Dorothy again. We've always been pals. Besides, I thought that the engagement of Eleanor to this chap Mountjoy would sort of put me out of the running, and I shouldn't be harassed any more by her attentions. So I came.'

He paused again.

'Yes?' breathed Mrs Bradley, so softly that he could scarcely hear the word.

'Well, that's about all,' said Bertie gloomily. 'All was as right as rain until Monday evening after dinner, and then she found me in the alcove in the drawing-room, and started leaning against me and—oh, damn it!—trying to hold my beastly hand! It was awful.'

'Monday!' exclaimed Mrs Bradley. 'Are you positive it was Monday? The day before the—before Mountjoy died?'

'Positive,' Bertie asserted. 'As a matter of fact, although it sounds most frightfully callous and all that, after the death business on Tuesday I remember thinking, "Well, there's one comfort—Eleanor will surely have more sense of decency than to come and maul me tonight."'

He paused again. Mrs Bradley, feeling certain there was more to come, said nothing to break the spell of the young man's confidences.

'It *was* all right on Tuesday night,' he continued slowly, and with evident reluctance, 'but on Wednesday, that is, last night——' He stopped speaking, and stood still in the centre of the gravel walk which they were traversing.

'Look here, Mrs Bradley,' he said, 'I feel a pretty frightful bounder telling you all this about the poor girl, but I think some woman ought to know about it. On Wednesday night, yes, last night, Eleanor came into my bedroom at about half-past twelve and—and wanted to stay there! I thought it was a ghost at first. I had terrible difficulty in getting rid of her. In fact, I had to get out of bed and shove her outside and lock the door. Choice, isn't it?'

After a long time, during which they resumed their measured pacing round the lawn, Mrs Bradley spoke:

'Of course you will lock your door tonight,' she said.

'You bet I shall,' said Bertie fervently, 'and nothing short of the house catching fire is going to persuade me to open it.'

'Yes, well, leave everything else to me,' said Mrs Bradley. 'Shall we go in?'

They went in without further words—Bertie wondering whether he had done well or ill to confide in this reptilian little woman; Mrs Bradley turning over in her mind the one strikingly significant statement in Bertie's narrative, and determining to communicate it to Carstairs at the first convenient opportunity.

'Ah, here you are!' said Garde, as they entered the drawing-room. 'What about the light fantastic, Father? Shall we be treading on your corns—house of mourning and so on?'

'What's that?' asked Alastair Bing sharply, for he was becoming a trifle deaf and did not want anyone to know it.

'I thought we'd have some dancing,' said Garde.

'By all means, my boy, if the others would like it. Do exactly as you please. I shall go to my study.'

'I think I'll come with you, Father,' said Eleanor. 'I could look up your references for you in the library if you like.'

'I'm glad Sis has gone,' observed Garde truthfully. 'She hates dancing. What shall we have?'

'A foxtrot is the only thing I can manage,' confessed Carstairs.

'Foxtrot it is!' said Garde, choosing a record.

'I'll work the machinery,' said Bertie obligingly.

'No, you won't. Take Dorothy. She refuses to dance with me. Carry on.'

The gramophone, whirring forth the preliminaries, burst into full syncopated harmony. Bertie, grinning happily, swung Dorothy into the hot flood of negroid excitement, and Carstairs took Mrs Bradley into a dignified embrace.

'I suppose you like that weird old woman quite well?' said Bertie to his partner, as they swung out into the hall.

'Of course.'

'Well, I mean, you don't think she's the juicy jimmy who did in that Mountjoy, do you?'

'Good gracious!' said Dorothy. 'No!'

'Oh, all right. Only, to me,' pursued Bertie, negotiating a standard lamp with masterly ease, 'she looks the sort of Caesar Borgia Nero de Medici who would fluff out her own mother for the fun of it. Don't you think so?'

'She's a very gifted woman,' said Dorothy severely.

Bertie, steering miraculously between a Japanese lacquer screen and a potted palm, kissed her swiftly and precisely upon the mouth.

'Yes, that's what I say,' he averred, as they emerged into more open surroundings.

'Beast!' said Dorothy, laughing, and referring to the kiss. 'Don't you know that I'm on the verge of being married to Garde Bing?'

'More tomorrow,' said Bertie, smiling. 'In fact——'

'Not out here!' Dorothy removed her hand from his shoulder and put it over his mouth. Bertie paused in his stride, and, as she blundered against him, caught her about the waist and neck and kissed her with youthful zest.

'Let go, idiot!' panted Dorothy, when she could speak. 'Don't be a little cad! Oh!'

For at that instant she became aware of the prim disapproval of Eleanor Bing, who had emerged from the library with a clock in her hand, and was standing looking at them.

'I say, Eleanor, please go and ask Garde to shove on a waltz. I feel in the mood for it,' said the graceless youth, apparently not in the least taken aback by her sudden appearance.

'So it appears,' said Eleanor coldly.

'Tell him,' yelled Bertie, who felt that nothing could make things appear much worse, 'that I'll lend him his wench for the next dance but three! If he's a good boy, that is!'

'I loathe you, Bertie,' said Dorothy, putting both hands in front of her face. 'You make me blush. What a loathsome sex yours is, angel-face.'

Bertie swung her up in his arms and grinned at her.

'See?' he shouted ferociously. 'I am the robber of the cave! Macbeth. No, Chu-Chin-Chow! See?'

'Yes, Bertie,' said Eleanor's voice from the drawing-room door. 'Chiefly stockings, that is one comfort!'

'Put me down, fool!' said Dorothy imperatively. 'Quick, or I'll tell my young man. Such goings-on!'

Bertie lowered her to the ground.

'There, pretty one,' he observed, smoothing her ruffled dark hair with exaggerated tenderness.

Crash!

Both, laughing, turned to see what Eleanor had dropped. It was the clock.

'*My* clock, you bad girl!' cried Dorothy, running to pick up the ruins.

'Don't be daft, Dorothy! You'll cut yourself on the broken glass!' shouted Bertie.

'Any damage?' asked Carstairs, appearing in the open drawing-room doorway.

'Hard luck!' said Garde, appearing beside him.

'Your clock? Never mind! It can be mended,' said Mrs Bradley, poking her head out and immediately withdrawing it in a disconcerting and tortoise-like manner.

'Good heavens! What a fuss!' snarled Alastair Bing, emerging, ruffled as to hair and temper, from his lair. He went back, slamming the door irritably behind him.

'If you loved Susie, as I love Susie!' bawled the gramophone, blatantly indifferent to clocks and their fate.

'Did you ring, sir?' asked a servant of Garde.

'Yes. Have this mess cleared up, and send the clock to be mended,' said Garde, giving his arm to Dorothy. 'Come along. Let's go back into the drawing-room while they clear up.'

'I'm sorry, Dorothy,' said Eleanor correctly.

'Don't mention it,' said Dorothy. 'It really doesn't matter a scrap. . . . Although why she should be carrying my clock about the house is more than I can fathom,' she added, in low tones, to Garde as they passed through the drawing-room doorway.

'Dorothy dear!' Mrs Bradley called after her, in honeyed tones.

Dorothy let Garde pass on, while she herself turned back at the sound of Mrs Bradley's voice.

'Did you say it was your clock? Do you mean it is your own actual property?'

'Yes.' Dorothy laughed in a slightly embarrassed fashion, and played with the fringe on her frock. 'It sounds silly, but I love that old clock. I've had it for six years, and I always take it with me when I visit people. It's like a friendly voice if I wake up in the night. Eleanor laughs, and calls it "Dorothy," because she says it and I are like twin souls. But still I can't imagine what she was doing with it.'

'What were you doing when she dropped it?' asked Mrs Bradley.

'I wasn't doing anything,' laughed Dorothy, blushing a little. 'That ass Bertie was trying to kiss me. He doesn't mean anything by it,' she added hastily.

Chapter Ten

A Troubled Night

'DOESN'T mean anything by it,' mused Mrs Bradley. 'I see. And now I want you to do something for me. I am proposing to make a little experiment tonight, and if it is to be successful you will not be able to use your own bedroom. Would you mind that very much?'

'Yes,' replied Dorothy, 'especially if it means I have to tell Eleanor I want my room changed. She hates having the domestic arrangements upset.'

'I don't see why they need be upset,' said Mrs Bradley. 'Why shouldn't you occupy the other twin bed in my room just for one night?'

'Oh, I had far rather not trouble you,' Dorothy hastily began, but the older woman cut her short.

'I will see to it,' she said promptly. 'It will not be any trouble. Only, you must not tell anyone that you are coming. Do you understand?'

'Not even Garde?' asked Dorothy. 'The fact is,

Mrs Bradley, that ever since the—the murder, I don't feel that I am safe in this house with anyone except Garde. You don't mind my saying this, do you? I don't mean to be personal or—or anything, and, of course, I am *certain* you were not the—the dreadful person—although one could say that about everybody, couldn't one? It has puzzled me ever so much. The only person who had any reason, you see, was the most unlikely of any of us to do such an awful thing. I mean, she is so quiet and sort of—sort of prim, isn't she?'

'Who?' asked Mrs Bradley keenly.

'Why, Eleanor,' whispered Dorothy, with troubled eyes. 'But I'm sure she couldn't have done it.'

'What made you say she had a reason?' asked Mrs Bradley quietly.

'Oh, I don't know. She was engaged to Mr—no, Miss Mountjoy, wasn't she? And I know she wasn't altogether happy about it, because she came into my room weeping most terribly, and all she could say was, "Oh, Dorothy, Dorothy! What shall I do about it? What shall I do about it?"

'And I said, "Do about what, Eleanor?"

'And she said, "Mountjoy! Mountjoy! I don't know how to bear it! I don't know what to do!"

'I didn't really know what she was talking about, but I felt compelled to say something, so I said:

'"If you feel unhappy about your engagement, Eleanor, I think you ought to break it off, before it is publicly announced."

'And she said, "But the shame of it, Dorothy! Think of the shame of it! Oh, no! I shall have to go through with it now! But how hateful! Oh, how more than hateful my situation is!"

'Of course, Mrs Bradley, you can guess what I thought she meant, although even then I could scarcely imagine the fastidious, prudish Eleanor getting herself into *that* sort of a muddle, but now I know she couldn't have meant that. Instead she must have——'

'Yes?' prompted Mrs Bradley, her eyes gleaming hard.

'Well, I think she must have found out about Everard Mountjoy's sex,' said Dorothy quietly. 'So really it was a blessing he—no, she—*was* drowned before the engagement was made public, wasn't it, from Eleanor's point of view.'

'Yes. I expect that *was* Eleanor's point of view,' said Mrs Bradley dryly. 'But there is more in the thing yet than meets your innocent eye. *Will* you sleep in my room tonight?'

'If I must,' said Dorothy, laughing unwillingly.

'Good!' said Mrs Bradley. 'And you are going to tell Garde Bing what we are going to do? Nobody else, mind, or my experiment will not work.'

'But what are you trying to prove?' asked Dorothy curiously.

'Never you mind! Let little girls be seen and not heard,' said Mrs Bradley, with her ghoulish chuckle. 'Now, listen while I tell you what to do.'

'All right, Celestine,' said Mrs Bradley to her maid. 'That will do.'

'How sweet of you to come and bid me good

night, Dorothy dear,' she added, for the maid's hearing, as the latter, with a quiet: *'Bien, madame. Bonne nuit. Bonne nuit, mademoiselle,'* prepared to quit the room.

'I must not stay long, though,' Dorothy replied, as they had arranged she should.

The maid's footsteps died away.

'Now, my angel,' said Mrs Bradley softly, but in an authoritative voice, 'you must go to your own room and undress. Get quite ready for bed, and be sure to put on a nightdress of which you have a duplicate. Understand?'

Dorothy drew a deep breath.

'I'm scared to death,' she whispered. 'Can't you tell me what is going to happen?'

'I don't know what is going to happen, I am thankful to say,' Mrs Bradley truthfully replied. 'I have not been cursed with the gift of second sight. Well, are you going?'

'I suppose so,' her fellow-conspirator answered half-heartedly. 'I must just go and say good night to Eleanor first, though.'

'I'll come with you,' said Mrs Bradley promptly. 'I almost wish it were the custom for us to go and say good night to the young men also. I should like to be certain that everybody fully intends to go to bed tonight.'

Dorothy raised her eyebrows, but, as Mrs Bradley did not intend, apparently, to satisfy her curiosity, she shrugged her slim shoulders, plucked up her courage, and sallied forth. To Eleanor's bedroom they went, but, as the room was in darkness and the door wide open, they correctly assumed that the occupant was not there, so Mrs Bradley departed again, and Dorothy, whistling gaily to keep up her spirits, walked along the landing to her own room.

The house was built in four storeys, the lowest of which contained the dining-room, drawing-room, library, morning-room, Alastair Bing's study, and, at the back, the kitchen and servants' hall.

On the first floor were the bedrooms allotted to Dorothy, Mrs Bradley, Eleanor herself, and the ill-fated Mountjoy, the last of which had remained unoccupied since the fatal day of her death. Adjoining, but not opening into, Dorothy's room, was the bathroom where the crime had taken place. This bathroom had been studiously avoided for the first few hours of the day succeeding the discovery of the corpse, but first Mrs Bradley, then Eleanor, and finally Dorothy, had put aside their superstitious repugnance to the room, and had gone on using it for the sake of convenience.

Dorothy switched on all the lights she could possibly pretend she needed, and, having locked the door, prepared for bed. Then, following Mrs Bradley's explicit instructions, she chose a pair of pyjamas like the pair she had donned, stuffed several pairs of stockings into each leg of the trousers, filled out the rest of the garment with a woollen sports coat, hung the coat upon a coat-hanger, filled the sleeves with her bathing-costume and a towel, buttoned the coat round a pillow, and, laying the whole dummy outfit in the bed, tenderly tucked it in. Then she drew from its hiding-place under a pile of folded silk underclothing a cunningly fashioned head, made out of a Guy Fawkes mask, a stuffed sponge-bag, and a quantity of dark brown darning-wool fixed on to represent hair.

Swiftly and cleverly, Dorothy arranged this monstrosity with the face half-hidden in the bedclothes, and the dark hair well showing. Then she stepped across the room, switched off the lights, and, greatly daring, unlocked the door, walked back to the bedside, and gazed down upon her effigy. The fitful, deceptive moonlight, shining down upon the lay figure, made her shudder. There was something horribly human about that half-screened face, that dark bobbed head.

Softly Dorothy tiptoed to the door. Barefooted, for, to complete the illusion, she had been warned to leave her bedroom slippers in their usual place, and, feeling uncomfortably naked, for, in obedience to the same decree, she had left her dressing-gown hanging over a chair, and her silk pyjamas were thin, she ventured into the darkness of the passage.

Then a thought struck her. These sinister preparations might as well be as complete as human thought and foresight could make them.

She tiptoed back again, pulling the door close behind her. She went across to the dressing-chest, and, aided by the greenish, eerie gleams of the moon, searched the top drawer. Her fingers encountered what she sought. Closing the drawer, she walked steadily across to the bed, clenched her teeth, and adjusted on the dark head of what her brain would terrifyingly insist upon calling 'The Corpse' a rose-pink shingle-cap!

Then she ran noiselessly to Mrs Bradley's door, and, without knocking, admitted herself.

Mrs Bradley, even less attractive in bed than she appeared out of it, was propped among her pillows. She held a volume of modern poetry in her claw-like right hand, and with her left was in the act of turning a page as Dorothy entered. She signalled to the girl to approach the bed.

Dorothy, closing the door quietly, came near. Mrs Bradley motioned to her to bend down. Then she breathed into her ear:

'Finished everything?'

'Yes, everything,' Dorothy whispered, 'and I'm—I'm cold.'

'No, scared,' said Mrs Bradley, grinning fiendishly. 'Never mind. You look charming. But get into bed now. Wait a minute. I'll turn over with a loud creaking noise. Oh, *I* shan't creak; it will be the bed. While it is creaking you must get into your bed and lie down, under cover of the noise I make. Do you understand? It is tremendously important that no one shall know you are here. If they do know, my experiment may be useless. Good night, my dear. I've drawn the beds very close together, so that if you feel lonely you have only to stretch out an arm and I'll wake up. But, whatever you do, don't say anything in your ordinary voice. Nobody is to suspect that you are here.'

'Very well,' whispered Dorothy, trembling with feverish excitement mixed with fear.

Mrs Bradley put an arm like a steel band round her shoulders and gave her a heartening little squeeze.

'Bed,' she breathed, releasing her.

Dorothy touched the clever, cynical face with slim, soft fingers.

'Good night,' she whispered; and glided round to the farther side of the other bed. With a creak and a groan, Mrs Bradley's mattress bore eloquent testimony to the way in which it was being ill-treated. Under cover of the noise, Dorothy insinuated her young graceful body between the sheets, gave a long, delicious wriggle under the clothes, and turned on to her side.

Then there was silence, save for the insistent ticking of Mrs Bradley's watch. To Dorothy's troubled mind the ticking seemed to grow louder and louder. The watch seemed to be two watches, each ticking at a slightly different interval. A bass note joined in, and the three sets of ticking seemed to hammer on to her brain. Then she slept.

It seemed to her that she wandered in and out of the vast rooms of a house. Suddenly she entered one that was empty save for a black and ivory throne placed at the far end of it. She tried to reach this throne, but always it seemed exactly the same distance away. Sometimes there was somebody seated on the throne; sometimes it was vacant. With all her powers she tried to reach it, but in vain.

Suddenly, her dream flashed and broke into a

thousand pieces. From somewhere in the house there burst an agonizing scream. It jerked her into sweating, shivering wakefulness, and clove the air with liquid fire. Brilliant green and blue lights flashed through her brain.

Regardless—indeed, totally forgetful—of Mrs Bradley's injunction, she sat up in bed, switched on the electric light, and, grasping that calm but fully awake guardian-angel by the shoulder, cried hoarsely:

'What was that?'

'That,' Mrs Bradley meticulously replied, raising herself on one elbow, and grinning broadly, 'was a scream. What did you think it was?'

'I—I—I know,' stammered Dorothy. 'You don't think—I mean—it isn't—you know what I mean!'

'Lie down again,' said Mrs Bradley.

'I can't! Oh, isn't it horrible?' said Dorothy, shuddering.

'Yes, it is,' Mrs Bradley coolly replied. 'Never mind. It might have been worse, I dare say.'

'What—what do you mean? Aren't we—aren't we going to—to—to do anything?'

'By all means, if it will give you any satisfaction, my dear. Incidentally, I think I may say that my experiment has been entirely successful.'

Mrs Bradley leapt lightly from her bed, pushed her feet into slippers, hustled her body into a dressing-gown of a surprising mustard hue, and ran a comb through her hair.

Dorothy crawled shiveringly out of bed, then

darted swiftly up to Mrs Bradley and clutched her by the arm.

'I'm not going to stay here alone,' she quavered.

'Well, you can't join in the fun looking like that,' Mrs Bradley pointed out, eyeing Dorothy's silk pyjamas with admiration. 'Here, wrap yourself in the eiderdown. Keep the ends from trailing or you'll get tripped up.'

The landing, which during the last few seconds had sounded like the meeting-place of armies, presented an unusual sight. Dozens of persons, in all stages of undress, from the ludicrous (in the case of Alastair Bing and the cook) to the semi-classic (in the case of Garde), the musical-comedy (in the case of Eleanor and Dorothy) and the sheerly pantomimic (in the case of Mrs Bradley and the butler) presented themselves to one another's startled gaze.

'What's happened?' said everybody to everybody else.

'Oh, it wasn't you screaming, then,' said Garde to Dorothy.

Mrs Bradley pushed her way through the hordes to where Carstairs, soberly clad in a dark brown dressing-gown and leather slippers, was interrogating Eleanor Bing.

Eleanor's usual calm had forsaken her.

She gesticulated wildly as she talked. Her voice seemed to shoot up two or three octaves now and again, as a boy's does when it is breaking.

'Now, calm yourself, Eleanor! Do please calm

yourself, and speak coherently,' said Alastair Bing, himself hopping about on the fringe of the crowd like a demented hen. 'Silence, please, all of you! Silence! And will the domestic staff please withdraw.'

The domestic staff moved back a few paces, and then stood huddled together at the top of the stairs. They seemed badly scared, and were inclined to look suddenly and shudderingly behind them.

'Now, then,' said Alastair, 'tell us what has happened.'

'I had neuralgia,' Eleanor said, trying hard to steady her voice, 'and I thought Dorothy might have some aspirin, so I went into her room to ask for it—and—and—well, go and see for yourselves! Oh, it is horrible! Too, too horrible!'

She covered her face with her hands and shuddered and shuddered.

Mrs Bradley beckoned to Garde.

'Don't leave Dorothy's side until I come back,' she whispered. Then she grasped Eleanor firmly by the arm.

'Come along,' she said, with quiet urgency. 'Come with me.'

Half guiding, half compelling Eleanor's faltering footsteps, she took her back to her bedroom, and caused her to lie down. There she left her for a minute, and returned shortly with a potent sleeping-draught.

'Good night,' she said, when Eleanor had taken it. 'Close your eyes, and you will be asleep in no time. I'll send somebody along to see how you are in a minute.'

'No, no! Don't send anybody,' said Eleanor faintly. 'I only want to be left alone. Please go now. Please go.'

Mrs Bradley returned to the landing to find the crowd beginning to disperse. Standing under the electric light where she had left them were Dorothy and Garde, earnestly talking.

'But I must see what has happened,' Dorothy cried, as Mrs Bradley approached them. 'Don't be aggravating, Garde! It's my bedroom, and I shall go into it if I choose.'

'Let her go if she wants to, young man,' said Mrs Bradley. 'In fact, we'll all three go. I don't see why we shouldn't share the fun, and find out what has happened.'

She led the way into Dorothy's room. Alastair Bing and Carstairs were standing at the foot of the bed, talking in low tones.

Bing turned as they entered.

'Ah, there you are,' he said to Mrs Bradley. 'Just look at this! I think we must be harbouring a maniac.'

On the bed lay Dorothy's dummy figure, as she had placed it some hour or two before. There was only one difference. The masked head was staved in as though from a terrific blow, and, just as it had been allowed to fall from some destructive hand, a heavy poker lay across the dainty coverlet.

Chapter Eleven

Another Mystery

'But—but supposing I had been lying there instead of—instead of—of that!'

Dorothy's grey eyes were black with terror as she stared wildly at Mrs Bradley.

Garde took advantage of the situation to place a comforting arm round her.

'Well, you weren't, so it's all right,' he observed, with admirable philosophy.

'But I should have been, if it had not been for Mrs Bradley,' faltered Dorothy.

'Eh? What's that?'

Alastair Bing barked out the question, his white imperial bristling fiercely.

'It's true,' said Dorothy, glancing fearfully behind her. 'I should have been sleeping here tonight if Mrs Bradley had not—had not——'

'But had you any reason—any inkling of—any— what shall I say?' demanded Alastair, turning fiercely on Mrs Bradley.

The lady grinned horribly.

'Just an intuition,' she said airily. 'Just an idea that came into my head.'

'Oh, rubbish! Rubbish!' snarled Alastair.

'Very well,' said Mrs Bradley placidly.

'At any rate, Father,' said Garde, with pardonable asperity, 'it seems to me that Dorothy and I owe Mrs Bradley something more than ill-tempered abuse. By the way—where's Sis?'

'Eleanor is in bed,' replied Mrs Bradley. 'I have given her a sleeping-draught, so I do hope that no one will have occasion to disturb her. Poor girl! I expect she has had a shock.'

'I have no doubt of that,' said Alastair Bing. 'According to what she told us before you came on the scene, Mrs Bradley, she went to the bed to awaken Dorothy, and after shaking that—that hideous effigy and receiving, of course, no answer, she turned on the lights, and that'—he pointed dramatically to the bed—'was what she saw.'

'Poker and all?' inquired Mrs Bradley unsympathetically.

Alastair Bing snorted.

'At any rate,' said Garde pithily, 'I consider Mrs Bradley has saved you from having another murder to report to the police.'

'To whom are you talking?' yelled Alastair, turning on his son.

'You,' said the god-like young man, unintimidated. 'Of course, you're rattled. So am I. But there's no need to be rude to Mrs Bradley. And I bet poor old Sis was rattled too,' he added grimly, 'when she came in and saw that lovely sight. My hat! what a blacksmith blow.' He closely inspected the head with morbid appreciation.

'Oh, these mask things dent very easily,' said Carstairs, joining in the conversation in his admirably modulated voice.

'Well, I'd like to know who bent it, anyway,' said Garde. 'And what they thought they were up to. I mean, say what you like, it was no practical joker who handed out that slosh, was it? What do *you* say, Mr Carstairs?'

Carstairs looked benignly at the wreckage on the bed, and gingerly prodded the unrecognisable mask with a sensitive forefinger.

'Upon consideration, I am inclined to agree with you,' he said. 'I think we are now looking upon one of the most ghastly attempts at murder I ever knew about. Oh—I am sorry I said that! How foolish of me!'

For Dorothy, with a little sigh, had lurched fainting towards the floor. Garde's arm, however, prevented her from falling, and, as the eiderdown fell from about her, he lifted her slim form in his arms and held her like a child against his breast.

'Your room, Mrs Bradley?' he asked, and, receiving a bird-like nod of assent, he bore his light burden along the landing.

'Which bed?' he asked, halting in the middle of the handsomely appointed bedroom.

'In here,' replied Mrs Bradley, drawing the bedclothes aside from one of the twin beds.

Dorothy opened her eyes, and smiled faintly as he laid her gently down.

'I'm awfully sorry,' she said.

'Darling!' said Mrs Bradley warmly.

'Think she's all right now?' asked Garde anxiously, as he ostensibly felt her pulse. Dorothy's soft fingers closed round his hand.

Mrs Bradley's left eyelid fluttered.

'You can stay a minute or two and see,' she said. 'I shan't go to bed any more tonight.'

She drew the folds of her hideous dressing-gown more closely about her, waddled over to the electric fire, switched it on, and seated herself in a roomy basket chair with a book of modern poetry upon her knees.

Garde sat down on the edge of Dorothy's bed and lovingly held her hand. They smiled at one another.

Mrs Bradley, covertly regarding them, sighed softly and sentimentally, abandoned the volume of modern poetry and the social conventions to their separate fates, and closed her eyes. . . .

When she opened them again, it was morning. Garde was seated on the floor, with his head against Dorothy's pillow. Her hand lay lightly upon his shoulder, for she had fallen asleep fondling his hair.

'A little lower than the angels,' quoted Mrs Bradley, under her breath. Then she tiptoed out of the room to prevent the admirable but gossiping Celestine from coming to call her, and so discovering the lovers.

This done, for she met the maid on the stairs, she repaired to the bathroom for her morning ablutions.

The bathroom door was locked. Mrs Bradley twisted the handle and pushed, but the door was fast.

'Eleanor, of course,' she said aloud.

'I beg your pardon!' said Carstairs, coming down from the landing above.

'I wanted the bathroom, but it is occupied, so I assume Eleanor Bing is inside. That is all,' replied Mrs Bradley. 'How did you sleep?' she continued. 'After the little contretemps last night, I mean.'

'I didn't sleep very much, I am afraid,' Carstairs admitted. 'That was a very queer business.'

'Very queer,' Mrs Bradley echoed, with a characteristic grimace.

'How did you come to—er—remove our young friend from the scene of the operations?' asked Carstairs. 'Dorothy Clark, I mean.'

'I had a hunch,' Mrs Bradley replied, 'and what had been merely a suspicion developed into an absolute certainty last night while we were dancing.'

'Did it?' asked Carstairs, interested. 'What gave you the idea?'

'The idea itself I had had for some time,' Mrs Bradley admitted. 'But it was the clock which clinched matters.'

'The clock?' Carstairs knitted his brows in a perplexed frown. 'The clock?' he repeated slowly.

'Yes, the clock,' said Mrs Bradley, thoroughly enjoying herself. 'There is an instance, but not as beautifully complete an instance, in the diary of Marie Bashkirtseff.'

She left a completely bewildered Carstairs shaking his head and returned to her bedroom chuckling ghoulishly.

At her entrance, Dorothy woke.

Mrs Bradley's quizzical glance at the still sleeping Garde caused a lovely blush to mantle the girl's cheek and brow.

'Darling child,' observed Mrs Bradley. 'How I wish I looked like that when I felt abashed! And how sweet that boy looks, doesn't he?'

Dorothy gave Garde's shoulder a rough shake. He woke, stared, then stretched cramped limbs, and at last stood up.

'Glory hallelujah!' he observed, taking in his surroundings. 'Did I go to sleep?'

'You did,' replied Mrs Bradley. 'Go away now. And don't let anybody see you going.'

Garde grinned at her, bent and kissed Dorothy before she could ward him off, and took his departure.

'I'll go too, and see if I can get into the bathroom now,' said Mrs Bradley, marching out in his wake.

The bathroom door was still locked.

'Bother!' said Mrs Bradley loudly, upon her return. 'How I hate washing in a bedroom!'

'So do I!' said Dorothy frankly. 'And, as nothing on earth will persuade me to go to my own awful bedroom and wash there, I suppose I shall sit here until you have finished.'

'Quite so,' said Mrs Bradley, grimacing.

Upon descending to breakfast, they found the men already assembled, and during the meal the topic of conversation which naturally excluded all others was the night's adventure.

'I thought the end of the world was come, and that we were listening to the last shriek of the damned,' said Bertie Philipson, spreading marmalade on toast with a sparing hand.

'So did I. Or that the Bolshies were really in our midst at last,' said Garde, following his example, but using about three times as much marmalade.

'Eleanor is apparently washing off the shock,' chuckled Mrs Bradley, nibbling dry toast and sipping hot water with apparent relish. She was more reptilian to look at than ever, in the clear light of morning.

'We ought to time her,' said Bertie, 'but, as we don't know at what time she usually comes down to breakfast, we can't do it. Poor Eleanor. Fancy expecting to find Dorothy, and seeing that damaged atrocity instead!'

'By the way, where were *you* while the fun was going on? I didn't spot you among the gathering of the clans,' said Garde to Bertie.

'Well, I did begin to get up, but when I saw the mobs of people on the landing below mine, I thought I might as well go back to bed. I took it for granted that somebody would rescue me if the house were on fire, or protect my possessions if burglars had broken in!'

He simpered idiotically at Dorothy as he spoke, but she elevated her chin and said nothing.

Unabashed, Bertie passed his cup for more coffee.

'You know what happened, though?' said Garde.

'You mean the damaged goods in Dorothy's bedroom, I suppose?' answered Bertie, in a fatuous voice which caused Dorothy to look more contemptuous still. 'Yes, I went in there this morning at the pressing invitation of Mr Carstairs, and had a good squizz at it. I'm rather surprised, I must say, that a big girl like Dorothy should still care for dolls. But there's no accounting for taste, of course. A cousin of my own, twice removed——'

'Oh, do shut up, you fool,' grinned Garde, 'and pass the marmalade.'

'Greedy youth,' said Bertie. 'Mrs Bradley, let us go and walk in the rose-garden. Dorothy can pour out his fifth cup of coffee. After all, she'll have to get used to doing it when they are married.'

'I don't want any more. I've finished,' observed Garde, folding a marmalade-smothered piece of bread and butter into halves, and depositing the whole amount in his mouth at once. 'Come on, Dorothy. Let's go and help them look at the dandelions.'

'Nobody is to leave the house and grounds!' said Alastair Bing, looking up from *The Times* and speaking in his dictatorial voice. 'The police will be here soon, and will want to question us.'

'The police!' Dorothy turned pale.

'Certainly,' said Alastair. 'If an attempt was made to kill you as you lay in bed—and Carstairs is determined to persuade me that such was the case—the sooner the police come and find the madman who seems to be living in our midst, the better. That is all I can say.'

'And very nicely said,' remarked Mrs Bradley dreamily.

Alastair glanced at her with the swift suspicion of one who imagines that his leg is being pulled, but her expression did not vary, and she appeared to be admiring the view from the window.

Alastair snorted with distrust and returned to *The Times*.

The others severally rose and made their way out into the beautiful garden, now a little past the height of its summer loveliness.

'You know,' said Garde to Bertie, 'it's all very well to jape about it, but I'm jolly glad Dorothy *was* sleeping with the old woman last night. I knew she was going to, of course.'

'Yes, so did I,' said Bertie rather surprisingly.

'Did you? Dorothy told me I was the only person who knew, apart from herself and Mrs Bradley.'

'I overheard the first bit of your conversation, and shamelessly listened to the rest,' Bertie confessed, grinning.

'The devil!' Garde grinned appreciatively. 'So you knew where she was all the time?'

'Yes,' answered Bertie. Then his face grew grave. 'But it's a beastly business,' he added soberly. 'I wonder what the explanation is?'

'You think somebody meant to do the kid in, I suppose, the same as I do?'

'What else is there to think?' asked Bertie. 'But who would want to do such a dastardly thing? I mean, Dorothy's such a topping girl. Anybody who wanted to put her out of the way would be absolutely mad!'

'That's it!' cried Mrs Bradley, joining them, closely followed by Carstairs. 'That's just what we've been saying, Mr Carstairs and I. Madness. That's just what it is!'

'Well, it does seem the sort of irresponsible destructive action one might expect of a homicidal maniac,' said Garde. 'Fancy trying to put somebody out with a poker! Nasty blighter, whoever it was!'

'I suppose that's why people have such a horror of the insane. They *are* irresponsible,' said Bertie.

'Well, yes, they are irresponsible in a way,' said Mrs Bradley, 'but they've always got an idea at the back of their irresponsibility, if you can only get at it, you know. And you'd be surprised to hear how logically some maniacs can explain their actions—actions which to us——'

At this moment they heard themselves hailed from behind. They turned, and were amazed to see Alastair Bing tearing after them across the lawn, his coat-tails flying, his hair standing straight on end, and in his face a blending of horror and fury such as none of them had before beheld, even upon his expressive countenance.

'Eleanor! Eleanor!' he gasped, and, with a choking cry, fell to the ground.

'Brandy!' said Mrs Bradley crisply. And, while the young men raced to get it, she knelt down by Alastair's side and quickly and skilfully loosened his collar.

'He'll be all right in a minute,' she said cheerfully. 'Don't look so scared, Dorothy.'

'But—but he said Eleanor's name,' faltered Dorothy, white to the very lips. 'You don't think——'

'I don't think anything for a minute,' returned Mrs Bradley. 'Here come those boys with the brandy. Go and tell one of them to go for a doctor. Although I don't think it is at all necessary. Still, one can never tell.'

'But Eleanor——' said Dorothy for the second time. 'Hadn't I better——'

'Wait a second. He is coming to,' interrupted Carstairs.

He supported Alastair, who showed signs of wanting to sit up, and the old man said weakly:

'Have they got her out?'

'Do you mean Eleanor? Where is she?'

'In the bathroom! That horrible place! I should have locked it up and disconnected the water. I realize now that I should have locked it up.'

'Good God!' said Carstairs, turning pale. 'Not another instance of foul play!'

He lowered Alastair's head to the ground, and

ran back to the house, calling as he ran to Bertie Philipson:

'Give the brandy to Garde, and come with me.'

Bertie obeyed, and neck and neck they sprinted across the lawn.

'What's the row this time?' yelled Bertie.

Carstairs, requiring all his breath for other purposes, did not reply until they reached the verandah steps.

'The lower bathroom?' he then gasped. 'This is an awful business.'

They entered the breakfast-room, where the scared servants, who had come to clear away, were clustered together as though for mutual protection.

'You may clear,' said Carstairs shortly, indicating the littered breakfast-table as he and his companion hurriedly passed it on their way to the door opening into the hall.

The servants, however, loitered uncertainly, and whispered among themselves.

'Please, sir,' began the butler, stepping forward, 'what about Miss Eleanor? She hasn't appeared yet, and—oh, sir, I do hope there's nothing wrong.'

'Of course not, Mander,' said Carstairs, with unusual abruptness, as he wrenched open the door. 'Get on with your work and don't think about anything else.'

He slammed the breakfast-room door behind him, and the two men mounted the stairs, their feet making no sound on the thick pile of the carpet.

The bathroom door was closed. Carstairs knocked on the panels loudly. Then he turned the handle and pushed, but with no result. He put his shoulder to the door and heaved. The door remained fast closed.

'Here, help me, Philipson, will you? When I say "Three!" fling all your weight against it. Ready?'

'Yes,' replied Bertie, gritting his teeth.

'Then, one, two, three?'

The lock yielded before their double onslaught, and the door swung open so suddenly that both men pitched forward, and were saved from falling full-length only by the opposite wall of the room, against which they both crashed.

'Hurt?' gasped Bertie. 'Oh, heavens!' he cried, without waiting for a reply from Carstairs.

Clad in her dressing-gown, and lying over the side of the bath with her feet on the floor, her head touching the bottom, and the chain of the wasteplug twisted round and round her left hand, was Eleanor Bing.

'Good God!' said Carstairs slowly. 'She's drowned! Although there's no water remaining in the bath now.'

He placed his arm round the woman's body and heaved it upright. Eleanor's wet head fell heavily against his shoulder.

'Take the feet, Philipson,' he said hoarsely. 'Better take her into Miss Clark's room, I should think. That's nearest. Face downwards on the floor. That's it.'

Slowly they bore their burden into the pretty bedroom, and, under Carstairs' directions, laid it down. With heavy hearts, for both imagined that their efforts were in vain, they attempted artificial respiration for the resuscitation of the apparently drowned.

For half an hour, taking turns about every few minutes, they toiled, but with no result.

Carstairs, whose turn it was, rose slowly to his feet, and shook his head. His face was grey, although great drops of perspiration testified to the genuineness of his efforts to bring poor Eleanor back to life.

'It is of no use, I am afraid,' he said.

The sound of a car on the gravel below caused him to look out of the window leading on to the balcony.

'The doctor!' he cried, and, opening the long window, he stepped out, and, making a trumpet of his hands, hailed the doctor as the latter stopped his engine and alighted.

'Yes? Hallo! What is it?' the medical man called out.

'Come up here as soon as you can!' bellowed Carstairs.

He came back into the room, and again knelt beside the inert woman.

'One more try,' he said, bending to the grim work.

Bertie watched his untiring efforts with the tremendous concentration of one who has received a great nervous shock. Carstairs glanced up at him once, and said kindly:

'Go downstairs and get yourself a peg, old chap. You looked knocked up.'

'I'm all right, thanks,' said Bertie heavily, with the ghost of a grateful smile. 'Shall I have another go at that to relieve you a bit?'

'No, it's all right. It's wasted labour, really, I am afraid, but one feels as though one can't remain still. And I can't face Bing yet.'

'Oh, Lord! Of course he has to be told.' Bertie whistled apprehensively. 'I say! How frightful it all is! First that poor chap Mountjoy—I can't think of him as a woman, somehow!—then that dastardly attempt upon Dorothy last night—and now, this! It makes one wonder who'll be the—well, the next victim, doesn't it?'

'No,' said Carstairs soberly. 'I'll swear there will be no more victims. I fancy this is the last. Poor, poor woman,' he added, with overwhelming pity, gazing down upon the apparently lifeless body.

A tap at the door heralded the doctor's entrance. He was followed by Mrs Bradley.

'Where's Bing?' demanded Carstairs, swift as a flash.

'Downstairs. His son is with him.'

'Oho!' said the doctor, taking in the situation with his keen, professional glance. 'What's happened here?'

'Drowned, I fear, doctor.' And Carstairs briefly outlined the circumstances so far as he knew them.

The doctor knelt beside the body.

At last he stood up, dusted the knees of his trousers, and spoke abruptly.

'Somebody shout for young Bing,' he said.

Then he resumed his seemingly thankless task.

'I'm here,' said Garde's voice at the door. 'Who sent for me?'

'I did. Understand this pumping game?' asked the doctor, without pausing in his steady work.

'I guess so.'

'Take the arms, then. I'm done. Nice mess here for somebody to clear up. Now, man, put your guts into it.'

With this last implicit instruction Garde nobly complied.

'Pretty work,' said the doctor appreciatively. 'I think we've pulled her through. Take his place somebody, and then I'll have another turn. Ah, she's coming. She's coming! That's it! I thought so.'

Eleanor was certainly manifesting signs of returning animation.

'She'll do! She'll do!' said the doctor, with professional approval. 'I'll take another turn now.'

At this point, when Eleanor, by deciding to return to life, had somewhat alienated public interest, Bertie Philipson created a diversion by suddenly falling prone across her body in a dead faint.

'Silly fool,' said the doctor pettishly. 'Haul him off, Bing. Might cause the poor girl to bite her tongue clean off, falling all over her like that just when she's coming round.'

Chapter Twelve

Interrogation

As the Chief Constable had stated, the proceedings at the inquest on the body of Everard Mountjoy were brief, and no witnesses were called except the doctors and such persons as were deemed necessary to identify the body. Little surprise was manifested by the general public when it was known that the jury had found for wilful murder. A detective inspector was officially placed in charge of the case, and, accompanied by the Chief Constable, he presented himself at the front door of Chayning Place just as the recovered Eleanor was being assisted into bed by Mrs Bradley and her maid.

'Keep her quiet,' was the doctor's parting injunction, 'because she has had a bad shock, you know.'

'How do you think she came to fall into the bath like that?' asked Alastair, who accompanied the doctor to the door, and so was on the spot to greet the Chief Constable and the inspector upon their arrival at his house.

'No business of mine, and I don't intend to hazard a guess,' replied the doctor. 'Sudden faintness, giddiness, anything of that sort might have been the cause.'

'But I should have thought the water would have brought her quickly back to consciousness,' said Alastair to the Chief Constable, with a puzzled frown.

'As I am unacquainted with the circumstances which occasion your discourse,' said the great man, twinkling, 'I am afraid I cannot pretend to join in the discussion with any tremendous enthusiasm. Don't tell us that something else extraordinary has occurred in your house, my dear Bing!'

The doctor hastily took his leave, and Alastair led the two officials into the hall.

'Come to my study, and I will tell you all about it,' he said.

They heard him to the end without interruption.

'Well,' said Sir Joseph to the inspector, 'well, Boring, what do you make of it?'

The impassive inspector knitted his brows.

'If I understand you to mean, Sir Joseph, what bearing do I think the events of the night and the awkward accident to Miss Eleanor Bing in the bathroom this morning have on the case we are investigating, well'—he paused, and frowned heavily—'I say, no bearing at all.'

'What!'

Alastair Bing's voice rang out like a pistol-shot.

'Do you mean to say that the dastardly attempt on Miss Clark's life and the extraordinary accident to my daughter have nothing to do with the fact that we have a criminal—yes, a murderer in our midst? Nonsense! Nonsense!'

Alastair's little white imperial quivered with rage.

'I beg your pardon, sir, but it is my opinion, and I intend to stick to it until it is disproved,' said the inspector quietly. 'Now, see here gentlemen. This poker and Guy Fawkes business upstairs. Has it been disturbed in any way?'

'By my express injunction,' said Alastair proudly, 'everything was left entirely as we found it. But come with me. You shall see for yourselves, and then possibly the inspector may see fit to modify his opinion.'

He led the way upstairs into Dorothy's room, which had been put tidy by the maids after Eleanor's recovery and exit, but in which the bed had been left untouched.

'Here we are. Poker, you see. Dummy figure. Smashed mask. It doesn't look like a joke to me.'

'Well, sir, I must disagree with you,' said the inspector stubbornly. 'To begin: who had a grudge against the young lady. According to you, no one. Well, I can find out more about that later on, so we'll leave it. Secondly: it is a chancey thing, you know, to aim a slosh at a sleeping person by

moonlight! Suppose you missed killing her, but she
had time to recognize you and yelled out! Risky,
very. You see, you wouldn't dare switch the light
on, would you, to see her better, and so direct
your aim? Third: it's a brutal way of going about
matters, isn't it, now? Imagine it for yourself. An
East End drunk or a mental defective might do a
thing like that, but remember you are virtually
certain that someone in your own household did
it. Can you fix on any one out of the whole crowd
who would slosh a pretty girl over the head with a
poker? Think of the nasty sight she'd present with
her head battered in and lots of blood everywhere!
Think of the sound of crunching bones! Think
of——'

'Good heavens, man, be quiet!' shouted Alastair,
the veins standing out visibly on his forehead.
'You—you horrify me beyond measure.'

'And rightly, sir. That's what I'm saying. It would
horrify anybody, wouldn't it? See?'

The inspector permitted himself a fleeting smile,
and continued, with scarcely a pause:

'Now, look at the other side of it. Two young
men—very young, very high-spirited—both under
a strain following on the death of Mountjoy—
what more likely than that they should think of
playing a rather unpleasant practical joke, eh? The
dummy figure, the Guy Fawkes mask, yes, and that
ridiculous silk net arrangement on the head—why,
it is exactly the sort of thing two young fellows
would think of! I've got two young sons of my own
studying at London University, and I know exactly

the sort of thing young fellows think funny. And then, again——'

'Oh, very well, very well,' snarled Alastair. 'If that's the police view, I can't help it, I suppose. After all, no harm's been done, that's one thing.'

'It is this Mountjoy business that has got on your nerves, sir, if you don't mind my saying so,' said the inspector soothingly. 'Now, that's a matter which *does* need to be carefully investigated. No practical joke there.'

'Well, now, about your daughter, Bing,' interposed Sir Joseph. 'Is she in a fit state to be interrogated? You see, the circumstances of her accident, although totally unlike those which caused the death of Mountjoy——' He broke off, as though expecting that Alastair would ask a question, but the latter did nothing of the kind, and merely answered carelessly:

'Question her by all means. She says she felt faint and must have been half-drowned before she recovered.'

The two police officials followed him to Eleanor's room. Eleanor, slightly pale but obviously in full possession of her faculties, was reclining against pillows. She was attired in a dressing-jacket of pale blue and white, which did little towards improving her extraordinarily plain appearance. Her summer nightdress appeared to be cut fairly low in the neck, and she had huddled the jacket about her as though for warmth. The day, however, was unusually fine and hot, so that this proceeding appeared particularly unnecessary.

The inspector coughed apologetically and advanced to the bedside.

'I hope you feel better, Miss Bing,' he began.

'Quite, I thank you,' replied Eleanor, with her most prim expression.

'Glad to hear it. Well, if you feel equal to doing so, we should like you to answer a few questions. That is, if you've no particular objection.'

This feeble attempt at jocularity died a sudden death before Eleanor's contemptuous gaze.

'First——' said the inspector, in desperation.

'First,' interrupted Eleanor dispassionately, 'I should like to request my father to descend to the study for a copy of one of the Latin authors.'

'Which Latin author, my dear Eleanor?' enquired Alastair in a solicitous tone, which drew a slight but ironical smile from his daughter, so unlike was it to his usual snarling utterance.

'Any one you like,' replied Eleanor, with affected weariness, 'but don't return with it in less than a quarter of an hour. I imagine these gentlemen will have concluded their inquisition by that time.'

Alastair, gasping like a landed fish, and, for once in his life, utterly bereft of speech, walked out of the room.

The Chief Constable tiptoed to the door and closed it.

'Now, Miss Bing,' the inspector resumed, seating himself, producing his note-book, and licking an anticipatory pencil, 'we want you to tell us what caused you to fall head-first into the bath this morning.'

'I was overcome by a feeling of extreme faintness,' replied Eleanor coldly, 'and was unable to call for assistance before I was wrapped in complete oblivion. The only wonder is that I am alive to tell the tale, or so I am informed by those who rescued me.'

'Yes. Yours is a devoted family circle, Miss Bing,' said the Chief Constable casually. He had strolled over to the window and was looking out.

Eleanor swung round at the sound of his voice, and, in so doing, loosed the folds of the dressing-jacket from about her neck for a full second. The angry reply she seemed about to make died on her lips, however, for the inspector suddenly cried:

'Come now, Miss Bing! There's no need for us to fence! Who are you shielding? Who attempted your life this morning in the bathroom?'

Clutching the dressing-jacket about her once more, Eleanor turned back on to her right side, and exclaimed:

'Fence! Shielding! Pray explain yourself.'

'Who attempted to murder you in the bathroom this morning?' repeated the inspector, with brutal directness. 'Come, now!'

Eleanor regarded him with lofty contempt.

'My dear inspector,' she said, with ineffable scorn, 'you are talking the most utter nonsense! Nobody attempted any such thing. I fainted, as I have told you, and was lucky enough to be rescued in time. That is all I can say. And, as I am still weak, and feel somewhat fatigued, I feel sure that you will relieve me of your presence as soon as possible.'

The inspector opened the door for the Chief Constable. Eleanor ironically smiled them out.

'Well!' gasped the inspector. His chief chuckled.

'Of course, she's lying,' Boring went on.

'You mean?' The Chief Constable raised his eyebrows interrogatively.

'Sir, somebody half throttled that young woman, and then pushed her into the bath and left her for dead. I spotted the bruises on her neck.'

'You sound sympathetic,' said the Chief Constable, smiling slyly.

'Well, I can understand his feelings, whoever he was,' said the inspector gloomily. 'Not,' he hastened to add, 'that I'm likely to commit a crime, I admit. But there's some young women that are past all bearing, and, if you'll excuse an entirely unofficial opinion, sir, would be better out of the way; and Miss Eleanor Bing is one of them. Now I wonder who the man is that she's shielding. If we could find him we might be laying our hands on the Mountjoy murderer, sir.'

'I rather doubt that, you know,' said Sir Joseph quietly. 'But we shall see. Yes, we shall see. What do you propose to do next?'

'Just what I was going to ask you, sir.'

'Oh, you're in charge of the case now. It is for you to decide. I'm only an onlooker at present. Besides, being an acquaintance of the family, I inspire a certain amount of—what shall I say—well, I help to allay those feelings of apprehension which your purely official presence would be certain to cause.'

'Make them less guarded, like,' said the inspector hopefully. 'Yes, there is that. Well, what do you say to a little general interrogation, sir? We could commence with the attempt on Miss Bing and work back to the Mountjoy business.'

'Carry on,' said Sir Joseph. 'Although, as I said, I don't think the two hang together.'

'Both in the same bathroom. Rather suggestive, sir, don't you think?'

'Far too suggestive,' said the Chief Constable thoughtfully. 'If you really want my considered opinion, I say far too suggestive altogether. Calculated to mislead, in fact, Boring. Do you think people learn nothing from criminals like the great George Smith?'

'I don't follow, sir,' said the inspector apologetically. 'The man who drowned his wives and collected the insurance, wasn't he?'

'Something of the sort,' the Chief Constable answered, with a reminiscent chuckle. 'Yes, well, Smith made the great mistake which clever criminals so often do make. He believed that there is no sense in improving on a good thing. Five times be got away with it, but the sixth repetition laid him low.'

'Yes, I get that all right, sir,' said the inspector lugubriously, 'but exactly what bearing——'

'Well, suppose I am a criminal. I commit a murder by drowning a woman in the bath. I am not found out. In fact, nobody appears to suspect me. If I want to commit another murder, what do I do?'

'Anything except drown the second one in the

bath, if you've any sense at all,' said the inspector, almost animatedly.

'Quite. Profiting, as I say, by the sad example of the late George Smith, I don't repeat myself. The second time I may make the one mistake which they say all criminals do make at some time or another, and so both murders may be brought home to me. But now, supposing a successful murder has been committed in a certain bathroom in a certain house, and somebody else wants to commit a murder also.'

'He'd imitate the first one as near as he could in the hopes that anything which did go wrong would recoil on to the first murderer instead of on to himself,' said the inspector, slowly working it out. 'Yes, I see your point, sir.'

'That's what I think may have happened in this house,' concluded the Chief Constable, 'but, of course, we cannot lose sight of the theory that this murderer may be another George Smith, who can't leave a good thing alone, but must duplicate it. The craftsman, in fact, instead of the artist.'

They had descended to the foot of the stairs, and were there carrying on their low-toned conversation, when Garde Bing came by.

'Oh, Mr Bing, we want to put a few questions to the family and so on,' the inspector began.

'I'll put the library at your disposal,' said Garde promptly. 'Oh, Mander,' as the impeccable servant appeared in response to his ring, 'I want you to be on duty here for a time. These gentlemen require

your services. You had better place yourself entirely
at their disposal for the time being. Find the people
they require, keep the door shut, and pay particular
attention to their instructions.'

'Very good, sir.'

'I shall be in the morning-room if I am wanted.
Do you know where to find everybody?'

'I think so, sir.'

The butler followed his young master's retreating
form with an eye of sympathy.

'Not much love lorst between 'im and Miss
Eleanor,' he thought to himself, 'but, still—it's been
a nasty shock to 'im.'

'Ask Miss Clark to be good enough to come to
the library.' The inspector's voice broke in upon his
musings, as the two men followed Garde into the
library, from which the young man immediately
emerged and retired to the morning-room.

'Very good, sir.'

Dorothy, white and more nervous than ever,
presently appeared, and was asked to sit down.

'Miss Clark?'

She nodded. The official pencil wrote.

'A sad business this, Miss Clark.'

Dorothy found her voice, after a tremendous
effort.

'It is awful,' she said, in little more than a whisper.

'What do you mean? I want you to be very frank
with us, Miss Clark. What is awful?'

'Well'—the girl made a plucky effort to collect her
thoughts —'first there was poor Miss Mountjoy—but
you know all about that?'

Her grey eyes sought those of the Chief Constable, and he nodded.

'Then it seems as though somebody tried to—tried to——'

'Tried to?' The official voice was keen but kindly.

'Tried to kill me!' said Dorothy, with a gulp and a shudder.

'Really? And what then?'

'Why, and then poor—poor—poor Eleanor! She was all but drowned!'

At this recollection, Dorothy broke down utterly.

'She might have died! We all thought she was—she was——'

'Poor child,' said the Chief Constable, patting her shoulder in a fatherly manner. 'There, now. Don't cry! Just try to tell us all that you know about last night. Will you? Come, be a brave girl, now!'

Dorothy lifted her head from the table, dabbed at her eyes, and smiled apologetically.

'I had a motor accident,' she explained, 'and it left my nerves in an awfully stupid state. What do you want to know?'

'Chiefly,' said the inspector, 'the story of what happened in this house last night. Tell us in your own words all that you can remember, and we will ask you any questions that we want answered. Now, then! Fire away!'

Dorothy rested a bare arm on the table, stared at a space between the two officers' heads, and began:

'Well, Mrs Bradley knew I was feeling nervous about poor Miss Mountjoy's death, and so she invited me to sleep in her room. But before I went I had to do what seemed to me an awfully queer thing.'

'Oh? What was that?' It was the Chief Constable who asked the question. The inspector was busily taking notes.

'I had to make up a dummy figure—the one you saw in the bedroom, in fact—and lay it in my bed, and place it, as far as possible, in the position in which I usually sleep. And, to make it as much like a human being as possible, we even put a mask on its head to look like a—a face, you know.'

The Chief Constable nodded, glanced at the inspector, and with his lips formed the words: 'Not the young men after all!'

'And I—I even put a shingle-cap on its head to make it as much like me as I possibly could. It was a horrid experience,' concluded Dorothy, shuddering involuntarily at the recollection.

'What is a shingle-cap?' inquired the Chief Constable gravely, for the inspector was writing in his note-book as though for a wager.

'Oh, it is a kind of silk net which we wear on our heads at night. It keeps your wave the right shape, and keeps your hair lying flat instead of its getting sort of bent up and funny, and looking peculiar in the morning,' Dorothy explained. 'They drive you mad the first night or two, but you get used to them,' she added naïvely.

'Thank you. Your exposition is most clear,' said

the Chief Constable gravely, while the inspector, who had finished writing for the moment, openly grinned.

'Yes, you placed the—er—the hair-net upon the model. And then?'

'And then I put my dressing-gown where I always put it, and my bedroom slippers in position—to carry out the idea that it was really myself in the bed, you know—and then I walked along to Mrs Bradley's room and slept in one of the twin beds there.'

'I see. Was Mrs Bradley in bed then?'

'Yes, she was sitting up in bed, reading. But when she had spoken to me—just a casual word or two—she lay down, and, I suppose, went to sleep. It was the horrible scream that woke us both.'

'I see. Now, Miss Clark, I want you to think very carefully before answering my next question.'

Dorothy steeled her nerves, for, although the tone was quiet and urbane, the remark had a sinister ring. She recollected, with a chilly feeling about her shoulder-blades, that this kindly grey-haired man who sat opposite was the representative of the law. She drew a deep breath.

'Yes?' she inquired, moistening her lower lip with the tip of her tongue.

'Have you any idea whether Mrs Bradley remained in the room all the time from when you both went to bed until the scream aroused the house?'

Dorothy wrinkled her brow. 'I am sure she did,'

she answered slowly. 'As I said, my nerves have
been in such a silly state since that smash I was
in that the very slightest sound wakes me. And I
did not wake up. And I drank nothing to make
me sleep, nothing at all. And Mrs Bradley's door
makes a grating sound over the carpet as you pull
it open. And my bed was near the door. And her
bed creaks when you sit up or turn over, or move
about on it. And——'

The Chief Constable interrupted her, laughing.

'I think you have proved your point, Miss Clark,'
he said. 'I am willing to believe that Mrs Bradley
did not leave the bedroom between the times that
I mentioned. Now, about that scream. It frightened
you, I dare say?'

Dorothy sat bolt upright in her chair.

'Frightened me?' she cried. 'It was too horrible
for words. I nearly died. I believe I *should* die if I
heard it again. It was a scream of most dreadful
terror.'

'Was Mrs Bradley scared?'

'She woke up, of course. But, if she was scared,
she did not show it. She just got out of bed and
went to see what had happened.'

'And you?'

'Oh, I went with her. I didn't want to go in the
least, but I just felt I couldn't bear to be left alone.
Do you know the sort of feeling?'

'I can imagine it,' replied the Chief Constable,
hiding a smile.

'Well, what did you both see?'

'Oh, nothing but a crowd of people—servants

too, you know—who were collected round Eleanor and were all trying to talk to her at once.'

'Oh, yes. And you joined them?'

'I followed Mrs Bradley. Father—Mr Bing, I mean—ordered the servants away, and we were able to hear what poor Eleanor had to say.'

'And what had she to say?'

'Oh, just that she had been into my room to ask me for some aspirin tablets for her neuralgia, and that I was not there, and that she had seen something which frightened her, and that she ran out screaming.'

'Oh, she said that, did she? Got it down, inspector?'

'Yes, sir.' The inspector finished his notes and handed the book to his superior.

'Yes, that's it. I'd like you to hear it, Miss Clark, and then you will be able to tell us if we have your statement down correctly.'

He read it aloud to her, precisely, accurately, and without any expression in his voice at all.

'That is correct?' he asked, when he had finished.

'Yes. That is quite correct,' answered Dorothy.

'You would be prepared to swear to all this in a court of law?'

'Will it be—surely it won't be necessary, will it?'

Then as the two policemen made no verbal reply, she added:

'It is all quite true, so far as my knowledge goes.'

'And your memory,' said the inspector, with a little smile at his chief.

'Yes,' said Dorothy, 'I haven't forgotten anything.'

'Very good. Well, now, Miss Clark, we come to the point. Who, in this house, had any reason to wish you dead?'

The girl, shocked by the bluntness of the question, half-rose, sat down again, bit her lip, swallowed, turned red and then white, and at last burst out:

'You mustn't ask me! You mustn't ask me! Really, I don't know! It was only my fancy! I ought never to have mentioned it!'

'Come, now, Miss Clark!'

The official voice was stern. The official eye bored into her brain.

'Answer me. The truth, mind!'

Dorothy stood up and thrust back her chair from the table. Her slender hands were clenched at her sides.

'It can't matter now,' she said, in a curious voice totally unlike her own. 'I will tell you. It was Eleanor who hated me. She always has. But she didn't try to kill me last night. I'm sure she didn't!'

'And why are you sure?' asked the Chief Constable.

'If she did! Oh, but she didn't! She couldn't have done! She couldn't! It would be too horrible!'

'Yes, I agree, Miss Clark,' said the inspector, in a peculiar tone. He glanced at his chief. 'Finger-prints might settle the matter, sir.'

'On the poker, you mean? Well, yes, perhaps. Dangerous evidence, though. Very dangerous evidence,' murmured the Chief Constable. 'Still, we will see.'

He walked to the door and held it open for Dorothy to pass out. Then he rang the bell, and, upon Mander's appearing, sent him to fetch Garde Bing.

'Ah, sit down, Mr Bing,' he said when Garde entered.

Garde sat down.

'Strongly attached to your sister, Mr Bing?'

Garde sat up with a jerk, stared into the Chief Constable's eyes, and decided promptly to tell this man the truth.

'No,' he replied curtly.

'No?' repeated the police officer. 'Before or after you knew of your sister's inimical feelings towards your fiancée? Miss Clark is your fiancée, I believe?'

'Oh, Dorothy—yes. I didn't know that Eleanor didn't like her. That is news to me, I assure you. Sis is never demonstrative, you know.'

The Chief Constable glanced at the inspector.

'No, thank you, sir,' the latter said, in answer to the unspoken question. So Garde was politely dismissed.

'Oh, and by the way, Mr Bing,' the inspector called after him down the hall.

Garde retraced his steps.

'You won't let anyone handle that poker, will you? You know the one I mean. I expect we shall want to take it away with us.'

'I will see that it is not touched,' the young

man promised. 'I don't think anyone has handled it so far.'

The next victim was Carstairs.

'Ah, Mr Carstairs!' The Chief Constable shook hands with a smile. 'I am sorry to have to question you about this affair, but my duty must be done.'

Carstairs smiled.

'I am entirely at your service,' he said, seating himself.

'Well, now, Mr Carstairs, who killed Mountjoy?'

'To the best of my knowledge,' said Carstairs, in his precise, dry way, 'Mountjoy was the victim of an accident.'

'Is that really your opinion?' said the inspector.

'It is—now,' replied Carstairs quietly.

The two policemen looked at him, but Carstairs merely smiled at them urbanely, and volunteered no further statement.

'Hum! Thank you, Mr Carstairs,' said the Chief Constable, hiding his disappointment.

Carstairs rose to go.

'And yet, Mr Carstairs,' said the inspector, 'I could swear that yesterday you thought very differently.'

'A scientist,' said Carstairs, with his hand on the doorknob, 'hardly ever thinks exactly alike two days running.'

He nodded cheerfully to them and went out.

'Of course,' said the Chief Constable thoughtfully,

'he won't be able to shuffle like that in the witness-box.'

'You think it will come to that, sir? So do I,' said the inspector. 'So does he, if the truth were known,' he added, 'and, for all his cheerfulness, he doesn't care for the thought one little bit.'

'I think we'll have Mrs Bradley next,' said the Chief Constable. 'Perhaps she will be good enough to tell us why she took that girl to sleep in her room last night.'

Mrs Bradley was more than willing to tell them that, and quite a lot in addition.

'To begin with,' she said, 'I would like to make a statement. You can question me about it afterwards.'

Feeling ridiculously like a very small boy in the presence of his teacher, the Chief Constable bowed.

'Take it, inspector, will you?' he said.

'I am making this statement quite voluntarily,' Mrs Bradley began, 'because I feel that my duty as a citizen compels me to do so. I am a member of the electorate of this country,' she added impressively.

'Quite so,' murmured the Chief Constable, trying to accustom his eyes to the rainbow hues of Mrs Bradley's jumper, and at the same time to compose his mind to listen to what she was saying.

'I was invited to stay at this house by Mr Francis Garde Bing, whom I was instrumental in saving from police-court proceedings on the night of the Oxford and Cambridge boat race. The details, although intensely interesting and very instructive from a psychological point of view (I have incorporated them in my *Small Handbook of Psycho-Analysis*, to be published next month), are irrelevant here, so I will pass over them. The young man gratefully invited me to spend a holiday at his house, and, upon the invitation being confirmed by his sister, Eleanor Bing, I accepted it, and arrived here in the last week of July. Eleanor interested me from the first.

'"Here is a woman," I said to myself, "young, exceedingly healthy, but a slave to her father's house and to her father's hobby. What repressed desires, what unsatisfied cravings for enjoyment and for freedom lie walled up behind those short-sighted eyes?" I was intensely curious about Eleanor Bing, and intensely interested in her psychological make-up.'

She paused. The two men nodded.

'Staying in the house at this time,' Mrs Bradley continued, 'was, of course, the woman, Mountjoy. We all thought that Mountjoy was a man.

'Obviously Eleanor Bing thought so too, for, shortly after my arrival, they became engaged to be married. And, less than a fortnight later, Mountjoy met her death.'

She paused again. Then she turned to the Chief Constable.

'I think you had doubts yesterday as to the cause of that death,' she said, fixing him with her beady eyes.

'Frankly, Mrs Bradley, I think Mountjoy

was murdered,' Sir Joseph said quietly. 'My
investigations, and the very considerable help
rendered me by Mr Carstairs, made that conclusion
almost inevitable.'

'Thank you, Sir Joseph,' said Mrs Bradley. 'Then
if I tell you that I had cause to believe that the
murderer of Mountjoy had designs also upon the
life of Dorothy Clark, you will not be surprised
that, unknown to the rest of the household, I took
the girl into my room?'

'We should like to hear upon what assumption
you based your conclusion that the girl's life would
be attempted by the murderer,' said the Chief
Constable. 'And, of course, we should be interested
to know the identity of the murderer.'

Mrs Bradley smiled.

'I haven't any proofs which a jury would
consider evidence,' she said. 'But I'll tell you what
I thought. I am not easily shocked or intimidated,
gentlemen, and I will confess at once that when I
heard that Mountjoy was dead, my first feeling was
one of vague irritation. Deaths always signify an
outbreak of sickly piety, of hushed voices, of funeral
furnishings; they augur a suspension of gaieties,
of light conversation, of entertaining quarrels, of
intellectual argument.

'My next feeling was one of interest in observing
the reaction of various members of the household
to the news. Mr Carstairs was genuinely grieved.
The rest of the persons in the house appeared
not so much as to turn a hair. Very interesting,
gentlemen, don't you think?'

She glanced first at one and then at the other, with a bird-like motion of the head which appeared to disconcert them considerably.

'Very interesting,' said the Chief Constable feebly. 'Please continue.'

'Then along came Mr Carstairs with his conviction that Mountjoy had been murdered. He did a little private detective work on his own. Then we went to the police, the result of whose investigations you know better than I do.

'Mr Carstairs and I discussed the case, and I think I was instrumental in suggesting to him the identity of Mountjoy's murderer.'

'Ah!' said the Chief Constable, leaning forward. 'Who murdered Mountjoy, Mrs Bradley?'

'Until this morning,' said Mrs Bradley calmly, 'I should have said it was Eleanor Bing. Now I am not at all sure that anyone murdered Mountjoy. I think she was the victim of an accident.'

Chapter Thirteen

Revelations

THE Chief Constable tapped the table thoughtfully with the tips of his fingers.

'I should be interested to know how you fixed on Eleanor, and how you could have proved your point,' he said.

'I told you I could not prove anything,' Mrs Bradley reminded him. 'I could not prove it, but I could have suggested a motive.'

'Motive?' It was the inspector's turn to lean forward. 'That has puzzled me a good deal since yesterday—the apparent absence of motive.'

'I present to you,' said Mrs Bradley, 'the picture of a woman, twenty-eight to thirty years of age, intelligent and healthy, but emotionally starved. One day a man comes into her life. True, he is not the tall, mighty, god-like creature of her girlhood dreams, but he is a man, he is a scientist, he has explored the waste places of the earth, he has dared climates, diseases, wild beasts, and wilder men. They find mutual attraction in one another's society. And, one evening, the woman discovers her heart to the man, and Eleanor and Mountjoy became affianced.'

'The feature of this case which I have not yet been able to fathom,' said the Chief Constable slowly, 'is why the woman Mountjoy ever allowed herself to become formally engaged to poor Miss Bing. After all, it was a cruel thing to deceive a woman like that. And she must have known that marriage was an impossibility.'

'I have thought out two possible explanations,' said Mrs Bradley, 'either of which will cover the facts as we know them. It may be that Mountjoy was urgently in need of money. Eleanor Bing possessed a fairly comfortable little fortune, and the other woman may have intended to carry out the tragicomedy of marrying Eleanor, secure in the certainty that her unfortunate dupe's fear of ridicule would result in her keeping Mountjoy's sex a secret.'

The Chief Constable slowly nodded, while the inspector made rapid notes.

'The other explanation,' went on Mrs Bradley, 'may sound to you extraordinary, but it is more probably the correct one. Have you heard of sexual perversion?'

The Chief Constable nodded.

'Not a pleasant subject,' he said briefly.

'I do not propose to discuss it,' Mrs Bradley assured him, 'but I do suggest to you that Mountjoy may have formed a very real and, for the time being, a very strong attachment to Eleanor Bing.'

'It is a possibility, of course,' said the Chief Constable in a tone which proved that he did not consider it anything of the kind.

'Whatever happened,' pursued Mrs Bradley, 'one thing must be regarded as certain. In some way or another Eleanor Bing soon discovered the truth about her lover.'

The inspector slapped his knee.

'Motive!' he almost shouted. 'Motive for the murder! Revenge on the person who had deceived her!'

'Exactly,' said Mrs Bradley placidly. 'That's what I should have said—until this morning.'

There followed a short but pregnant silence. Then the Chief Constable said:

'That is certainly a very ingenious theory, Mrs Bradley. It certainly provides a motive, and a strong motive for the crime.'

Mrs Bradley smiled in her reptilian manner.

'Did they tell you about the watch?' she asked.

'The watch?'

'The watch belonging to Mountjoy, which was discovered by me at the bottom of the washstand jug.'

'What about the watch, Mrs Bradley!' The Chief Constable looked puzzled.

'Drowned watch, drowned woman,' said Mrs Bradley cryptically. 'Just another little proof that Mountjoy was murdered and did not die as the result of an accident.' She cackled with grim, sardonic amusement, and then added: 'I think that concludes my voluntary statement, gentlemen.'

'Which means that if we want any further information, we must ask for it,' chuckled the Chief Constable. 'Well, thank you for your very enlightening remarks, Mrs Bradley. Now, just one question. Will you tell us exactly why you took Miss Clark into your bedroom last night? I gather, of course, that you thought someone might make an attempt on her life, but what gave you that impression? For I presume it was not mere guesswork or scare-mongering on your part.'

'Oh, I had my reasons,' Mrs Bradley answered. She stared absent-mindedly out of the window for a little while, and then turned basilisk eyes on the police officers.

'I knew that Eleanor would kill the girl if she could,' she announced calmly.

'But how could you know such a thing?' cried the Chief Constable. 'That is what we would like to know. What put the thought into your head?'

'Well, for one thing, Eleanor is quite mad, you know,' said Mrs Bradley kindly. 'And mad people do such queer things, don't you think?'

The Chief Constable moved restlessly.

'I think you are wrong. I have talked with Miss Bing this morning, and I never saw anyone who appeared more entirely in possession of all her mental faculties,' he said coldly.

'Well, then I need not say any more,' Mrs Bradley

pointed out. 'I thought you wanted to know why I took Dorothy to sleep in my room. That is all.'

'You say that you knew Eleanor Bing would make an attempt on her life?'

'Exactly,' Mrs Bradley beamed on him as upon a favourite pupil. The inspector grinned behind his hand.

'And I think the discovery of that dummy figure with its head staved in, and a heavy poker lying near, justified my assumptions,' she added.

The inspector hitched his shoulders irritably.

'I suggest that it is quite as likely you went in and did the damage yourself,' he said abruptly. 'It's not an impossible theory, is it?'

Mrs Bradley cackled gleefully.

'My word!' she said happily. 'That is a very clever thought of yours, now, isn't it! Of course I might! I never thought of that! But still, you know, there was the clock. You haven't heard about the clock yet.'

The inspector turned an unfortunately audible expletive into a hacking cough, and avoided his chief's eye.

Mrs Bradley, however, was perfectly serious.

'I didn't tell you how she smashed the clock,' she said. 'You'd like to hear about the clock, wouldn't you?'

'What clock?' The Chief Constable was becoming restive again.

'The Freudian clock. Dorothy's clock,' explained Mrs Bradley, waving her hands with what was intended to be an explanatory gesture.

'I am afraid I don't understand.' The Chief Constable was obviously becoming bored.

'No?' Mrs Bradley, more bird-like than ever, put her head on one side and pursed her little beaky mouth at him. 'You wouldn't. But you may take my word for it. Smashed clock, smashed woman. My dear man, she positively flung it on the ground when she saw them kissing! The most interesting thing I've ever seen! I shall incorporate the incident in my *Handbook of Psycho-Analysis*. Beautiful! Beautiful! The incident, I mean, not my book, although the latter will be half price to police officials, post free. Signed copies one guinea extra. Can I put your name down?'

She smiled in a terrifyingly mirthless way, and the Chief Constable rose.

'I think we are wasting time, madam,' he said shortly, going to the door and holding it open. 'I think, inspector,' he added, turning his head towards his subordinate, who had also risen and was finding it hard work to keep his countenance, 'that we had better apply for a warrant to search the house. I like to trust the evidence of my own eyes.'

'Beautiful! Beautiful!' sighed Mrs Bradley ecstatically, as she passed out of the room. But whether she was referring to the Chief Constable's eyes, or to something else, it is difficult to say.

When the door had closed behind her, the Chief Constable stared frowningly out of the window for a moment, and then turned briskly to the inspector.

'Let's go and have some food,' he suggested. 'That woman unnerves me.'

'You don't really think she placed the poker there after she herself had smashed in the dummy's mask, do you?' asked the inspector.

'Well, I cannot say until you have the finger-prints from that poker. We might learn something from them, although they are like figures, you know—a clever criminal can do almost anything with them. Still, we'll see whose they are before we start to generalize about them. If they do turn out to be Mrs Bradley's she had better look out for herself. Oh, and that is another thing. We ought, I think, to have a further interview with Miss Eleanor. That drowning business was certainly not accidental, because, apart from the rather conclusive bruises on her neck, surely anybody who felt faint would at least have the ordinary common sense to turn away from a bath full of water before she swooned; and if it was attempted suicide—well, it was a very queer way of going about the business. It would require some hardihood, you know, to bend over the side of a bath and hold your head under water until you were drowned. Besides, the bruises. The bruises ought to be conclusive.'

'Why should she attempt to commit suicide, anyway?' asked the inspector.

'True. There is that point to be considered. That is partly why I want you to search the house, as a matter of fact. Papers, letters, diaries—all sorts of things like that might give us a line to follow up. You see, the bother with people of this class is that

you can't bully them as you would the cottagers.
They are too well-educated, and too well-balanced,
and they know that the police are hedged in and
hampered and red-taped until it is a wonder we can
do any work at all in the detection of criminals. Oh,
it's silly! Silly! I know they know all about it, and
I know they won't tell us anything until you arrest
somebody on suspicion—and even that may not
open their mouths. Look at this Bradley woman, for
example. She may decide to make away with both
these other young women, and be planning to kill
a few more people for all we know.' He laughed
good-humouredly, but the inspector scowled.

'I don't like the look nor the sound of that Mrs
Bradley,' he said. 'And, unless I'm much mistaken,
she is a very cool customer and needs watching. That
statement of hers! A pack of lies from beginning to
end, I expect. Why else did she give it to us?'

'Oh, come, come!' said the Chief Constable,
smiling, 'we can't say that she's untruthful. At
least, not so far as we know.'

'Oh, everybody is untruthful nowadays,' the
inspector rejoined gloomily.

'What about the "Blue Boar" for lunch?' said
the Chief Constable soothingly.

Mrs Bradley found Carstairs in the orchard smoking
his pipe.

'Well,' he said, as she joined him under the trees,
'is the inquisition over?'

'The poor things don't know what to believe
and what to scoff at as incredible. They haven't

the least idea as to what is germane to their case, and what they can safely leave out. And they are now having bets with one another as to whether Eleanor was really a killer and tried to commit suicide because she knew she was going to be found out—or because she was overtaken by remorse; or whether a beneficent Providence nearly laid her low in her moment of supreme triumph; or whether I tried to kill her after having carefully faked evidence against her with masked dummies and pokers and incantations and moonlight flittings; or whether——'

Carstairs, laughing, interrupted her.

'I gather you are not greatly impressed by our guardians of the law,' he said.

'Oh, I dare say they are well enough,' answered Mrs Bradley, shrugging her shoulders. 'How they hate me, though! It is most astonishing. Besides, I told the truth, so far as I knew it.'

She cackled harshly.

'I am afraid this is not one of your lucky days,' said Carstairs, laughing. 'Who is the next victim of the inquisition?'

'I don't know. You, I should think. Although you are *persona grata* with the Chief Constable, aren't you?'

'I am his little ewe Iamb,' said Carstairs modestly. 'In fact,' he added, 'I could murder the whole lot of you, and, although I should be the only one left alive, Sir Joseph would think it so unfriendly to arrest me that I should get off scot free. As a matter of fact, I think he is a very clever man.'

'Really?' murmured Mrs Bradley. 'That is what I am afraid of!'

'Oh, dear! What a nuisance! Here comes Alastair,' interrupted Carstairs.

'Feeling much better,' said Mrs Bradley dryly. 'What hypocrites these parents are!'

Alastair began to speak long before he reached them.

'The Police Are Continuing Their Investigation,' he said, with capital letters in his voice. 'I understand that they are going to take all our finger-prints.'

'And what are they going to do with them?' asked Carstairs, for the sake of saying something.

'I don't know in the least what they intend to do, either with the prints, or in any other way,' Alastair replied, 'but I am going to ask them to let me feel their bumps.'

At which statement Mrs Bradley was so overcome by a fit of choking that she was obliged to return to the house for a glass of water, leaving the two men alone.

As soon as she was out of hearing, Alastair Bing came very close to Carstairs, and lowered his voice to a conspiratorial murmur that was barely audible.

'I can't stand that woman!' he said. 'Do you know what I think? I think she tried to kill poor Eleanor! I do really! After all, why not? She looks a tigress, doesn't she? Doesn't she?'

His bony forefinger found Carstairs' short ribs and made him wince.

'My dear Bing! My dear fellow!' he exclaimed,

edging a little farther away. 'You must not say things like that to me. Mrs Bradley is not a very beautiful or even a very prepossessing looking woman, I admit, but one can scarcely call her a murderer on such slight grounds as those which her personal appearance affords. You really must not make these mischievous statements, you know. Of course, I would not dream of repeating them, but there are others who would, and you might easily damage the reputation of some perfectly innocent person.'

'But somebody tried to kill Eleanor,' Alastair Bing insisted, clutching Carstairs by the arm. 'I know that. She was a perfectly normal, healthy girl. Why should she be accidentally drowned? Why should she attempt to commit suicide? They are silly ideas, both of them. Utterly silly. And there's my book on *The Roman Antiquities of Dorset*. Who else could have looked up my references for me? Who would have done the typing? Who would have read the proofs and written to the publishers? It's all very well to talk about fainting fits and attempted suicides, but I've seen the bruises on her neck. And I want the murderer found. Do you hear! I want him found!'

He began to weep—a maudlin old man's tears. Carstairs comforted him as best he could, and, when he recovered himself, suggested that they should return to the house.

Here they found an interesting ceremony in progress. The inspector, assisted by a detective-sergeant, for the Chief Constable had not returned

to Chaynings after lunch, was collecting finger-
prints.

'Don't do the servants if you can avoid it,' said
Dorothy to the police officials as Alastair Bing and
Carstairs came in. 'If you do, poor Mr Bing won't
have a servant in the place next week.'

The proceedings were being watched with a
certain gloomy interest by the onlookers, who
included Bertie Philipson and Mrs Bradley.

'They've done everybody's now except yours,
Father, and Mr Carstairs,' said Garde, looking
attentively at the fingers of his own large brown
hands, 'so come along. Roll up. No charge is being
made. All the fun of the fair!'

The sergeant glanced at Carstairs' hands and
shook his head.

'I shan't need to take yours, sir,' he said. 'It's a
thumb-print that's clearest on the poker, and I can
tell at a glance that your thumbs, with the whirl
almost in the centre, are nothing like the print I've
taken, nothing at all. I understand, sir,' he went
on, turning to the inspector, 'that there's a young
lady in bed upstairs whose prints we haven't taken,
and that it is just possible she was the last person
to handle that poker. Could we——'

Alastair Bing glowered, and led the way to
Eleanor's room. He tapped at the door, put his head
round, and in a few words informed his daughter
of what was about to happen.

'Just take this card between the thumb and
first finger, please, Miss Bing. No, the other hand.
That's it.'

They bore the card away with them, and the inspector quietly closed the door.

'Well!' he said. 'Comparisons unnecessary, Toddie, I guess?'

The sergeant grinned.

'You're right, sir. Miss Eleanor Bing was certainly the last person to handle that poker, I fancy. Where's the powder?'

'Hum! Somehow, I rather expected as much, although how it affects the case, as the case stands, I can't quite say,' said the inspector later on. 'You see, we're out to find the murderer of Everard Mountjoy, not to discover why Miss Bing walks about the house at night bashing Guy Fawkes' napper with a poker. Which reminds me,' he went on, almost without a pause, 'of a small duty I ought to perform. Go and dig out one of the ladies, and ask her to accompany me up to Miss Eleanor's room again. I want to have a look in her medicine cupboard. Now, what excuse shall I make? Bit of bandage for a cut finger!'

He drew out a small penknife. 'Just as well to have a little real blood while we're about it,' he said, almost gaily. 'Never tell a lie if it's just as easy to be truthful.'

Chapter Fourteen

Mrs Bradley Explains

'You're looking very jovial this morning, sir, if I may say so,' said Inspector Boring to Carstairs next day.

Carstairs, out for an after-breakfast stroll in the grounds, had encountered the long-faced police officer and had stopped to chat with him.

'Yes, I am going to a wedding in about an hour's time,' Carstairs somewhat surprisingly answered. 'Mr Garde Bing and Miss Dorothy Clark are getting married by special licence in Wavertree.'

'Are they, by Jove!' said the inspector. He lowered his voice. 'What's the little idea, sir?"

Carstairs smiled slightly and shook his head.

'Oh, come now, sir,' persisted Boring, almost pleadingly. 'It is a bit out of the ordinary, you must admit. Yesterday we take their finger-prints, and today they go and get married. There must be something in it.'

'I don't see why, inspector.'

Carstairs was frankly amused, and did not trouble to hide the fact.

'What have the two things to do with one another?' he asked.

'Ah!' said the inspector, in the tone of one who has a grievance. 'What have all the facts in this case to do with one another? That's what I'd like to know, hanged if I wouldn't! Do you know what the Chief Constable said to me this morning? He asked me if I'd like to call in Scotland Yard.'

Carstairs whistled softly.

'Yes, that's what he asked me. Of course, it may come to that yet, sir. Now, look here, Mr Carstairs, why don't some of you ladies and gentlemen come across with what you know? It would help me considerably, and, what is more, you know, sir, it will save some of you the sight of a lot of trouble in the witness-box later on.'

'What do you mean?' asked Carstairs.

'I mean I'm going to find out who killed Everard Mountjoy. You know the verdict of the coroner's court! The coroner, guided by us, summed up so that it was utterly impossible to leave the word "murder" out of it. But I can't prove murder, you see, sir, and yet I know, the same as you know, that murder was done.'

'But I *don't* know that murder was done. As I told you and Sir Joseph yesterday, I felt certain at first that Mountjoy was deliberately drowned, and I imagined I knew the identity of the murderer. But I've changed my mind.'

'You and Mrs Bradley seem to think alike upon

most subjects,' said the inspector, with a grin of distaste at the mention of Mrs Bradley's name.

'Upon most subjects we do *not* think alike,' Carstairs observed, 'but in this case——' He left the sentence unfinished, and cocked an eye at the inspector, but the latter would not allow himself to be drawn.

'Very well, sir,' he said, with more good-humour than might have been expected from him, 'you mean you won't help me. Well, the police get used to that attitude. Still, I should have thought that a clever gentleman like yourself would have come across with any information he might have in his possession, if only to save awkwardness for himself later on. Especially'—Boring paused, as though carefully weighing his words—'especially,' he repeated, with slow and solemn emphasis, 'as I have removed your name from the list of suspected persons.'

'That's very good of you, I'm sure, inspector,' said Carstairs with his quizzical smile. 'To what, in particular, am I indebted for the honour?'

'Oh, to yourself, chiefly, and, of course, on the strength of a tip from the Chief Constable. Said you were a member of his London clubs, or something.'

Carstairs chuckled.

'See what it is to have respectable haunts,' he said. Then the smile left his face, and he went on very seriously:

'Look here, inspector! I liked Everard Mountjoy, and I am as keen as you are to find her murderer.

I'll tell you who I thought it was, and I'll tell you why I've changed my mind.'

'I'll tell *you* both those things, sir,' interpolated the inspector. 'You thought it was Miss Bing, and you've changed your mind because you suspect what we know for a fact, namely, that it was no fainting fit, but a cold-blooded attempt at murder which caused Miss Bing to be found nearly drowned in the bath yesterday morning.'

'You are quite right,' said Carstairs. 'That is what I thought. So there we are. And I'm forced to the conclusion that Mountjoy's death was an accident.'

'Come, come, Mr Carstairs!' The inspector's tone was reproachful. 'You are not handing me that, surely! If Mountjoy was not murdered, why did someone try to kill Miss Bing? *Somebody* still thinks she was the murderer, if you don't! And why, in the name of goodness, are those two people in such a hurry to get married? If they knew what I know,' concluded the inspector darkly, 'they'd think twice. Special licence, indeed! What for, Mr Carstairs? What *for*?'

Carstairs shrugged his shoulders carelessly.

'Impetuous youth,' he said, with half humorous sadness. 'Or perhaps they think Miss Clark stands in need of a husband's protection.'

'Protection?' The inspector ruminated on this for a time, and then exclaimed:

'Mr Carstairs, you've hit it! They are afraid of another attempt on her life! I was wrong about the Guy Fawkes! It was not a practical joke. We

realized that when we heard that Miss Clark and
Mrs Bradley had rigged it up between them, and that
the young fellows, Bing and what's-his-name?—
Philipson—had had no hand in it. That means
they can guess pretty nearly who the poker-fiend
was, and have some idea he may try again. Half a
minute before you say any more. I'll just get that
idea down clearly. There's a lot in it.'

He took a newspaper from his tunic, unfolded it,
placed it on the ground, and seated himself. Then
he produced his note-book, licked his pencil, and
wrote busily for several seconds. Carstairs seated
himself on the edge of a stone garden ornament
and hummed softly.

The inspector finished writing, and rose, tidily
picking up the newspaper as he did so. 'And
that brings us back to Eleanor Bing,' he placidly
observed.

'How do you mean?'

Carstairs was obviously startled.

'I mean this.' And from his tunic-pocket the
inspector drew a little bottle more than half-filled
with small round white tablets. He extended the
bottle so that Carstairs could decipher the chemist's
label upon it, but did not offer to relinquish his
hold.

'Aspirin,' said Carstairs. 'What's the point,
inspector?'

The inspector returned the bottle to its place.

'Exhibit One,' he replied contentedly, 'to prove
that Miss Eleanor Bing is a very poor liar.'

'Eh?' Carstairs was still puzzled.

'Didn't she tell all of you that she went into Miss Clark's room that night for aspirin tablets to relieve her neuralgia? Well, I found this bottle in the very front of the little cupboard in her own room. It ought not to be difficult to find out whether it was bought yesterday, and, if so, who has had—let's see!'

He took out the bottle again.

'It ought to contain fifty, according to the label. It actually does contain'—he removed stopper and cotton wool, and shook out the tablets on to his hand—'thirty-one. Well, it's fairly safe to assume that she hasn't taken nineteen of them since the night before last, so, if I can prove that nobody else has had nineteen out of this bottle since then, I've got reason for saying that Miss Bing told a lie when she said she went to Miss Clark's bedroom for aspirin. This, taken in conjunction with the fact that the finger-prints on the poker are those of Miss Bing, justifies me in assuming that she dealt the blow to that Guy Fawkes. Now, the snag will be to prove whether she thought she was trying to kill Miss Clark, or whether she knew it was only a dummy, and, if the latter is the case, why she wanted to do such a darn fool thing—especially in the middle of the night.'

He paused, and drew breath.

'I hope I haven't been boring you,' he said apologetically. 'I don't usually say off a whole long piece like that at once, but I wanted to get the hang of my ideas.'

'Inspector, you belie your name,' said Carstairs,

laughing. 'Boring you may be, but boring you are not.'

They walked up to the house together.

Breakfast was on its last legs, as Garde observed to them when they entered by the French windows. That was to say that Eleanor, who found herself sufficiently recovered from her experiences of the day before to resume her usual position as mistress of ceremonies at the breakfast-table, was pouring out a last cup of coffee for the indolent Bertie, who never dreamed of appearing at breakfast until everyone else had finished. This habit, which would not have endeared anyone else to Eleanor, elicited from her, in this case, nothing more than a long-suffering moan of motherly reproachfulness.

The inspector came to the point in his blunt but effective way.

'I hope it isn't the aspirin habit that makes you sleep so sound, Mr Philipson,' he observed, with heavy jocularity.

'Aspirin? Good Lord, no! I leave that harmless, unnecessary drug to the ladies,' said Bertie, laughing.

'Indeed,' retorted Eleanor, rising swiftly to the bait, 'I am sure, Bertie, that you have no reason for saying so when I am the only member of my sex present. Personally, I rarely, if ever, have recourse to such a means of inducing sleep. In fact, I only keep aspirin in the house at all for the sake of the maidservants, in case they should suffer from aching teeth, or some such affliction common to the lower classes. I am constantly saying to Mabel,

"Why don't you have your teeth properly attended to? You are an insured person. It will cost you nothing. I will arrange your work so that you can visit the dentist at a convenient time!" But no!' cried Eleanor, warming to one of her favourite subjects. 'The lower classes have no forethought! Mabel became quite impertinent. I was obliged to pull her up very sharply.'

'Do you *never* take aspirin, Miss Bing?' pursued the inspector. 'When did you purchase the last amount of it?'

'I am at a loss to understand your interest in the subject, inspector,' observed Eleanor coldly, 'but, since you ask, I will tell you that I purchased the last bottle of aspirin tablets——' She pulled at a gold chain, which, in defiance of feminine fashion of the moment, she wore suspended round her neck, and which terminated in a large flap-pocket in her house-frock. A small, black, stiff-covered book came into view. She consulted it, and then gravely announced: 'On May 15th I bought a bottle containing fifty aspirin tablets at the chemist's in Wavertree.'

'And you've purchased none since?' the inspector persisted.

Eleanor returned the little book to its place, pursed her lips, shrugged her shoulders, and, ignoring the inspector entirely, asked: 'More coffee, Bertie?'

Carstairs and the inspector returned to the garden.

'Well, sir,' said Boring at last, when they had

traversed the gravel path round the lawn, 'what
do you make of her?'

'I think she has forgotten she went to Miss Clark's
room that night with the poker,' answered Carstairs
deliberately.

'Forgotten she went there?' The inspector was
incredulous.

Carstairs smiled ruefully and nodded.

'You see, it was fairly obvious,' he said, 'that your
questions about the aspirin touched no responsive
chord in her mind.'

'Or else she's deeper than you think, sir,' the
inspector pointed out. 'It's wonderful how some
of these people refuse to give themselves away,
you know.'

'Yes,' admitted Carstairs, 'that is true, I think. All
the same, I had a good deal of experience during
the war in interrogating people. I speak German,
and so I was given the job of interviewing German
prisoners, and I learned to detect, almost infallibly,
whether a man was concealing anything from me.
Now, I watched Eleanor Bing very closely while
you were speaking to her, and I feel certain that
your questions irritated her simply because she
considered them pointless.'

'You said just now that she has forgotten she
ever went into Miss Clark's room that night,' said
the inspector, wrinkling his brow. 'Do you mean
she is suffering from loss of memory?'

'Not exactly. I think it likely that the shock
resulting from her being nearly drowned has not
yet worn off, and the incidents which produced

the shock are filling her mind to the exclusion of everything else.'

'Then you mean she might have obtained aspirin since then and forgotten she did so?' pursued the inspector.

'I think nothing is less likely,' pronounced Carstairs, filling his pipe. 'To begin with, it seems that she keeps a record of her purchases in that small book which we saw her produce from her pocket, and, to go on with, as she was in bed all day yesterday, she could not have gone out and bought anything, could she? All you have to do——'

'Thank you, sir. No need to teach me my business,' chuckled the inspector. 'I'll go and find out what parcels were delivered at the house yesterday and the day before, and who went out shopping and what they bought. No, I don't smoke when I'm in uniform, sir, thanks very much.'

Left to himself, Carstairs retired to the summer-house for a quiet smoke, and found the little building in the possession of Mrs Bradley, who, rather to his surprise, was reading, with a frown of concentration, the best-selling novel of the month. She put the book down when she saw him, and grinned fiendishly.

'Good morning,' said she. 'At what hour are we due to start for the church? You see me attempting to get my mind in tune with the great event. Dear young people! I hope they will be very, very happy together. And how hugely delighted our dear Eleanor is, isn't she? Have you observed that fact?'

'No,' replied Carstairs, 'I can't say that I have. Rather a curious attitude on her part, if all that I suspect about her is true.'

'On the contrary,' contradicted Mrs Bradley, with spirit, 'it is absolutely in line with all her behaviour throughout these curious proceedings.'

'Expound,' said Carstairs, 'for, behold, we have an hour and forty minutes before we need start for the church.'

'Of which period of time I shall require to spend the hour in donning my wedding garments,' remarked Mrs Bradley. 'But the forty minutes is completely at your disposal. First of all, I wish you would tell me your version of all that has occurred since last we talked together.'

'I don't think I have one,' Carstairs began. 'I thought Eleanor killed Mountjoy, and I'm sure she intended to kill Dorothy Clark. But since then somebody has certainly tried to kill Eleanor herself, and so I am forced to the conclusion either that Mountjoy's death was an accident—which I am not prepared to believe for a single instant, in spite of what I've said to the inspector—or else that the murderer is a homicidal maniac who accounted for Mountjoy, attempted to kill first Dorothy Clark, and then Eleanor Bing, and, for all I know to the contrary, may be lurking at the back of the summer-house at this very moment waging to make an attempt on you and me. The only question is, who is it?'

Mrs Bradley cackled.

'And you, brave man, sit here calmly talking about it,' she jibed. 'Run for your life! Run!'

'Well, if you know a more feasible explanation, give it,' said Carstairs, laughing. 'But, first of all, there is just one point about the whole affair that I can't get clear in my mind. It's trifling, I admit, but it worries me considerably.'

'Ah!' said Mrs Bradley, with quiet relish. 'I thought you'd notice the scream.'

'You *are* a witch! I've always thought as much, and now I know it,' said Carstairs. 'What on earth gave you the clue to my thoughts?'

'Nothing. After all, the scream *was* the extraordinary part of the business, so why shouldn't you notice it?'

'Passing over your quite unique habit of reading my mind,' said Carstairs, 'I admit at once that you are right. Why *did* Eleanor scream like that?'

'Well, why do women usually scream?' asked Mrs Bradley.

'They scream because they are in agony, or because they are in danger, or because they are badly frightened.'

'Well, let us say because they are suddenly frightened,' corrected Mrs Bradley. 'Very well. We can dismiss the idea that Eleanor was in agony, I think. She seemed quite remarkably healthy both before and after the scream.'

'She said she had neuralgia,' Carstairs interpolated.

'Yes, she *said* so,' Mrs Bradley agreed, 'but, even if that were true, people don't usually give one loud, terrifying scream that wakes the whole household when they have neuralgia. Besides, if she did scream with pain, she could have said so. There was no reason against saying so.'

'That leaves us with the alternatives of danger and sudden fright,' said Carstairs.

'Exactly. Let us examine them. The view that she was in danger in that bedroom must not be lost sight of, and the view that something in the bedroom frightened her is undoubtedly true. She admitted it herself, but her explanation of what caused her sudden fright is amazingly thin. She said that when she turned on the light she saw that dummy figure in the bed, when she had expected to see Dorothy Clark. Now I contend that Eleanor was not telling the truth. To begin with, a glance should have sufficed to tell her what the dummy was. To go on with, although I grant it may have startled her, I very seriously doubt whether it would have startled anyone except an extremely hysterical person into screaming at that pitch. Now, Eleanor is not an hysterical subject, for, if she were, the probabilities are that she would have gone on screaming, aren't they?'

Carstairs nodded.

'Go on,' he said. 'Like Portia's, your exposition is sound. The sight of the dummy figure did not cause her to scream. The question is, what did?'

'Let me conclude my argument about the dummy figure,' said Mrs Bradley. 'I think Eleanor told a lie when she said she turned on the light. Her fingerprints were on that poker. The head of the dummy was staved in by a heavy blow. The inference is that

Eleanor struck that blow. The poker is a particularly weighty one, which is, or rather was, used and kept in the dining-room. What was Eleanor doing with it in the middle of the night? She must have intended to kill Dorothy Clark with it. Would she have risked turning lights on, if she had had this purpose in her mind? No! no! The moonlight, she judged, was sufficient to guide her aim. She struck the blow, and then——'

'Screamed,' said Carstairs. 'But why?'

'Because somebody was hiding in Dorothy's room that night,' said Mrs Bradley, quietly, 'and this person sprang out and confronted Eleanor immediately she struck that heavy blow. It was this person who switched on the light. It was at sight of this person, it was at this sudden, utterly unexpected appearance, and his fierce, almost murderous attitude and expression, that Eleanor emitted that fearful scream. Not only did she realize that someone had seen her kill Dorothy, but she thought her own life was in danger from the eye-witness.'

'But she *didn't* kill Dorothy,' said Carstairs feebly.

'No, but she thought she had. It was not until the unknown person pointed to the bed that Eleanor realized her own life was safe.'

'But—but I'm hanged if I see where you are getting your facts from,' said Carstairs. 'It's all out of my depth.'

'These are not facts. This is only my reconstruction of what must have happened that night. You admit that it accounts for Eleanor's dreadful scream as no mere sight of a dummy figure could do, don't you?'

'I admit that it is a clever reconstruction,' said Carstairs, smiling.

'Yes, but don't you see that it also accounts for the attempt made on Eleanor's life? If Eleanor had struck Dorothy instead of the dummy figure that night, she herself would never have left that room alive. But because Dorothy was safe the unknown witness allowed Eleanor to go. Later on, however, he thought better of allowing her to escape scot-free and remain at liberty to injure Dorothy on some future occasion, so he entered the bathroom next morning, and, as he thought, drowned Eleanor in the bath.'

Mrs Bradley broke off, and emitted another of her hideous yelps of laughter.

'I expect he worked tremendously hard yesterday morning trying to bring her round,' she observed. 'It must have been a staggering shock to him when she recovered, and he realized that he had taken all that trouble and run all that risk in vain.'

Carstairs frowned.

'You say "him," and that means you are certain you know the identity of this unknown person,' he said.

'I am not certain of his identity, although I could make a guess at it,' said Mrs Bradley. 'But I am sure he is a man and not a woman, because we can all account for Eleanor, and Dorothy and I can account for one another, because we slept in the same bedroom, and, as I don't think it was one of the maids,' she added, cackling, 'that leaves, besides the menservants, yourself, Alastair, Garde, and Bertie Philipson. Come along. Take your choice. Which one will you have?'

Carstairs pondered.

'Garde Bing is the likeliest,' he said slowly, 'but you won't persuade me that he was the unknown witness if you try from now until my dying day!'

He spoke with some heat. Mrs Bradley shook her head. 'A fair guess,' she said, 'but, I think, a mistake. Try Bertie Philipson.'

Chapter Fifteen

A Confession

'BERTIE PHILIPSON?'

Carstairs laughed heartily.

'That is where your excellent reconstruction falls flat,' he said.

'Very well,' agreed Mrs Bradley, quite unruffled. 'Then perhaps you'll tell me why, of all the members of the household, servants included, Bertie was the only person who did not join the rest upon the landing outside Dorothy's room.'

'Wasn't Bertie there?' asked Carstairs slowly, although his own retentive memory had answered the question almost before the words had left his lips.

'You know he was not. Don't you remember at breakfast next morning Garde teased him about his non-appearance? Besides, I counted up, and I know he was not there. He was hiding still in Dorothy's room. Naturally he could not step out and advertise his whereabouts. Young men don't usually spend the night crouching behind the head of someone else's bed, especially that of a young unmarried woman. Besides, there was the heavy poker and the dented mask to be accounted for. So Bertie, when he heard the pandemonium following on Eleanor's startled scream, went to earth again. And small blame to him,' added Mrs Bradley, chuckling. 'I could wager that he spent a remarkably uncomfortable half-hour, too; for, besides the discomfort of his crouching position, he could not be sure that some one of us would not spot him. He wondered, also, whether Eleanor would give him away.'

'Yes, if what you say is true, why didn't she?' asked Carstairs. 'She would not have needed to alter a word of her own story, and it would have made her screaming appear the most natural thing under the circumstances. Even the finger-prints on the poker need not have proved an insurmountable difficulty, for she could have said that Bertie used some sort of a holder for it and that she had handled the poker last—snatched it away from him, or something, after he had struck the blow.'

Mrs Bradley shook her head at him playfully.

'There is a master of sensational fiction lost in you,' she said.

'I like that,' said Carstairs warmly. 'Who devised this whole remarkable account of the proceedings on that interesting night, pray?'

'Not guilty, my lord,' responded Mrs Bradley. 'This is not of my devising. It is the simple truth.

Test it in any way you choose, and see how well it all hangs together. There is not a flaw that I can detect.'

'You pointed one out to me only a minute ago,' said Carstairs dryly. 'Why didn't Eleanor give Bertie away?'

'She is in love with him,' said Mrs Bradley simply; and she recounted to the astonished Carstairs the story Bertie himself had told her; the story which had begun two years before, and which was now moving to its astounding conclusion.

'Well,' said Carstairs, when she had finished, 'I should like to think the whole affair out again in the light of what you have told me——'

'Exactly,' agreed Mrs Bradley complacently. 'One increasing purpose runs through the whole of these unhappy but interesting affairs, and the theme is Eleanor's desire for Bertie Philipson. Forgive me, but I really must go and dress. Who did you say the other bridesmaid was to be?'

'A girl named Pamela Storbin,' Carstairs answered. 'A nice girl. Her guardian is a friend of mine, and I have known Pamela since she was three.'

'Is she coming here first?' asked Mrs Bradley keenly.

'I believe not. The arrangements for the wedding have been fixed up at such very short notice that I fancy Pamela is to meet the others at the church, and will come back here to lunch.'

'I—see,' said Mrs Bradley, in such a thoughtful tone that Carstairs was moved to ask:

'There is no reason why she shouldn't, is there?'

'It is almost a pity that Bertie is such a charming squire of dames,' was Mrs Bradley's cryptic, and therefore disquieting, reply. 'And that, by the way, brings us back to the beginning of our conversation. You said you had not noticed how pleased Eleanor is at the news of this wedding.'

'No, I haven't noticed,' said Carstairs. 'But if she *is* pleased, I understand the significance of her pleasure. The marriage finally separates Bertie and Dorothy, doesn't it?'

'It does,' replied Mrs Bradley. 'And now I really must go and dress. Are you coming too? How very nice.'

But Carstairs was not to be allowed to dress in peace. He was in his bedroom, attending to a refractory tie, when a sharp knock at the door arrested his attention.

The detective-inspector stood outside.

'Any inside information for me, sir?' he asked keenly. 'I saw you hobnobbing with Mrs Bradley in the summer-house, but the partition was too thick for me to catch much of what you were saying. Still, I heard enough to know that Mrs Bradley was parting with valuable information. So come, sir! Spill me what you know!'

Carstairs laughed heartily.

'But I don't know any more than I did an hour ago when we talked together,' he said. 'Mrs Bradley was giving me a fanciful, highly coloured reconstruction of the events of the last two or three days so as to include all the known facts and a few which, I think, she has made up out of her own head.'

The inspector looked disappointed, but was too wily to press the point.

'Not much use in theorizing at this stage, sir. We haven't collected enough facts to start theorizing about them. And, by the way, sir,' he broke off, 'there's just one snag in the whole affair that I can't get over anyhow.'

'What's that?' asked Carstairs.

'Well, look here, Mr Carstairs, you know Miss Bing better than I do, so you may be able to explain things to me which I haven't had a chance to observe for myself. Does she seem to you, sir, the sort of young woman who would climb in at the bathroom window and drown a naked person? Seems to me she's such a prim sort of young woman she'd hardly like to *think* about people with no clothes on, never mind coming in where they were and murdering 'em! You see my point, sir, don't you? It isn't in the picture, that isn't. And I've learned to beware of things that don't fit.'

'You knew Everard Mountjoy was masquerading as a man, and that Eleanor Bing was formally engaged to her, didn't you?' asked Carstairs.

'Good Lord, sir. Yes, of course! I was losing sight of that fact,' cried Boring. 'Well, that gives us a motive at once, as the Chief Constable seemed to think.'

'So Mrs Bradley thought,' said Carstairs. 'The idea is that Eleanor found out the truth about her lover, and couldn't bear it.'

'Wait a minute, sir. Don't harp on it. Let me get down the facts from a fresh point of view. Can't have too much light on a dark subject.'

Out came the note-book and pencil, and the inspector methodically re-tabulated the evidence against Eleanor Bing.

'Of course,' said Boring, when the note-book was again stored safely away, 'she didn't go to the bathroom to kill Mountjoy, but to sort of have it out with her—the bathroom, in these modern times, being one of the very few places where you can reckon on being undisturbed. Then, her feelings in the matter overcoming her judgment, Miss Bing——'

He made a suggestive movement and Carstairs nodded.

'Easiest thing in the world,' said the inspector, with serious interest, 'to drown a person in the bath. I wonder more murderers don't do it. No incriminating weapon, no marks of violence, nothing but the body, which you don't even have the trouble of getting rid of, because there's always a big chance of the coroner's jury bringing in a verdict of Accidental Death. For that's usually the bother in a murder, sir,' he went on, warming to the subject in whole-hearted fashion, 'what the 'ell to do with the corpse. Look at Crippen! Look at Patrick Mahon! Oh, it's the very devil to the murderer, the corpse is! Talk about the albatross what hung round that fellow's neck in the poem we learnt at school! Well, a corpse is that same bird to the murderer, nine times out of ten. They burn

'em up with lime, or set fire to the house where
they've left 'em, or carve 'em up so that the king's
own butcher would be hard put to it to name the
joints, but'—the inspector nodded solemnly—'we
get 'em in the end, sir!'

He nodded, and passed out.

Carstairs, with a sigh of relief, returned to his
tie, finished dressing, and ran downstairs, to find
the rest of the party waiting for him.

The ceremony was soon over. Eleanor and the
brown-haired, youthful Pamela Storbin were the
bridesmaids, Bertie Philipson acted as best man, and
Dorothy's father, summoned, with her mother, by
telegram, gave the bride away. These casual and
modern parents then refused to return with the
wedding party to Chaynings, but, having bestowed
a kiss and their best wishes on their daughter,
and shaken hands with their new son-in-law, they
departed for Aix-les-Bains without further delay.

The second bridesmaid, young Pamela, was very
easily prevailed upon to return to Chaynings, and
Bertie promised to drive her home, a distance of
twenty miles or thereabouts, soon after dinner.

This well-laid plan, however, fell through owing
to a sudden, violent thunder-storm accompanied
by a deluge of rain.

'Thought it seemed a bit oppressive this afternoon
while we were playing tennis,' Bertie observed.
'Never mind. Let's see what it's like after dinner,
Blue Eyes.'

But after dinner the storm seemed at its
height.

'You can't go home in this,' said Garde.

'Of course not! Of course not!' cried Alastair Bing fussily. 'Quite impossible!'

'Well,' said Bertie, wrinkling his brow, 'if it's all the same to everybody, I'd just as soon *not* take my little old bus out in this.'

'I doubt whether you'd get across Handleigh Bottom after all this rain,' said Dorothy. 'It will be flooded down there.'

Pamela glanced at Eleanor, but her hostess, beyond remarking, 'I must go and see about the rooms, then,' vouchsafed no wish for her company.

'What's bitten Eleanor?' asked Garde, slightly put out by the discourteous lack of hospitable feeling betrayed by his sister.

'Your sister is tired after a long day,' replied his father, with obvious insincerity, and more for Pamela's information than that of his son.

'Well, I hope she's fixed up our room all right,' remarked Garde. 'Come on, Dorothy! Let's go and see the bridal chamber.'

'I am afraid, Garde is apt to be coarse at times,' said Eleanor, who happened to catch the tail-end of her brother's remarks. 'If you will accompany me, Miss Storbin, I will show you your room.'

'Oh, thanks ever so much,' said young Pamela, turning away from the window, through which she had been watching the jagged lightning above the trees.

'Shall I come with you, darling?' said Bertie, in his most fatuous manner.

A jar of red roses by Eleanor's elbow crashed to the ground.

'Dear me,' Mrs Bradley mildly observed, 'what a disaster!'

Eleanor irritably pressed a bell for a servant, and, turning her head over her shoulder, said:

'Come along, Miss Storbin, please.'

Unobtrusively, and almost unnoticed by everybody but Carstairs, Mrs Bradley slipped out after them, and returned in less than ten minutes with Pamela in tow.

'Dorothy dear,' she said, 'you might lend this small child a nightdress. I don't think it has occurred to Eleanor that she'll need one.'

'Of course!' cried Dorothy, who, needless to say, had not accepted her husband's invitation to inspect what he was pleased to call the marriage bed. 'Come along, Pam! I expect you are put into my old room, aren't you?'

This proved to be the case, so, turning out the contents of Dorothy's charming wardrobe upon the bed, the two girls spent a delightful hour in talking of clothes and their own mutual acquaintances and circle of friends.

'And may I really borrow this one? Isn't it a duck?' cried seventeen-year-old Pamela, enraptured with the dainty garment.

'You can keep it if you like,' said Dorothy good-naturedly. 'It isn't one of a set. There's a boudoir-cap somewhere to go with it. Here you are. Yes, it suits you better than it does me.'

'Dorothy, you're a perfect angel,' cried Pamela.

'Oh, and I do hope you'l! be ever so happy with Garde! Can you cope with him? He looks kind of fierce to me. Now, that angel Bertie Philipson——Oo, Dorothy! What was that?'

'Can't hear anything through the thunder,' said Dorothy, turning suddenly very pale; for, although she could not hear, it was easy enough to see, and the 'that' of young Pamela's startled question had been a rustle of clothing and a stifled cough, and, following the direction of Pamela's eyes, Dorothy had caught sight of the glinting spectacles of Eleanor through the crack of the door.

'Whether you heard anything or not,' said Pamela, tossing her delightful brown head, 'I'm going to open the door and find out what it was. Why, Dorothy, you look nearly sick with fright! Is this one of those old ghostly houses? What screaming fun!'

But Dorothy leapt between her and the door and flung it open. The landing was empty, but somebody was descending the stairs.

'Oh, it was only Eleanor,' said Dorothy, in what she hoped was a light and casual tone; but Pamela's eyes were keen, and her ears sympathetic.

'You're as scared as you can be!' she cried, putting her arms round Dorothy and giving the older girl a heartening hug. 'And I'm going right now to tell your fierce husband so, and make him take care of you.'

'No, don't tell Garde! He'll think me silly. I'm going to tell Mr Carstairs. Promise you won't say anything to Garde, Pam!'

'See that wet——' began Pamela promptly. Arm in arm, they descended the stairs.

'Is Mr Carstairs your nerve specialist, then?' asked Pamela. 'We all heard about that fearful motor smash you were in, and I don't wonder your bearings have all worked loose, you poor kid.'

Without vouchsafing any other explanation to the child Dorothy sought out Carstairs, who had slipped into the billiard-room for a quiet smoke, and haltingly told him her fears.

'Eleanor hates this kid. I don't know why. Mr Carstairs, I'm as scared as I can be. You don't think—I mean, it's an awful thing to suggest——'

'Then don't suggest it, my dear,' said Carstairs, with the special avuncular smile he kept for Dorothy. 'Make your mind easy. I quite understand, and I promise you that all possible precautions will be taken.'

'Oh, thank you. You are always so—so lovely to me!' said Dorothy, half-smiling, half-tearful. To Carstairs' mingled gratification and surprise, she put her arm round his neck and kissed him.

'You couldn't quietly hint to Mrs Bradley that I'm in here and that it seems quite a nice place for a confidential talk, could you?' he asked, as she prepared to open the door.

Seven minutes later, Mrs Bradley, in a magenta-gold-and-green evening frock, which for sheer ugliness could scarcely have been equalled, slid coyly into the billiard-room and softly closed the door.

'I have made all the arrangements,' she remarked,

so softly that even Carstairs' quick ears could scarcely catch what she said. 'Listen. I take Pamela into my room, as I did Dorothy. You take Bertie Philipson into Dorothy's old room where Pamela is supposed to sleep, and, if there are any'—she paused for a suitable word—'any manifestations during the night, you deal with them as you think best. I shall spend the night fully dressed and wide awake, so if you want me you have only to tap three times on my door.'

'Good!' said Carstairs. He laughed self-consciously. 'How mad it all seems,' he said, passing a hand across his brow. 'I feel as though I am living in a dream.'

'Well, I suppose you are,' said Mrs Bradley tritely. 'I beg your pardon. My philosophy is about on a level with that of the lamented Polonius.'

She smiled sourly.

'I'll make a wager with you,' she said. 'I am willing to bet—let me see—fifty thousand pounds that, while you are keeping your vigil tonight with Bertie, he will tell you the same funny little tale that I told you in the summer-house this morning.'

'I refuse to bet on a certainty. He will do nothing of the kind,' answered Carstairs. 'What about candles and our prayers?'

Dorothy, instructed by Mrs Bradley, whispered to Pamela, as they went up the stairs:

'Eleanor has had to change your room and doesn't like to tell you, so she asked me to do so. Don't say anything to her about it, will you? She's so extraordinarily touchy where things to do with

the household arrangements are concerned. You'll
have a room-mate. It is only Mrs Bradley. She
probably won't go to bed all night. Sits up and
reads. But don't let it disturb you. She's an awfully
good sort.'

Pamela obediently followed Mrs Bradley into the
room containing twin beds.

'Sweet dreams, my dear,' said the old woman.

Less than twenty minutes later, Pamela lay curled
up in bed, fast asleep.

Mrs Bradley set the bedroom clock right by her
watch, drew up the blinds, and watched the moon-
drenched sky. The storm had cleared away, except
for an occasional rumble and mutter far away to
the south, and the night was lovely in its luminous
calm.

Mrs Bradley sighed sentimentally, tiptoed to the
door, listened a full two minutes, and then, shaking
her head, walked back to the window again.

Later she switched on an electric reading-lamp,
opened a volume of verse, and sat motionless,
except for turning the pages, for over an hour. A
quarter past twelve chimed from the church steeple;
the moon was lower in the sky. Somewhere in the
house a mouse scratched and nibbled.

Mrs Bradley read on. At last she arose, laid
down her book, crept across to the dressing-table,
opened a drawer, and withdrew from its interior
a cup and saucer and a thermos flask. She poured
out half a cup of coffee from the flask, drank it,
and returned to her book.

Carstairs and Bertie were the last to go upstairs.

When everyone else had disappeared, and even Eleanor had popped her head in at the billiard-room door to bid them good night, Carstairs said casually, replacing his cue:

'I hope you're not feeling sleepy, because I've got a job of work for you.'

'Oh,' said Bertie, stifling a yawn, 'how dashed annoying of you! I thought all my friends understood that my beauty sleep is indescribably precious to me, and that even the guns of Flanders could scarcely persuade me to forgo it.'

'Flanders?' said Carstairs, surprised. 'You're not as old as that, are you?'

'Thirty last birthday,' grinned Bertie. 'But now to the work! What is't thou would'st have me do?'

'Help me keep watch in Dorothy's old room, where the young girl Pamela Storbin was to have slept,' said Carstairs calmly.

'Keep watch—here, I say! What's the game, sir?'

The young man looked so startled that Carstairs wondered whether Mrs Bradley's queer story could possibly be true.

'And if so,' thought Carstairs humorously, 'I hope the young beggar won't want to start trying to murder me!'

Together they went up the stairs, repaired each to his own room, counted five hundred slowly (this was Carstairs' idea), and then, in stockinged feet, crept down the flight of stairs which divided their landing from Dorothy's own.

'Hate going about with only my socks on my feet,' confessed Bertie. 'Always feel so bally nervous and helpless without my shoes. I've brought them in my hand, though, as you said.'

'You can put them on now,' said Carstairs, 'as long as you don't make too much row. Now, look here. I've moved the bed out about another four inches, so that we shall be more comfortable hiding behind the head of it than you were when you hid in here last time.'

This shot in the dark had immediate effect.

'So you know,' said Bertie, his fresh-coloured face going white. 'What do I have to do? Shut your mouth for you, or give myself up to the inspector Johnny for attempted murder?'

'Not much good killing me,' said Carstairs, smiling disarmingly. 'Mrs Bradley knows, and I've more than a feeling that the inspector has his suspicions.'

All this he confided in a whisper.

Bertie followed his example, and replied: 'Are you two going to give me away?'

'Of course not,' said Carstairs simply.

'Good man!' said Bertie feelingly. 'I'll tell you all about it. It will be quite a relief to get it off my chest. Well, it happened this way.'

'Keep your voice low,' urged Carstairs. 'We don't want anybody to know we are in here.'

'Rather not,' agreed Bertie. 'By the way, what's the little idea? I mean, why *are* we in here?'

'I haven't the least idea,' said Carstairs, not quite truthfully. 'Our stunt is wait and see. Want another cushion behind your back? Now, then, fire away.'

Chapter Six

Night Alarms

BERTIE began to talk. He was a trifle awkward and diffident at first, but gained confidence and power of expression as he proceeded.

'Of course, you know I'm fond of Dorothy,' he said. 'I always have been, but she liked Garde better. That isn't a bit surprising, I know. Well, I'd always felt that I'd—well, that I'd do anything on earth for her. You know the sort of thing. I knew her when we were kids, you see, and even then I used to tell lies for her and get her out of scrapes, and all that.

'Well, to make the yarn brief, Dorothy had hardly arrived here, when she sort of got a beastly feeling that Eleanor hated her, and she was in a horrible funk, not on her own account so much—although, of course, it is not the pleasantest thing on earth to know that someone hates you!—but because she was horribly scared about Garde. Garde, you know, is by the way of being one of those strong, silent coves who land people a doughboy first and think afterwards, and then are frightfully perturbed at the coroner's nasty tactless remarks. You know the sort of chap? Well, Dorothy jolly well knew that, if Eleanor went for her, Garde would pretty well settle Eleanor's hash for good and all. In fact, he had said as much, in decorated Gothic—so to speak—to us both. So I thought things had better not come to a head.

'Well, Mrs Bradley knew which way the wind was blowing that night, and, as you remember, she took Dorothy to sleep in her room.

'Well, I got wind of the careful preparations; the dummy figure which had to be made so life-like; the secrecy with which it was assembled, and all that; and I was jolly keen to find out what was going to happen. Up to this point, I must say I was actuated by curiosity. Can you understand what I mean?'

'Perfectly,' replied Carstairs.

'Yes, well, I do hope you can,' said Bertie, grinning shamefacedly, 'because what I did next requires some charitable comprehension. Frankly, I was so keen to find out what the game was, that I crouched on the second landing, and watched until I saw Dorothy trail along to Mrs Bradley's room, and then I tiptoed down the stairs, sneaked into Dorothy's room—I say, I know this sounds pretty rotten and cheap, but, at least I did know that Dorothy wasn't likely to come back there that night—and hid myself behind the head of the bed, as we are hiding now. It is formed of a good stout slab of mahogany, isn't it? Quite a fruity little dug-out, in fact. I had my dark brown dressing-gown on, and I had retained my socks, so it was not bad at all behind there.'

Carstairs drew in his breath. What a fool he had been even remotely to suspect that Mrs Bradley had been romancing. Clever woman! He felt that he owed her an apology.

'Well, of course, after an hour or so—just as I was beginning to get a bit bored and fidgety, and to think that bed wasn't a bad sort of idea, and to remember that curiosity killed the cat—along toddled Eleanor, complete with poker.

'I don't mean to be flippant. Honestly, it was the beastliest thing I ever saw! The moon was fairly bright, so she didn't turn up the light. She just stood there for a full minute, I should think, perfectly still, with the moonlight flooding all about her, and that heavy poker grasped firmly in her right hand. I'm sure her eyes gleamed in the darkness like those of a cat.

'She must have heard my breathing, I am sure, and I should think she heard my heart thudding too, but I suppose she thought it was only Dorothy, sound asleep in the bed.

'Anyhow, just as I was getting so worked up that I thought I'd have to come out and say something just to relieve the tension, she did the trick!

'My God! but it was horrible! She raised that heavy poker above her head with both hands, and as she brought it down on that still, apparently sleeping head I distinctly heard her chuckle. I tell you, I could have bellowed at her with sheer horror. For she was mad at that moment! She was a homicidal maniac!

'Scarcely had the poker crashed down upon that dummy head, when I made my spring. I leaped upon her from the side, and at that instant she screamed.

'You people thought that scream pretty blood-curdling, I know, but if you'd only heard it at close range as I did! It was ghastly, I can tell you that. It was perfectly frightful. It nearly scared me stiff. I had no idea anybody could make such a hell of a noise.

'I loosed her, and she ran out into the passage, dropping the poker across the foot of the bed as she went.

'In a moment I heard voices, doors opening, and the sound of feet on the stairs. I don't know why—I had nothing to fear—but, for some unearthly reason, I felt it would be most damnably awkward to explain myself to you all, so I crouched down again behind the head of the bed, and hoped for the best. At the time it seemed the only thing to do. I intended to indicate that I had been sleep-walking, should I be discovered there.

'I had a fine time for the next quarter of an hour or so. The whole house was in an uproar. I could hear all your voices, and I even heard Garde ask where that lazy devil of a Philipson was. Of course, next morning, you remember, I pretended that I had heard the rumpus, but had decided, after a cursory inspection, that it had nothing to do with me, and that I had crawled back into bed.

It was queer, really, how none of you seemed to suspect me.

'Well, I nearly had fits, as you can imagine, when you all came in to admire the débris on the bed and to goggle at the poker; especially as one of you *did* turn the light on, and I expected every minute some one would observe my shadow on the wall, and haul me out of my hiding-place.

'However, luckily for me, Dorothy, poor kid, was on the verge of hysterics, and demanded most of your attention.

'At last you all went away, and I waited for about twenty minutes, and then decided to make a dash for it back to my own room.

'I arrived safely, but I guess I didn't sleep much.'

Carstairs stirred in his place. He was wondering if, after all, his first impression of Mrs Bradley's reconstruction of these events had been the correct one, and that her version had been the merest romantic story, utterly false and wrong.

'That's a very interesting statement, Mr Philipson,' he said, a trifle weightily for a man with a sense of humour. 'It is very interesting indeed.'

'There is more to come, Mr Carstairs,' said Bertie, in a low voice.

Carstairs metaphorically sat up with a jerk.

'Indeed?' he asked, in as quiet and ordinary a tone as he could manage, considering his sudden excitement, and the fact that they were both speaking in whispers.

Bertie went on:

'I—can't—I shall not attempt to explain what happened next. It is almost too horrible to tell you about, but I've decided I must get the whole thing off my chest.

'I only want to say that, if I had the time over again, I should act in precisely the same way. I know I should. It was a horrible thing that I did. An awful thing. But it seemed to me then, and it seems to me now, the only possible course to have taken.'

'What did you do?' asked Carstairs. 'At last,' he thought, 'at long last, I am going to get to the bottom of this mystery!'

'Well, I decided that I must kill Eleanor before she could harm my Dorothy.'

The unconscious introduction of the possessive note was intensely pathetic.

'I stole from my room,' Bertie continued, 'very early in the morning. At about six o'clock, I think it must have been, although I don't remember looking at my watch. In my stockinged feet I descended the stairs on to this lower landing. Then I crept along until I came to this room again.

'Do you remember how you and old Mr Bing got me to crawl from Dorothy's balcony to the bathroom window that day?' he broke off.

Carstairs, unwilling to break the thread of the narrative, merely nodded into the gloom.

'Well, I repeated that stunt,' said Bertie. 'First of all, I opened those doors which lead on to the balcony and left them ajar. Then I stood behind this door leading on to the landing, and watched through the crack to see Eleanor come into the bathroom.

'She came to the bathroom early that morning. That was rather lucky for me. As soon as she had shut and locked the bathroom door behind her, I climbed from Dorothy's balcony to the bathroom window, hung on by my eyebrows, and looked in.

'Eleanor had just turned both taps on, so she could not hear me, and I crawled back to *terra firma* and waited until I judged the bath would be full enough for my purpose.

'Luckily for this purpose, Eleanor was a bit of a fresh-air fiend, even in the somewhat parky hours of the early morning, so that she had opened the window a trifle at the top. I observed that it would be easy enough to enter the bathroom without leaving my tracks behind me in the form of a broken window. I was glad of that.

'Now, at this point, I want you to believe me when I say that I was undecided what to do next. I am not a violent sort of cove, and, while waiting behind Dorothy's door for Eleanor to appear for her bath, it had struck me that I could quite satisfactorily arrange for Dorothy's safety without actually doing in Eleanor. I thought that if I confronted Eleanor suddenly in much the same way as somebody must have confronted poor Mountjoy, and also before she had had much time to make up a good lie about what she had been up to in Dorothy's room on the previous night, I might be able to scare her so much that she would leave Dorothy absolutely alone in the future. See what I mean? Sort of blackmail idea.'

Carstairs nodded, although the motion was imperceptible in the darkness.

'Well,' said Bertie, 'I had just got the bathroom window nicely open and was about to heave myself over the sill when rather a weird thing happened. I don't know to this day whether Eleanor saw me, or whether she was overcome by faintness from some other cause, but the fact remains that she flung out her arms with a funny little coughing moan, and crashed head downwards over the side of the bath, which was half full of water.

'What devil of wickedness seized me I don't know. But I sprang over the sill like a cat, and rushed at the girl, and with a terrific feeling of savage joy—I could have laughed and laughed aloud for the sheer, hellish pleasure of it!—I held Eleanor's head under water, while the two taps beat a devil's tattoo in my brain as they splashed crazily into the bath! Then, when I felt certain she must be dead, I twisted the chain of the waste plug round her hand and let the water run away. I left her lying there with her head over the side of the bath, and climbed back the way I had come, leaving the bathroom door locked. The luck of Beelzebub stuck to me to the very end. I met not a soul on the way back to my bedroom. I got into bed, and, when my man called me, I really and truly was sound asleep, and for half a second I couldn't think why my socks were damp when I pulled them on.'

Carstairs sighed softly into the darkness at the

conclusion of Bertie's narrative, and for ten minutes or more neither man spoke.

Suddenly Bertie lifted his head and whispered: 'What's that?'

It was a queer shuffling sound, and it was coming along the landing. As suddenly as it had begun it ceased, and, with tense muscles and eyes fixed on the door, the two men waited, straining their ears to catch the next sound. Carstairs laid a restraining hand upon Bertie's arm in case the younger man should precipitate matters by emerging from his hiding-place too soon.

Still as stone, they waited and watched. Then they detected the sound again, and candlelight gleamed through the crack of the floor.

Again there followed a pause, while Carstairs counted thirty to himself. Then the candlelight moved forward, and the door was pushed slowly and softly open. Carstairs' fingers closed painfully on Bertie's arm. The tension was extreme.

Framed in the open doorway and looking the picture of maniacal, avenging fury, stood Eleanor Bing. The candle, whose flickering, uneasy radiance illumined the scene, was held in her left hand. In her right she gripped an enormous carving-knife.

'Good God!' said Bertie, between clenched teeth.

Eleanor stopped short, and listened with a kind of ferocious intentness. Gone were her puritanical expression and her prim demeanour; gone her faintly derisive smile and her neat Victorian coiffure. This was Fury incarnate which stood before them;

Fury of the French Revolution; Fury of the Russian
famine; Fury of Furies—wild-eyed, streaming-
haired Fury loosed from hell!

She laughed; and the blood froze in Carstairs' veins.

'She's mad,' he whispered, gazing with fascinated
repulsion as Eleanor advanced towards the empty
bed with the carving-knife raised high in the air.

Quietly he began to worm his way out from
behind the bed's head, and round the walls, keeping
carefully outside the circle of fitful candlelight.
Bertie, divining his intention, followed his example,
but took the opposite side of the room.

'Now!' yelled Carstairs suddenly, as, with a shriek
of wild-beast rage, Eleanor, beholding the empty
bed and knowing herself foiled of her prey, slashed
and slashed again at the bedclothes, ripped open
the eiderdown, cut and sawed the blankets, and
tore the sheets into strips with the knife and her
own cruel, strong hands.

Carstairs grasped her round the body, imprisoning
her arms, while Bertie snatched the powerful knife
from her fingers.

Eleanor fought and struggled, while from the
lips which were accustomed to employ the most
trite and correct of expressions there poured forth
a stream of the most foul and abominable filth
which ever disgraced the name of language.

'For heaven's sake stop her!' cried Bertie
frantically. He himself tried to place a hand over
her foaming mouth, but received a bite for his
pains which caused him quickly to desist.

Someone switched on the electric light.

'Now then!' said Mrs Bradley's voice, in accents neither man had heard before.

The fighting, struggling Eleanor gave a little whimpering cry like that of a dog which expects a beating, and attempted to shrink away from the newcomer and to efface herself behind Bertie Philipson.

'Come, now!' said Mrs Bradley, in the same tone. 'What are you thinking of! You're tired. You want to go back to bed. Come here! This way!'

She advanced towards the demented girl as she spoke, and grasped her firmly by the arm.

'No nonsense!' she said. 'This is very, very foolish! Back to bed at once!'

The two men followed them out of the room and along to Eleanor's own chamber.

'Just in case of accidents,' said Carstairs quietly to Bertie, 'I think we had better stand by.'

Eleanor, however, seemed to recognise in Mrs Bradley a master mind, and shiveringly but mutely obeyed her commands.

'No need for you to stay out of bed any longer,' Mrs Bradley told the two men. 'I'll get her into bed, and I'm going to give her a fairly powerful sleeping-draught. I'll just stay with her while she drinks it, and then I'll lock her door on the outside when I come away. Good night. Thanks very much for your help.'

A low, distracted moan from the chair on which Eleanor had seated herself cut short her remarks.

'Yes, yes. All right now. Quite all right now,' the men heard the older woman murmur.

They waited outside for a minute or two, but, hearing no further sounds except the creaking of Eleanor's bed, followed by the chink of a glass, they tiptoed away.

'I expect the dementia spasm, or whatever it is, has passed by now,' whispered Carstairs. 'Good night. Your room is next to mine, so if there should be anything else happening and you are needed, I will knock three times on the wall.'

'Right you are. Good night,' responded Bertie; and they retired to bed.

About five minutes later, Carstairs, who had undressed as far as his shirt and trousers, was startled by hearing an urgent tapping at his bedroom door. He opened it to find Alastair Bing, closely followed by Garde and Dorothy, confronting him.

'Oh, here you are, Carstairs! Is anything wrong? Awful amount of noise going on in the house. Shocking amount of noise going on in the house,' cried Alastair, bristling fiercely. 'I hope there's no foolishness going on.'

'Good heavens!' cried Carstairs. 'Whatever is that row?'

'That row, as you call it, is the noise I refer to,' said Alastair. 'It comes from my daughter's bedroom. She says she can't get out. Why can't she get out? Why not? *Why* not?'

'Tell you later,' replied Carstairs, clutching his dressing-gown from its peg and hastily swarming into it. 'Send Dorothy back to bed, and you two come with me.'

Outside Eleanor's door they encountered Mrs Bradley, and a moment later a tousle-haired Bertie descended the stairs to join them.

'I think I had better go in to her,' said Mrs Bradley. She produced the key of Eleanor's bedroom door from her dressing-gown pocket and cried loudly to drown the rattling and banging of the occupant:

'All right! All right! We are here!'

Eleanor was out of bed and clad only in her night-dress. She fell back against the bed when she saw Mrs Bradley and began to whimper.

'Get into bed,' said Mrs Bradley. 'Go to sleep. So tired, aren't you? Yes, ever so tired!'

She assisted Eleanor into bed again, and tucked the bedclothes round her.

'But what—what—what's the matter?' cried Alastair Bing. 'Is the girl ill?'

'Bad case of nervous breakdown,' answered Mrs Bradley, thanking her stars for that polite and modern phrase. 'You'll have to call in a specialist tomorrow, I'm afraid.'

'All these horrors! All these abominations!' cried Alastair Bing. 'No wonder the poor girl's brain is affected! I wonder we are not all gibbering maniacs! To bed! To bed!' he suddenly broke off, waving his arms at them all as though they were poultry. 'Get along! Get along!'

At this point, however, Eleanor in a drowsy voice asked for a drink, and Garde volunteered to go downstairs for a cup and saucer, as Mrs Bradley observed that she had some coffee left in her thermos flask.

'Rather a pity to give her coffee, isn't it?' Carstairs ventured to ask. 'I mean, it is a stimulant, not a sedative. Wouldn't a little warm milk be better?'

'This coffee is nearly all milk,' Mrs Bradley replied. 'I'll go and get it.'

She was absent less than ten seconds, and returned with the identical flask from which she had poured her own half-cup of coffee some hour or so earlier.

Garde groped blasphemously in the kitchen to find the electric switch, turned up the light, and soon returned with a large white and gold kitchen cup.

Mrs Bradley poured a generous amount of coffee into it, and Eleanor drank to the dregs.

'She'll be all right now,' said Mrs Bradley contentedly, gazing benignly down upon Eleanor's still form.

When she appeared to be sleeping soundly, they left her, but again Mrs Bradley took the precaution of locking the bedroom door on the outside.

'You'd better have the key, as it is your house,' she said seriously, handing it to Alastair Bing.

'Do you think we had better get a medical opinion tonight?' asked Alastair.

'No. Unnecessary tonight. Besides, she is asleep,' replied Mrs Bradley. When Alastair had been persuaded to retire, Carstairs crept to Mrs Bradley's door and tapped softly. She herself opened it.

'Did you—tell Alastair?' asked Carstairs.

Mrs Bradley, looking like an exceedingly ruffled eagle, shook her head.

'I have nothing to tell him. Eleanor is not insane, if that is what you mean.'

'Not—not insane?' cried Carstairs. 'She seemed absolutely like a maniac to me.'

'I don't believe a specialist would certify her,' said Mrs Bradley, shaking her head.

'But—but damn it!' cried Carstairs. 'She's—she's dangerous.'

'Yes, I know,' Mrs Bradley answered. 'But she's only dangerous when anybody takes a liking for Bertie Philipson. Even Mountjoy was safe until Bertie arrived, I fancy, but Eleanor's motives in that case must have been mixed. She wanted Bertie. She also discovered that Mountjoy was a woman. The two things together may have unbalanced her mind as neither of them separately would have done. Then she attempted Dorothy Clark's life when she discovered Bertie's infatuation for Dorothy. Now tonight Bertie addresses this child Pamela in carelessly affectionate terms, therefore Eleanor determines to annihilate Pamela. And so it will go on until she gets herself hanged for murder. It's an awful—an impossible situation! Still,' she added, with her horrid cackle, 'we must hope for the best.'

Carstairs, little comforted by this pious suggestion, retired to bed. His dreams were chaotic, and he awoke feeling tired and unrefreshed.

At a very early hour he heard sounds from the adjoining bedroom indicating that Bertie Philipson was also astir. Carstairs tapped on the wall, and Bertie unlocked the connecting door between their rooms and entered.

'I say,' said Bertie, 'did we really see Eleanor with the carving-knife last night, or did I dream it?'

'I was inclined to ask you the same thing,' said Carstairs. 'The frightful question is, what are we going to do about it? Of course, they'll call in a doctor today, I've no doubt. By the way——' He hesitated, wondering how best to introduce the subject uppermost in his mind.

'Yes?' said Bertie, prompting his hesitating tongue.

'Well—er—I suppose—that is—— Look here!' cried Carstairs desperately. 'Why don't you take Pamela home this morning and stay with the Storbins for a bit?'

'I'd thought of it myself,' Bertie moodily answered, 'but I don't suppose this damned inspector will hear of one of us going before he's completed his beastly case.'

'Oh, I don't know,' said Carstairs. 'He's got nothing against any of us. Besides, he can always have us watched and shadowed.'

'I'll see him after breakfast,' said Bertie. 'Meanwhile, I'm for a bath and shave and a nice little walk in the grounds. This nightmare house is beginning to get on my nerves.'

He retired to his own room for his towel and other accessories, and descended the stairs, saying over his shoulder:

'Even Eleanor can hardly be using the bathroom at the unearthly hour of six-fifteen in the morning.'

That, however, was exactly what Eleanor was

doing, as they discovered an hour later, for Bertie waited and waited, and, at length, impatience overcoming courtesy, hammered and hammered. At last, becoming thoroughly panic-stricken, he ran for Carstairs, and, with him, shouted and shouted until the whole household came running to find out what was the latest terror to fall upon the ill-fated mansion.

They burst the newly repaired door down and found her.

She was lying almost full-length in the bath, and when they lifted her out she was colder than the cold water in which she lay.

Chapter Seventen

The Inquest

THE inquest on Eleanor Bing's body was held in the large, pleasant morning-room of Chayning Place, and the sunshine, which appeared the more brilliant in contrast with the gloomy clothes and pale, strained faces of the family and guests, seemed strange and incongruous.

The jury were sworn in, and the medical witnesses went upstairs to make formal examination of the body, although by this time everyone present knew that the verdict of the local doctor had been confirmed by a great London specialist, and that there was no doubt as to the cause of death.

'Not drowned?' Alastair Bing had cried. 'What was it, then, doctor? Heart-failure?'

'Mr Bing'—the doctor was very grave—'you will have to know. I am distressed to tell you that I cannot certify the cause of death without an autopsy.'

'But—but—surely——' Alastair had begun to stammer.

'I am sorry,' the doctor repeated. He hesitated, and then said: 'And I should like to call in another opinion. The fact is—I hardly know how to—that is, you must prepare yourself for a shock. Mr Bing, I believe your daughter died from the effects of poison!'

The first witness called was Bertie Philipson, who was questioned about the finding of the body.

The medical evidence was then taken. 'You say that the deceased did not meet her death through drowning? What, in your opinion, was the cause of death?'

Death was due, the witness observed, to an overdose of a drug, and, in response to a further question from the coroner, testified that an autopsy had revealed traces of the drug called hyoscin-hydrobromide.

'In a sufficient quantity for there to be no doubt that it was the cause of death?' asked a juryman.

'The amount of the drug recovered from the stomach was one and three-quarter grains.'

He went on to explain, in answer to a further question, that one quarter to one half a grain of the drug would constitute a fatal dose.

Inspector Boring gave it as his opinion that the drug had not been self-administered. He had been present, he said, when the body was discovered, and had later searched the house for traces of poison.

'Before or after you knew the result of the autopsy?' the coroner inquired.

'Immediately the body had been removed from the bathroom,' Boring replied.

'But what caused you to suspect poison?' he was asked.

'Well, sir,' was the detective-inspector's dry comment, 'when there's a corpse whose hair isn't so much as damp, it would be a funny thing if she had been drowned.'

As the position of the body in the bath had already been minutely described by previous witnesses, the jury were not slow to appreciate the inspector's point.

'But why poison?' asked a juryman.

'Miss Bing had been laid up a day or so before, and had received medical attention. I particularly questioned the doctor as to the general state of her health, and he assured me he had never known a healthier person,' Boring stolidly explained. 'All the organs were in good order and everything about her was sound. Now, when the doctor examined the deceased he found no wound or other evidence of a violent death, so that left me with the idea that she might have been poisoned.'

'The fact that the deceased died as a result of poisoning has been proved,' said the coroner. 'It remains for the jury to find whether the poison was administered by the deceased herself, and, if so, whether she took it in error or with intention to commit suicide, or whether it was administered by another, person, and, if so, whether by accident, in error, or by design.'

The remainder of the inspector's evidence confirmed the latter view. He reiterated that he had searched the house and had discovered, in the bedroom of the deceased, laudanum, witch-hazel, and a bottle of disinfectant, and he knew that the deceased had bought aspirin at various times. The poison which had caused death was not one of these, and, moreover, a further careful search, when he had been made acquainted with the doctors' verdict, had failed to produce any trace of hyoscin. It was unlikely, the inspector led them to understand, that the deceased could have obtained possession of such a drug, and it was impossible, he asserted, for her so to have hidden the receptacle which had contained it that his methodical search had failed to bring it to light.

Recalled, the medical witness declared that death would have followed quickly upon the taking of so large a dose of the drug, and therefore that it was unlikely the deceased would have had time or opportunity to destroy all traces of the receptacle which had contained the poison.

The wineglass into which Mrs Bradley affirmed she had poured a sleeping-draught had been recovered from Eleanor's bedroom, and a girl named Cobb, the second housemaid, observed that she had collected a used cup from the same small table.

'How was it that you took up the cup and left the dirty wineglass?' asked the coroner.

The girl replied that Miss Eleanor had always been 'such a one to go on at us if we broke anything that I was afraid to take the wineglass away knowing as it was one of a set, so I left it where it was and hoped Florrie would see it when she dusted, and would take it down to the kitchen. But the police officer came before Florrie got around as far as that, and took it away with him. But the cup being only an ordinary white and gold common sort of a cup that the cook uses for breaking eggs into and such-like, I took it downstairs and it got washed up with the other things.'

'Where is that wineglass now?' asked the same juryman who had made the other inquiries.

Inspector Boring, appealed to, remarked that it had gone to have the residue of its contents analysed, and that he hoped to obtain the analyst's report in a day or two.

Mrs Bradley was then called, and was put through a searching catechism as to her movements on the night of Eleanor's death.

Her story of Eleanor's freakish behaviour was corroborated by Carstairs and Bertie Philipson. Mrs Bradley admitted that she had administered a sleeping-draught to the deceased, and, keenly pressed, testified that it had consisted of a harmless bromide compound such as was usually prescribed for sufferers from insomnia.

She was then questioned about the cup of coffee.

She observed that the cup was a clean one, procured from the kitchen by Garde Bing (who, later, confirmed this statement), and that she had poured out the coffee from her own thermos flask under the eyes of several witnesses.

The inquest was finally adjourned by the coroner, who remarked that it was impossible for the jury to give a verdict until the residue of the contents of the wineglass had been analysed, and the analyst's report read.

By the time the proceedings were over, Inspector Boring was a keenly interested but distinctly puzzled man.

His first task was to interview the Chief Constable and inform him of all that had taken place.

The Chief Constable heard him to the end, and then remarked:

'Mr Bing said Mrs Bradley gave the key of Eleanor's door to him, and therefore he could not see how it was possible for his daughter to leave her bedroom and go into the bathroom that morning.'

'Yes, Sir Joseph.' The inspector nodded. The point had already occurred to him.

'Well,' said the Chief Constable, eyeing the inspector's long, solemn face keenly, 'I think I should go and ask Mr Bing for that key, if he still has it in his possession. You'll find that key worth thinking about, Boring.'

Boring allowed his saturnine features to relax into a faint grin.

'You mean, I suppose, sir, that I shall find——'

'Not one key, Boring, but two keys; or, if only one key, then probably that it will not fit Miss

Eleanor Bing's bedroom door; or, if it does fit, that it is not the key which Mrs Bradley handed over to Mr Bing; or, if it *is* the key which she gave him, and it *does* happen to fit, that nobody bothered to try the door to see whether she really locked it.'

'You think, then, sir——'

'Boring,' said the Chief Constable, eyeing the ceiling and bringing the tips of his fingers together, 'I don't think—I am sure. But proof, Boring, proof is another matter.'

'Yes, sir,' said Boring, preparing to take his leave. 'I'll find out about the keys. Thanks for the hint, sir. And I want an interview with that young girl who stayed the night—Storbin, I think her name is.'

'I'll manage that interview,' interposed the Chief Constable firmly. 'Just tell me what you want to ask her.'

'Oh, chiefly, sir, where and how Mrs Bradley spent the night after she had given Miss Bing the coffee.'

'Very well,' said Sir Joseph, rising. 'I have to see Sir Thomas Storbin on a matter of business, so I will take the opportunity of questioning Miss Pamela for you at the same time.'

Boring thoughtfully returned to Chaynings in the side-car of a motor-cycle combination driven by his sergeant.

'Put me down just outside the gates,' he said. 'I'll walk the rest. There's no reason to announce the fact that I'm in the bosom of the family once more.'

The sergeant grinned comprehendingly, and drew

up where a growth of sturdy shrubs at a bend in the gravel drive would prevent their being seen from the house.

'You'd better come back for me about five,' the inspector observed. 'Wait down the road a bit, not at the lodge. I may leave by the wall door. You know it? Good!'

He walked briskly towards the house, and the sergeant drove away.

The first person Boring encountered was Bertie Philipson. The young man greeted him with a rueful grin.

'Well, inspector, got the handcuffs nicely polished?' he said.

The inspector smiled.

'Perhaps I have, sir. Perhaps I have. We shall see presently.'

'I suppose the police know who did it?' suggested Bertie still grinning, but with a tinge of anxiety of which the inspector was immediately aware.

'Maybe they do, sir, and maybe not. Where can I find Mr Bing?'

'Oh, I say! You're not going to worry poor old Bing yet!' cried Bertie. 'Why, the unfortunate old lad is all to bits, you know. You ought to have more decency, inspector, than to come along harassing a man in his condition.'

Bertie's indignation was not assumed. The inspector shrugged his shoulders.

'Duty, sir, is duty,' he sententiously remarked, 'and I have to do mine. It's no good shirking it because it's unpleasant. And after all, you know, although the old gentleman, I'm sure, is as cut up as you say, yet he'd be the first to want his daughter's murderer discovered.'

'Yes, but look here,' broke in Bertie eagerly, 'don't you think the poor girl committed suicide? That's our opinion, the whole lot of us, except——'

'Except?' said the inspector, quick to detect the note of hesitation.

'Except Mrs Bradley,' concluded Bertie. 'She swears Eleanor must have been murdered.'

'Oh? It's rather interesting to me, sir, that Mrs Bradley should say that. What does she base it on? Or is it just one of the lady's opinions, based on nothing but intuition?' said the inspector, grinning sarcastically.

Bertie giggled.

'She says Eleanor could never have got hold of such a poison, and that, anyway, she had enough poison in the house to kill herself twenty times if she wanted to commit suicide. Oh, and she talked a lot of psychological stuff about Eleanor not being the type that does away with itself, and quoted books and things, mostly by American and German authors, I believe, to prove her point. I know it sounded an awful lot of bosh to me, but then I can't make head or tail of that sort of stuff.'

'Nor me, either, sir,' replied Boring. 'Do you know whether Mrs Bradley has ever been in America, sir?' he inquired suddenly.

'Yes, I believe so,' Bertie answered carelessly, 'but I don't really know anything about her, you know.'

'I see. Well, I must be getting along,' said Boring. 'Are you coming back to the house, sir?'

'As far as the garage,' Bertie answered. 'I thought I'd hop over to Storbin's place and have a look at young Pamela. Probably stay for tea. No objection on the part of the police, I presume?'

'You presume right, sir,' the inspector half-humorously replied, 'but I expect the police will know all that you do, and most of what you talk about, over there.'

'Thanks for the hint,' grinned Bertie, parting from him at the end of the terrace. 'My lips will be sealed.'

Boring walked up to the French windows and peered in. Mrs Bradley was alone, and was deep in a book. The inspector walked away, and disappeared round a corner of the house.

'Ha, ha!' observed Mrs Bradley, not laughing, but pronouncing the two syllables in careful accordance with their spelling. 'The eye of the law is upon us once more.'

She smiled, and went on reading. Inspector Boring, who fancied he had seen Alastair's coat-tails disappearing round the angle of the house, found that he had not deceived himself.

'Mr Bing, I want a word with you,' he said.

Alastair turned his head, halted, and allowed the other to approach.

'Oh, it's you, inspector! Well, what is it? Be brief. I'm in no mood to be questioned.'

'Of course not, sir,' said the inspector smoothly.

'I only wondered whether you'd still got that key Mrs Bradley gave you.'

'Key?' repeated Alastair, frowning. 'What key? Oh, you say the one Mrs Bradley gave me? No, I haven't. The fact is, inspector'—he coughed and glanced swiftly behind him—'the fact is, I'm afraid I've mislaid it.'

'Oh, that's a pity, sir,' replied the inspector, 'because it's going to take some of my precious time finding it. I wonder if you'd let the maids have a look for it, sir? I rather want that key.'

'They *have* looked! They *have* looked!' snarled Alastair, his temper, as usual, overcoming, or perhaps expressing, his emotion.

'Oh, well, I must have a look myself, then,' Boring casually observed; and, without another look or word, he walked into the house by the servants' door.

'Oh, cook!'

The buxom genius who presided over the Chaynings' kitchen threw her eyes heavenwards.

'For the land's sake, inspector, you ain't going to march me off to gaol, are you?' she cried. 'I never did it. Honest I didn't.'

'Not yet,' said the inspector, with his sardonic grin. 'Not just yet. I really want to see the two housemaids. Look here, you girls,' he went on, addressing the scared and semi-hysterical maids, 'I want to know where the key of Miss Eleanor Bing's bedroom door is.'

Mabel, the younger, turned on Florrie, the older.

'Go on, Florrie! You can be put in prison if you don't tell!'

Thus enlightened, Florrie, dabbing her eyes, informed the world that she hoped no harm would come to the master through her, as he was a good enough master when he was not in one of his tantrums, but, as she was a born woman, she had seen him throw something, which chinked when he dropped it on the stone slabs, into the round pond, and that was this morning, as ever was, directly after the inquest.

'Does he know you saw him do it?' Boring asked.

Mabel, in spite of her terror of the police, giggled hysterically, but, under Boring's quelling eye, hiccoughed and again dissolved into tears.

'Oh, no, sir!' cried Florrie. 'Why, I shouldn't be alive to tell the tale if he knew I see him! Such a *temper!*' Words failed to express her conception of Alastair Bing's temper, and she concluded with: 'He's got a devil in him, I do believe, when he's roused!'

A short time later Boring was regarding with interest a medium-sized key. Sacrificing his personal dignity, he had lain on his stomach and salvaged the key from the round pond, an ornamental pool some ten inches deep and nine feet in diameter, after fifteen minutes of blasphemous groping on the mud-covered bottom.

'Now,' said the inspector to himself, 'does it fit, or doesn't it? And why did Alastair Bing throw it away? And why did he throw it away in a place where he could get it again pretty easily if he wanted to? And I wonder what sort of terms he was on with his daughter.'

Meanwhile the unfortunate relations and guests of the late Eleanor Bing were paying the penalty of having notoriety, if not greatness, thrust upon them by the suddenness and the mysterious nature of her death. All, with the exception of Mrs Bradley, who looked more briskly bird-like than ever, were moody, ill-at-ease, worried, harassed, and bad-tempered. Even Carstairs' sanguine temperament could barely cope with the inevitable nervous reaction following the events of the past few days. As for Alastair Bing, he could scarcely bring himself to say a civil word to anybody. The others, however, recognized in his savage gruffness an underlying sense of grief and shock, and bore with him, but relieved their feelings by quarrelling with one another.

'I say,' said Garde, rendered morosely furious both by the news he had to impart and by the fact that he and Dorothy had quarrelled and she had wept. Garde hated to see her in tears. In common with most men, he felt that a good cry was woman's method of hitting below the belt.

'I say, the beastly affair is in all the papers, of course, with Eleanor's name in the headlines as large as life. And some brute has published a photograph. I chased two local reporters off the premises this afternoon. I bet they'll be here in swarms tomorrow, and, if they come and pester Father, he'll murder one of them, and that will tear it properly. Why on earth,' went on Garde, bitterly— '—why on earth we should have been plagued like this I can't imagine. It's not, dash it, as though we'd ever done anybody much harm. All we ever asked for was a bit of peace and quietness, and now—all this damned nonsense——!'

He bit his lip savagely, and stared moodily at the fireplace.

'Well, we haven't found the key yet that your father has mislaid,' observed Mrs Bradley, by way of changing the subject. 'It almost looks as though it must have been swept up and thrown away. If so, a careful search among the ashes might reveal something. They have not been removed this week yet.'

'That will be a nice, choice sort of job,' said Garde, recovering a little of his cheerfulness. 'Are we all going to be taken to bits and disinfected afterwards? I vote we let the inspector look for it, and then——'

'Be quiet, Garde,' said Dorothy. 'You are going to say something objectionable in a minute, and I hate you when you are vulgar.'

'Cheer up,' growled Garde, moodily kicking the hearthrug. 'And go to bed! You look yellow and bilious.'

'Very well,' replied Dorothy, ominously taking him at his word and going towards the door. 'Good night.'

Garde lit his pipe and puffed away fiercely.

The next morning the entire household was kept busy trying to get rid of hordes of journalists and reporters who wanted first-hand stories of the crime, photographs of the house, private and uninterrupted views of the bathroom, the life story of each member of the family, especially of Eleanor, and biographies of the deceased Mountjoy, and of Mrs Bradley.

'Look here,' said Garde, interviewing about the fiftieth earnest young man who had called that morning. 'Will you jolly well hop it, and take all your damned friends and relations with you?'

The reporter, a large, untidy young man 'from whom perspiration was pouring in streams, for he had sprinted the half mile or so from the station in a vain attempt to be the first upon the scene of operations, mopped his face and glared reproachfully at Garde.

'It is for your own sake I'm talking,' the son of the house went on. 'If my father catches sight of any more of you fellows, he has threatened to shoot. And we're fed up with corpses in this establishment. So hop off, there's a good chap. Cultivate a little decent feeling!'

'But look here, Mr Bing,' began the reporter, drawing a large, elastic-bound note-book from his pocket.

'Nothing doing,' said Garde firmly. 'You make your get-away while the going's good, because it jolly well won't be in another minute.'

'But look here, Mr Bing,' began the reporter again, opening his book and licking his pencil in a business-like manner.

Garde thrust his face near to that of the newspaper

man. They were much of a height, and their eyes were on a level.

'Will you hop it, or shall I ruin your appearance for good and all?' he said menacingly.

'Gently does it,' replied the reporter, grinning and withdrawing from the argument. 'I'm to be married on Sunday, and I can't go into the bonds of matrimony with a black eye.'

'Married? God help you,' said Garde piously, for he was still sore from his overnight quarrel with Dorothy.

He shook the large, moist hand of the reporter and patted him on the shoulder with melancholy sympathy.

'Our prayers go with you, my poor brother,' he said, and walked with his undesired visitor to the gate to make sure he took his departure.

The methods of the servants were different, but seemed equally effective. The cook openly menaced all strangers with the rolling-pin. Mander elevated his nose and informed all and sundry that they had been 'misled as to the address of the 'ouse.' Chaynings, near Birmingham, was what they wanted. He then wished them an aloof but civil good-day.

The young reporter whom Garde had conducted to the gate met a comrade at the station.

'Too late, my lad,' he informed the new arrival. 'Full house already. No seats, and money being turned away at the doors. Standing not allowed. And, if you ask me, I should say every one of them is a killer, servants and all. You should have seen the matey way I was bundled out!'

'You don't mean it?' said the other, whose horn-rimmed glasses gleamed with the earnest light of a tiger's eyes seeking prey. 'Turfed you out? You?'

'Me,' replied the other. 'And, what's more, I'm going to stay put. Little Eddie isn't looking for lead, oak, or elm yet awhile. You take my advice and keep away from Chaynings. It isn't a healthy neighbourhood for quiet young fellers like you and me. I'm going into that pub over the road what has got a real sanded bar-parlour, and I'm going to sit me down and write up details of the absolutely exclusive interview I've just obtained with Mr Garde Bing. You'd better do the same. Got anything good for the three-thirty? Spill it, then, and I'll give you a description of the bloke.'

Chapter Eighteen

An Arrest

INSPECTOR BORING, bicycling over to interview the Chief Constable, encountered that gentleman in his car along the road, for the Chief Constable was on his way to Chaynings.

'Ah, Boring,' said Sir Joseph, stopping the car, 'give your bicycle into Thompson's charge, and take his place at the wheel. I want to see you.'

The chauffeur vacated the driving seat, and Boring climbed into the car.

'I was coming over to hear the adjourned inquest,' said Sir Joseph. 'Has any other evidence cropped up, do you know?'

'Well, they've received the analyst's report on the residue in the wineglass,' replied Boring, 'but it is in Mrs Bradley's favour. The glass had contained an ordinary bromide sleeping-draught, just as she said.'

'Oh, really!' said Sir Joseph. 'What did you think it had contained?'

'When I heard that the coffee cup had been washed up and the wineglass left to be discovered by the police, I knew what to expect, sir, and so I'm not disappointed,' replied Boring morosely. 'If only we could have got on to that dirty cup, sir!'

'Oh, come,' chuckled Sir Joseph, 'you mustn't assume that an analysis of the residue in that coffee cup would have revealed traces of the poison, Boring. What happened about the key of the bedroom door, by the way?'

'Oh, that's got me properly puzzled, sir. You see, Mr Bing—the old gentleman, not the young one—threw it away.'

'Threw it away?' Sir Joseph's eyebrows lifted in astonishment. 'That looks rather bad, Boring. Let me take the wheel a minute, while you tell me about it.'

'Well, sir, that's what I thought. It did look bad, I said to myself. But I discovered the key, sir, through one of the maids being busybody enough to spot her employer throwing it into that little ornamental pond they've got on the right front of the house. I tried it in the lock of deceased's bedroom door directly I'd fished it out, dried, and cleaned it, and, sir, it would not fit!'

'Aha!' said the Chief Constable. 'Queer thing, that. Why did he throw it away, I wonder.'

'Well, I nabbed him alone, and taxed him with throwing it away, sir, without telling him I'd found it.'

The Chief Constable nodded.

'Wanted to see whether he knew it was the wrong key, I suppose?' he asked.

'Yes, sir. Well, he became confused and annoyed, and in the end confessed that he'd thrown it away in a fit of panic after hearing the evidence at the inquest. Apparently it never occurred to the poor simp that his daughter might have been given the poison *before* Mrs Bradley locked the door and handed him the key. I believe him, too, sir. He's just the sort of impulsive old fool to go and do a silly thing like that; always flying off the handle about something, as you know.'

'That brings us back to Mrs Bradley,' said Sir Joseph thoughtfully. 'I'll pull up on that grass patch a minute, and we'll have a sandwich and a smoke, and work this out.'

He leaned back in his comfortably padded seat, and commenced to expound his ideas.

'First of all, there's the question of motive. Of course, assuming—as, between ourselves, we may, although no word of our suspicion must leak out until the proper time—assuming that Mrs Bradley is the guilty person, I can guess the motive. But it's a motive that won't do to offer a jury, Boring. The British public doesn't believe in disinterested actions, and it is just as well it should be so. An absolutely disinterested action with an altruistic motive is a very unusual thing. In this case I think the criminal was actuated by two motives. On the one hand, she wished to save the lives of we cannot say exactly how many women and girls, and she also wanted to save

Eleanor Bing from being hanged—or confined in Broadmoor.'

'Then you think that yarn of theirs about Miss Bing and the carving-knife was true?' asked Boring incredulously. 'It sounded more like the meaty bit out of a shilling shocker to me, sir.'

'I know. That's why I'm sure it is true,' said the Chief Constable. 'You see, Boring, the two people who told us this tale are neither of them of the type which cares about the shilling shocker or the more lurid Sunday papers. Left to himself, either of them would have invented a far less highly exciting tale—and I should not have believed it!'

'Then you believe that the Guy Fawkes business was another attempt at murder? Miss Clark that time—that is, Mrs Garde Bing?' asked Boring.

'Don't you?' asked Sir Joseph. 'And, what's more, I know why Eleanor screamed. She saw somebody watching her that night.'

'Mrs Bradley?' said Boring. 'If so, sir, I suppose it was Mrs Bradley who tried to drown her in the bath next morning, but it didn't come off. Now she's had another go, and it *has* come off.'

'Too fast, Boring. Much too fast,' laughed the Chief Constable. 'Have you formed such a poor estimate of Mrs Bradley's character and capabilities that you realiy imagine she would bungle a job like that, and let the victim recover? If Mrs Bradley did it, why didn't Miss Bing say so when she recovered?"

'Fear?' suggested the inspector.

'Maybe. Personally, I'm more inclined to think

Eleanor Bing was shielding someone she was fond of. Don't say a name, Boring,' he concluded, laughing, 'or I shall have to institute an official inquiry, and I'm not a bit keen, really, on charging a perfectly harmless person with attempted manslaughter. So let us allow sleeping dogs the repose they have earned, and get back to the matter in hand.'

'Very good, sir,' replied Boring, well fortified by the Chief Constable's sandwiches, flask, and tobacco. 'What do you make, sir, of the fact that the key was a dud?'

'Well, Mrs Bradley had to get back into Eleanor Bing's bedroom if she was to carry out her plan to dispose of the body in the bath,' said Sir Joseph thoughtfully, 'and also——' He broke off, and, after screwing up his eyes a moment, went on: 'You really ought to get hold of that girl, Mabel, who collected the coffee cup, and pump her a bit more. Didn't she say at the inquest that she heard Eleanor Bing's voice answering her from within when she knocked on the bedroom door to rouse her in the morning?'

'Yes, sir. She did say that, but I've met that type of girl before. They say the first thing that comes into their heads without ever stopping to think. If Mabel Cobb had thought before she spoke, she'd have known she was thinking of the previous day, not the morning of the murder.'

'Why?' asked Sir Joseph, smiling.

'Well, sir, to begin with, Eleanor Bing wasn't in the bedroom. She was in the bath. Secondly, wherever she was, she was dead. The medical evidence established that, sir. You see, they found her less than an hour after the maid's usual time for calling her in the morning, and, although doctors are always a bit shy nowadays of tying themselves down when it's a case of the time death took place, yet none of them thought she'd been dead for as short a time as that. So I say the maid couldn't have heard her voice from the bedroom, sir, when she called her.'

'Yes, Boring, that's exactly what I'm trying to get at,' said Sir Joseph patiently. 'Mabel Cobb couldn't have heard Eleanor's voice, because Eleanor was dead. Therefore, whose voice did she hear? I'll tell you. She heard the voice of the murderer.'

'But, look here, sir——' Boring began, feeling utterly unconvinced by the Chief Constable's hypothesis.

'Just a minute. I'll give you the gist of what I gleaned from my interview with Miss Pamela Storbin, and then you'll see my point, perhaps. Briefly I elicited the following facts: First, that Mrs Bradley took Pamela Storbin to sleep in her room. She made an excuse which must have been a lie, because Pamela had to promise not to mention the change of room to Eleanor. Well, we know all about the reasons for the change. Pamela had to be protected from Eleanor.

'Secondly, I learned that Mrs Bradley did not retire to bed that night, but that, on confused sounds being heard in another part of the house not far removed from her own bedroom, Mrs Bradley slipped out of the room and was absent some minutes. The sounds woke Pamela, apparently, and, being frightened, she did not fall asleep again for about an hour and a half.

'Thirdly, I obtained the information that Mrs Bradley re-entered her bedroom after a few minutes' absence, sat down in the same chair she had occupied before and picked up a book, but that about five minutes later, further noise and a confused shouting caused her to depart once more. Very shortly afterwards she re-entered the bedroom again, picked up her thermos flask, and departed. She did not return to the room any more that night, neither was she there when Pamela awoke in the morning.'

'That's interesting, sir. May I ask a question or two?' said Boring, who had drawn out his friend the note-book and was engaged in scribbling down what Sir Joseph had related.

'By all means. One or two suggested themselves to me when I heard Pamela's story, and I put them to her. I expect yours will be much the same questions, so carry on.'

'Well, sir, how long did it take Mrs Bradley to get the thermos flask and go out again?'

'I asked that, and Pamela was certain that Mrs Bradley came in so hastily that she knocked her arm against the wardrobe, snatched up the flask, which was on a small occasional table near her chair, and was off again immediately.'

'Hum!' said the inspector, in a disappointed tone. 'I was hoping Miss Storbin might have seen her tampering with the flask in some way.'

'I pressed the point,' said the Chief Constable, 'but the girl remained firm.'

'How was it she could see all this in the bedroom?' was the inspector's next question.

'Mrs Bradley was using an electric reading-lamp,' replied Sir Joseph. 'It did not shine on Pamela's face so as to interfere with her slumber, but its light was sufficiently diffused for her to see Mrs Bradley and observe her actions.'

'And—most important, sir—how can Miss Storbin be sure that Mrs Bradley did not return to the bedroom after getting the flask?'

'I asked her that, and she said she was feeling frightened, and, as Mrs Bradley had not returned after what seemed to her a long time, she got out of bed and put a chair against the door. The chair was still there in the morning, and she was still alone in the bedroom.'

'Hum! Seems conclusive to me, sir. I don't know what you think.'

The Chief Constable shook his head sadly. He had detested Eleanor Bing.

'I certainly will question Mabel Cobb about the voice that answered her, sir,' said Boring, after a short pause. 'If she really did hear it, it's a fairly valuable bit of circumstantial evidence. It eliminates all the men, I suppose, and that leaves Mrs Bradley, Miss Storbin and Mrs Garde Bing. Well, we can eliminate Miss Storbin. It's hardly probable that it was Mrs Garde Bing, as she slept with her husband for the first time that night, and so, I suppose, was hardly likely to leave him and climb into Eleanor's bed before six-thirty in the morning; and that leaves us with Mrs Bradley again.'

'It seems so,' the Chief Constable assented, without noticeable enthusiasm. 'Well, we'd better drive on. I expect I've missed the resumed inquest proceedings altogether. With luck we might be there in time to hear the verdict.'

'They won't start without me, sir,' grinned the inspector as he started up the car. 'I'm one of their chief witnesses.'

'By the way,' said Sir Joseph, as they drove along, 'the fact that the key did not fit the bedroom door is in Alastair Bing's favour, isn't it? A guilty man wouldn't have thrown the wrong key away. He'd have kept it, to show that he couldn't get into Eleanor's room with it. By the way, did you notice anything about the key of the bathroom door when they forced it open?'

'When I arrived, sir, there was no key in the bathroom door on either side,' said Boring, consulting his note-book, for the Chief Constable had again taken the wheel.

The car turned in at the gates of Chayning Place.

'And yet the bathroom door was locked, and they had to break it down to get in,' said Sir Joseph pensively.

'Yes, sir, and the key that won't fit Eleanor Bing's room fits the bathroom door,' said the inspector, with sly triumph.

'And the locks of the upper and the lower bathrooms are identical,' concluded Sir Joseph.

Boring's face fell, for a moment, to think that he had overlooked this interesting fact, but soon brightened again.

'Then Mrs Bradley could have handed Alastair Bing one bathroom key, and used the other herself, while still keeping possession of Eleanor's bedroom door key!' he cried exultantly.

Upon the inspector's arrival, the adjourned proceedings took their course. Carstairs, who had given what further evidence was required of him, and then gone out into the garden, now re-entered the house, and walked into the morning-room just as the jury filed out. The coroner scowled at him, and Carstairs sat down as unobtrusively as possible. Mrs Bradley leaned across to him and whispered loudly enough for everybody in the room to hear:

'That silly little man thinks I did it.'

Carstairs fought down an overmastering impulse to giggle like a schoolgirl, and glanced involuntarily at the coroner, who, of course, had heard the remark, and, scowling more fiercely than ever, tapped irascibly on the table and said irritably:

'Silence, please, silence.'

In the midst of the silence that followed, in trooped the jury, after an absence of two minutes. The foreman, who, under ordinary circumstances, was the local butcher, rendered the verdict in the voice he usually kept for advertising the more luscious portions of his stock. 'Wilful murder against some person or persons unknown.'

Carstairs drew a deep breath. 'And death was

due to poisoning, not drowning,' he said to himself.
'Hum! Doesn't sound very nice. I wonder why they
found for murder, though? It could just as easily
have been suicide, according to the evidence—or
lack of it!'

With her uncanny trick of reading minds, Mrs
Bradley, having drawn him into the garden, began to
talk about the very point that was puzzling him.

'Of course, that horrid little coroner told them
to say it was murder,' she stated. 'Otherwise, I am
certain they would have said suicide.'

'Told them?' questioned Carstairs, with an
amused twinkle in his eyes.

'Well, it amounted to that. His whole attitude was
a disgrace. We all know the ordinary law courts
are not impartial, but a coroner's court ought to
be. Those poor idiots would just as easily have
said suicide if he had encouraged them. But no!
He intended to have it murder, and brought in as
murder it is! It makes matters so very awkward for
me, you see, now that coffee cup has been washed
up. Of course the horrid little fellow fastened on
that, and there you are!'

Carstairs gave a long whistle. 'No wonder you
are perturbed,' he said. 'Good Lord! Yes, it's a pity
Mabel Cobb couldn't leave well alone!'

'Good Lord indeed!' said Mrs Bradley, with spirit.
'I shall find myself in the dock before many weeks
are out. You mark my words!'

Carstairs made sympathetic noises, but, as usual,
could think of no adequate reply.

'I shall plead not guilty,' said Mrs Bradley firmly,

'and I shall get Ferdinand Lestrange to conduct my case.'

'He is a very young man, isn't he?' said Carstairs doubtfully.

'He is thirty-nine, and was born on my eighteenth birthday,' Mrs Bradley promptly replied. 'Oxford 1908 to 1911, called to the bar in 1914, Great War 1914 to 1917. Invalided out in June, 1917. Now a K.C.'

'You seem to have followed his career with some minuteness,' said Carstairs, amused.

'Well, he is my son,' was Mrs Bradley's somewhat startling reply. 'By my first husband,' she added. 'A clever boy, Ferdinand. Besides, it will make an immediate appeal to the jury—the dutiful and anxiety-racked son defending his poor old mother against the monstrous, foul, and calumnious charge of being concerned in a murder!'

Her harsh cackle of eldritch laughter filled the summer air with hideous merriment.

Carstairs shivered in spite of the sun's warmth. Extraordinary woman!

'It seems to me that you are in an infernally awkward position,' he said slowly. 'If there is anything I can possibly do——' He stopped short. 'After all, you are not arrested yet,' he said hopefully.

'Am I not?' said Mrs Bradley, with her mirthless chuckle. 'Look!'

From the house two men were advancing. Both were clad in police uniform. At about twenty paces, the taller man halted. The other still advanced.

Carstairs and Mrs Bradley stood waiting, both outwardly calm, but Carstairs was conscious of the sickening thumping of his heart. It reminded him of his first tiger-hunt. He glanced at his companion. To his amazement he saw her dive into her capacious skirt-pocket and produce a small bottle and a large green-bordered handkerchief. Without, apparently, removing the cork, she tipped up the bottle on to the handkerchief and then handed the bottle gravely to him under the nose of the advancing policeman.

'You might thank Dorothy very much and tell her my head is much better,' she remarked quietly. Then, to the policeman, she said:

'Well, my man?'

'I arrest you for the wilful murder of Eleanor Millicent Bing,' gabbled the officer, 'and it is my duty to warn you that anything you say may be taken in evidence against you.'

'Thank you for the kindly, timely, and exceedingly thoughtful warning,' said Mrs Bradley, smiling. 'Good-bye, Mr Carstairs. I perceive the gallant inspector's hand in all this. That man has intelligence.'

'I will do everything I can,' said Carstairs, from the depths of his heart. 'It will be quite all right, I am sure. You can't possibly be convicted. I must get to work and find the real murderer. That will be the thing to do.'

He stood frowning thoughtfully, and gazing after the little procession. The police certainly had not wasted much time.

He became conscious that he was still holding the little bottle which Mrs Bradley had handed him. He looked at it curiously. It was a small, flat, dark-green bottle, with a famous perfume-maker's name on the label, and was marked 'Lavender Water.' Carstairs slipped it into his coat-pocket.

Chapter Nineteen

The Sleuth

AFTER the arrest of Mrs Bradley, Carstairs returned to his bachelor flat, and set himself solidly to the task of finding out the facts regarding the death of Eleanor Bing.

Rack his brain as he might, he could think of no one who might be guilty of the crime.

'After all,' he said to himself, 'it seems impossible to suspect Mrs Bradley, and yet, if she did not do it, who did? Young fellows like Garde and Philipson don't go about poisoning people. I don't pretend to know why it is so. They just don't do such things. Dorothy Bing wouldn't do a thing like that. Alastair? Well, he isn't above committing a murder if he felt angry enough, but I don't somehow see him poisoning anybody. It wouldn't be sufficiently violent or picturesque for his liking. I myself didn't do it. That brings us back to Mrs Bradley, unless it was a case of suicide after all. But there! I've thrashed that theory out in my own mind time and again. If Eleanor Bing had wanted to make away with herself she would have drunk laudanum, or overdosed with aspirin, or put her head in the gas-oven, or shot herself with Alastair Bing's revolver, or opened a vein with one of Garde's surgical instruments, but she would never have gone to the lengths of obtaining a drug like hyoscin for her purpose. Why, I doubt whether she knew such a poison existed.'

He took up his note-book, and wrote, one on each page, the names of the fateful house-party, and against each name put down what he knew of the person, and any evidence for or against his having committed the murder.

1. *Alastair Bing.*—Possible, even though deceased was his daughter, but not probable.

2. *Garde Bing.*—A strong case could be made out against this boy. It seems fairly certain that Eleanor attempted the life of his sweetheart. He is a medical student, and so might have been able to obtain the drug which poisoned his sister. *N.B.*—This might prove a big point in Mrs Bradley's favour. It looks as though Garde could have obtained the drug more easily than she could, although this requires proving. Moreover, there was ill-feeling between the brother and sister, although that would be scarcely strong enough to form a motive for murder. Against this must be set the important fact that G. is a normal, healthy, cheerful young Philistine; that is to say, not at all one's conception of a poisoner; also, he has a strong alibi.

3. *Dorothy Bing.*—Well, poisoning is quite as much a woman's crime as it is a man's—more so, perhaps, as a man tends to rely upon his physical strength more than a woman does upon hers. Nevertheless, the important aspect of character comes in again here. One cannot tolerate the thought of that charming little girl as a murderer. Still, the facts of the case must not be burked on that account. Dorothy Bing's life had been in danger from Eleanor. *N.B.*—I have not had the courage to ask her whether she knew that fact. I ought to have done so. In fact, I *must* do so. It would clear up a doubtful point. If she did know that Eleanor meant to kill her, she would have had a powerful motive for wishing Eleanor out of the way. Undoubtedly she has become a very different person since Eleanor's death.

4. *Bertie Philipson.*—I cannot understand this young man. He poses as a butterfly, but there is something deeper in his nature than he wants one to see. He was in love with Dorothy Clark, and he certainly was quixotic enough to want Dorothy's enemy to be out of the way. Of course, he has an alibi of a sort for that night when, presumably, the poison was administered, but that says nothing, because there is no evidence as to the exact time of death.

5. *Mrs Bradley.*—The evidence points a little more to her than to anybody else at present. The prosecution is bound to stress that point about the dirty coffee cup, unless the defence can put up a good show about the wineglass which was found.

At this point, Carstairs laid down his pen and laughed ruefully. Then he picked up his pencil, re-read his notes, looked at the clock, and determined to go for a walk and thrash the whole thing out again in his mind.

'Starting from the point that poor Eleanor Bing was undoubtedly mad,' he added, half humorously.

An hour's hard walking brought him no further light, and he turned into his usual place for lunch with the problem still bombarding his brain. To his relief, nobody of his acquaintance was lunching near him, for he felt in no mood for the usual urbanities. Just as he was drinking coffee, however, in came a man he had known fairly well for some years. He was a medical man, a specialist in his own line, which happened to be tropical diseases. Carstairs determined to ask him a few questions. He had his coffee taken to the doctor's table in response to a signalled invitation, and sat down there.

'What do you mean by lunching, when all your patients are clamouring for attention?' said Carstairs, smiling.

The other man grinned. He was tall, thin, and might easily have passed for an Oriental, so expressionless and dignified was his face, so urbane his manner, so charmingly polite and yet so absolutely non-committal his air.

'My wife's on holiday,' he explained. 'Must lunch somewhere, and I detest my own home when she isn't there. Beastly month for a holiday, September, I think. But the school vacations settle these matters for us, don't they?'

'I am not a parent,' said Carstairs dryly. 'How is your daughter?'

'Mavis? Oh, charming, charming! Of course, I very rarely see her. She is always out when I'm at home, or else in bed, or, as in this case, away with Phyllis. They've gone to Normandy. Do you know Normandy?'

'Yes. My old nurse lives there,' confessed Carstairs. 'She is one hundred and two. But look here, Woodford, do you mind answering a few questions?'

'My dear chap! Nothing wrong with you, I hope.' The doctor was all professional concern at once.

'No. Nothing wrong with me. But, Woodford, you have heard of the Bing case?'

'I should think so! Oh, of course, you were staying there at the time. Found hyoscin-hydrobromide in the viscera, didn't they? That's a queer drug for a lay murderer to get hold of. Reminds me of the Crippen case. Do they know where she got it?'

'Where who got it?' asked the startled Carstairs.

'Why, the woman they have arrested. Mrs Bradley, you know.'

'Look here,' said Carstairs. 'I wanted to ask you about that drug. You see, strictly between ourselves, the other people down at the house—Chaynings, you know—don't believe for an instant that this Mrs Bradley did it, and neither do I. There are various others who could equally well be suspected, as a matter of fact, but immediately the second inquest was over the police collared Mrs Bradley on very slight evidence (it seemed to us), and charged her with the crime. She is behaving rather madly, I think, by reserving her defence.'

'Oh? Is she doing that? Looks fishy, you know. Much better to make a frank statement to a magistrate or the coroner. The prosecution are certain to make a big point of that.'

Carstairs nodded gloomily. 'She will not be persuaded,' he said. 'But what I really wanted to ask you was this. You say it is a queer drug for a lay murderer to procure. What's your definition of a lay murderer?'

The other smiled.

'I mean, of course, someone who is not a medical man—or woman.'

'Thank you. Would a medical student be able to procure hyoscin easily?'

'Oh, I should hardly think so. Certainly not enough to kill anybody, I should imagine.'

'How much constitutes a fatal dose? It was given in the medical evidence at the inquest, of course, but I didn't make a note of it.'

'A fatal dose? Oh, a quarter to half a grain, I believe, but really, you know, it is out of my line. If you want to know all about hyoscin, an asylum for the insane is your objective. It is a calmative drug, often used for cases of nymphomania, I believe, and for violent cases—homicidal mania and so on. They use it a lot in America, if you feel inclined for a short sea trip.'

Carstairs left the doctor, feeling more downhearted than ever.

Hyoscin was a difficult drug to obtain. It was unlikely that Garde, the medical student, could have had any quantity of it in his possession. But it was used in the treatment of lunatics—and Mrs Bradley was a psycho-analyst and a specialist in mental and nervous diseases. She had visited asylums, both public and private, in America, where the drug was commonly used.

It looked a black, a horribly black, prospect for Mrs Bradley, if these facts came out in court.

'The thing to do,' Carstairs told himself glumly, 'is to return to Chaynings and hunt about to find some clue to Mrs Bradley's innocence which the police have overlooked.'

He arrived in the early afternoon to find Dorothy cutting roses and Garde seated on the verandah enjoying a cigarette.

'Why on earth didn't you let us know you were coming?' cried Dorothy. 'We could have met you with the car. What a long, dusty walk you must have had.'

'Can I see Alastair?' asked Carstairs.

'That is just what you cannot do,' said Garde, scowling. 'The silly ass has gone to Tibet.'

'Gone—where?' cried Carstairs.

'I don't wonder you're surprised,' said Dorothy, laughing to see Carstairs' look of bewilderment. 'No, Garde is not pulling your leg. It's the truth. He must have been quite prepared, and must have had all his arrangements cut and dried, because, the same day that the police arrested Mrs Bradley, off he went without a word to any of us. It was the inspector who found out where he was bound for, and the police are afraid they won't get him back in time for the trial. You see, they only found out for certain where he was going the day before yesterday, so he's had nearly a month's start. Of course he isn't an important witness, but still——'

Carstairs whistled softly.

'But surely he knew he would be wanted as a witness,' he said. 'I can't understand it.'

'I can,' said Garde. 'Lazy old devil! Didn't want to be bothered. Thought he'd get away before they could serve the papers on him. Well, I jolly well hope they catch him. And I jolly well hope the defending counsel makes it hot for him. Of course, Dorothy and I don't mind. It's quite jammy for us to have the house to ourselves.'

'I suppose, then, I can ask the favour of you that I'd intended to obtain from Alastair,' said Carstairs.

'Rather,' cried Dorothy. 'What is it?'

'Shut up, minx,' observed her husband, pulling her down on to his knee. 'No petticoat government here.'

'I want you to let me search the house and grounds to try and find any clue which will help to clear Mrs Bradley,' said Carstairs. 'As things are at present, it's a poor look-out for her, I'm afraid.'

'Do what you like, sir, of course,' said Garde warmly. 'I'll tell the servants to let you have keys and things, and, if we can do anything to help, you must be sure to let us know.'

'Thanks very much, old man,' replied Carstairs.

'Oh, and by the way, you might like to have a go at interrogating Mabel Cobb,' suggested Garde. 'I have a kind of notion that she's thought over what she said at the inquest, and has decided that she can add a bit to it. She's tried to sound me about what happens if a person tells less than the whole truth in court. I didn't see what she was driving at, and I'm afraid I frightened her a bit, so I haven't been able to get any more out of her. So you have a go. It may be important, or it may not.'

'And there's Eleanor's diary,' chimed in Dorothy. 'We can't make anything out of it, but you may be able to put two and two together.'

'This sounds too good to be true,' cried Carstairs. 'Mabel Cobb and Eleanor's diary! I suppose the police have seen it?'

'The diary? Yes. The Chief Constable and the inspector have both seen it, and have come to the conclusion that Eleanor certainly murdered Everard Mountjoy. But, as we had all come to that conclusion ages ago, it seemed a bit pointless to rake it all up again,' said Garde. 'However, the police haven't done any more nosing round in the house since they arrested Mrs Bradley, so, unless we've inadvertently disturbed them, your clues are all ready and waiting for you.'

Carstairs smiled.

'I don't really expect to have any luck,' he said. 'But I feel I must do something.'

The first thing he did was to send for Mabel Cobb.

Without any preliminary questions, and as a shot in the dark, he said:

'What did you do with the coffee cup on the morning of Miss Bing's death?'

'I picked it up and took it downstairs to be washed up,' said Mabel sullenly, and obviously prepared for a trap.

'Oh? And, look here, Mabel, who was it you saw on the landing in the morning on the day of Miss Bing's death?'

The shot told. Mabel gulped, turned red and then pale, and clutched the table as though she had received a blow and wanted to steady herself.

'I—I—I—never saw nobody!' she faltered at last.

Carstairs glared at her ferociously. 'That won't do!' he barked. 'Come, now!'

But Mabel had got over her momentary terror. Her foolish face was set like stone, and so had lost its foolish expression. Her hands were clenched, and she no longer held the table for support. Her voice was little more than a whisper, but what she said was short and to the point.

'You can go to Jericho wi' your old questions,' said Mabel, 'for I shan't answer any of 'em! Who be you?'

With which Parthian shot she moved with dignity from the library.

Carstairs bit his lip, choked back burning words, and finally laughed.

'I shall have to talk it over with Garde,' he

thought. 'But it can wait. Let's see what we have here.'

He picked up Eleanor's diary and opened it at the first page.

A good deal of the diary referred to household matters. It appeared that Eleanor used it as a memorandum for shopping, special cleaning, servants' holidays, their hours off, their illnesses, and the like; Carstairs skipped the first half of the little book, which held nothing to interest him.

At the end of May, however, the tone of the entries changed. The references to household matters were as frequent, but were jotted down in a very brief form, shorthand signs being used here and there, obviously to leave room for other and, it appeared, more pressing matters.

There was a reference under the date of May 28th which ran: 'Hodges. Windows. Din: 7. H. home wk-end. Father behaved scandalously. Cannot think what to do. Mabel notice. Could not sleep for thinking. Snake in the grass.'

'I wonder what Alastair's unfortunate lapse could have been, and what could have been its consequences,' mused Carstairs, smiling.

Other references were made (on several subsequent dates) to the same occurrence, and the writer stressed the necessity for 'getting rid of the dreadful girl at once.'

Farther on, Mabel was referred to as 'that brazen hussy,' and Alastair Bing as 'my father, a monster of iniquity.'

'She certainly seems to have taken something to

heart all right,' thought Carstairs, turning to the next entry with interest.

It read, under the date of June 17th: 'Father refuses to "shirk his responsibilities" as he (nobly!) calls them. The atrocity Mabel is to stay. Garde supports Father. I feel that it is pollution to be in the same house with them.'

'Fancy anyone being so stirred up,' thought Carstairs. 'Poor Eleanor! She seems to have taken things to heart far more than any of them gave her credit for.'

He read on, under the date of June 24th:

'Either that hideous snake or I must leave this house. I cannot and I will not remain under the same roof with her.'

At last there came the reference which Carstairs had been hoping to find. It appeared under the date of June 30th.

'Father has had the audacity to invite guests as though nothing had happened. For the credit of the family I cannot go away until their visit is over. Garde has invited a woman, a Mrs Lestrange Bradley. I remember her.'

This entry continued straight on through the next day's portion of this page.

'She is that horrid little woman who inspected us in France. She got Garde out of some scrape—an Unpleasant Episode, I expect, if the truth were known,' wrote the puritanical Eleanor, in highly suggestive capital letters.

Further on came the reference to Mountjoy.

'One younger man is here to whom I feel

curiously attracted. Everard Mountjoy is his name.'

Here the diarist had scribbled the name 'Everard' several times at the bottom of the page, and in one place had followed it with the surname 'Mountjoy,' and then, very faintly, but perfectly plain to be seen, the word 'Mrs' had been insinuated in front of the whole name.

Carstairs sighed.

'It is easy to see who desired that tragically terminated engagement,' he said to himself.

The announcement of the engagement itself followed in due course, and was recorded with a sober, and, as it seemed to Carstairs, a reverent pen. It was followed by these words: 'This solves all my difficulties.'

This seemed nothing less than the truth, for the next few entries were again devoted to details of the house-keeping.

From the date August 2nd onwards (the last entry, significantly enough, being under August 12th, the day preceding Mountjoy's death) the diarist seemed to have lost her calmed outlook, and to have been plunged into doubt and suspicion.

One entry read:

'We are engaged, but Everard has made no reference to marriage ever since. Perhaps he thought me bold in forcing him to speak.'

'That's illuminating,' thought Carstairs. 'She "forced him to speak." In other words, she proposed to Mountjoy rather than the other way about.'

'It is torture,' another entry read, 'to be with my

dear Everard as much as I am, and to know that he has no desire to caress me. One should be content, I suppose' (this entry took the whole of the next day's space as well as its own) 'with his beautiful platonic love, but sometimes strange desires come into my mind. I scarcely like to confess them, even to myself. I said to him something about leaving his tennis-shirt open at the neck as Garde and Bertie do, but he mumbled something, and kept it fast buttoned. He looked like that stupid curate we had three years ago. I want Everard to be manly and sunburnt.'

'Deuced awkward for Everard. I wonder why on earth she ever consented to become engaged to Eleanor,' mused Carstairs.

At the last entry he blinked, and closed the book with a snap. There was a fire burning in the room. He walked over to it, and consigned Eleanor's diary to the flames.

'The freedom of the modern girl,' said Carstairs, 'has its good points. I should say that poor Eleanor was making up for the self-imposed repressions of twenty-odd years when she wrote that last entry.' He blushed as he recalled it.

'Settles the Mountjoy murder right enough,' he muttered. 'After all that, to find that Mountjoy was a woman simply turned the poor girl's brain. Mrs Bradley was right—Eleanor killed Mountjoy—but who the devil killed Eleanor? Well, let's start a systematic search, and see what we can find.'

He determined to inspect first the bedroom that

Mrs Bradley had occupied during her visit, and then the room which had belonged to Eleanor.

Careful and methodical was the search, disappointing the result. At last, however, his eyes brightened.

He was exploring the recesses of the small medicine cupboard in Eleanor's room, and near the back of the bottom shelf, which was about on a level with his shoulder, he discovered a medicine-glass. Curiously enough, for Eleanor was a careful person, it contained a drop or two of liquid.

'Suicide?' said Carstairs, scarcely daring to breathe the word.

Without touching the glass, he went in search of Garde.

'Phone the inspector, and ask him to see about getting the contents analysed,' said Garde. 'Of course, it will turn out to be ammoniated tincture of quinine, or something, but, still, anything is worth trying.'

The inspector himself came over. He grinned with humorous resignation at Carstairs.

'What's this, sir? The usual red herring?' he said.

Carstairs smiled and shrugged his shoulders.

'I've a friend in durance vile, inspector,' he said, 'and I'm not missing any chances. I suppose you'll test this glass for finger-prints?'

'You suppose right, sir,' replied the inspector, 'and I'll promise to let you know the result. Good day.'

'And suppose the stuff in the glass is hyoscin,

and the finger-prints are those of Mrs Bradley, how
do we go then?' asked Garde.

'I have more faith in Mrs Bradley's common sense
than to suppose anything of the kind,' grinned
Carstairs.

Chapter Twenty

The Case for the Crown

MRS BRADLEY was enjoying herself. She had enjoyed being arrested. It was a new experience, and she had made special note of her psychological reactions to it, and had planned to incorporate them in her next book. She had enjoyed the talks she had had with her lawyer about the conducting of her defence, and she had enjoyed his intense exasperation when she resolutely declined, in spite of all his arguments and pleadings, to make a statement before the trial.

'I am reserving my defence,' she would tell the perplexed man, and, expostulate as he might, she would expose her teeth in a cat-like grin, and refuse to budge from what he called her 'criminally foolish attitude.'

'It looks so bad,' he explained to her more than once. 'I know it used to be considered the right thing to do, but it has gone out of fashion nowadays. The jury are certain to be influenced by it, either unconsciously or under instruction from the Crown counsel. You see if I am not right. It is certain to go against you at the trial.'

'Perhaps I want it to go against me,' was Mrs Bradley's cryptic answer.

She enjoyed the first day of the trial more than she had ever enjoyed anything. Her interests were mainly intellectual, and, although she was in danger of being hanged for wilful murder on the verdict of twelve 'good men and true,' she was able to set aside that aspect of the matter, and devote herself to a serious study of the psychology of the leading counsel for the Crown and his witnesses.

The court was crowded with people, and, as she let her eyes roam casually over the assembly, she picked out mechanically a dipsomaniac and two drug fiends, and was proceeding to classify the first two rows of spectators in greater detail when she was aware that the jury were being sworn in.

The leading counsel for the Crown was fat. She disliked fat men. Fat women were normal, healthy, good-tempered, well-balanced people, but fat men were an offence against nature. She hoped he would lose his case.

She glanced round the court again. She was pleased to see a full house!

Ferdinand Lestrange, her son, the leading counsel for the defence, looked distinguished, she thought. Nobody there knew she was his mother. Ferdinand wouldn't care a hang whether she were convicted or not, except in so far as his professional reputation was concerned, but he would take care not to let that suffer!

She looked at the fat prosecuting counsel and again at her son.

'Ferdinand will get me off,' she thought comfortably. 'Clever boy!'

She had thought of asking if she might take written notes during the trial, but decided that it might not be quite in order. Anyway, her memory, she thought, would serve her.

The voice of the clerk of the court, addressing her, once again cut short her musings.

'Beatrice Lestrange Bradley, you are indicted and also charged with the wilful murder of Eleanor Millicent Bing on the eighteenth August last. Are you guilty or not guilty?'

Mrs Bradley gazed at him benignly.

'Not guilty, my lord,' she answered, transferring her glance to the judge.

His lordship was a good chap. She had met him at Cowes one year, she recollected. The wig and robes suited him. She was glad she had made Ferdinand choose the bar. He would probably be a judge some day, too.

The leading counsel for the Crown, in a booming, plum-like voice which associated well with his girth, commenced his opening speech. It dealt chiefly with Mrs Bradley's past life, and she learned some things which surprised her.

'This man will make me blush in a minute,' she thought, as the learned counsel referred to her for the fourth time as this 'deservedly famous woman.'

'I suppose psycho-analysis is still new to some of

these people,' she thought. Her attention wandered to the jury. There was one, she felt certain, who possessed all the mental characteristics of the Emperor Caligula. The man fourth from the end was a neurotic type, with sadistic traits, perhaps. She wondered if it would be in order to object to his being on the jury.

'Still, if the other eleven want to let me off, he isn't the type to stick it out, that's one comfort,' she told herself.

She looked again at the crowded court. That woman at the end was Cora Mason, the society medium. A clever woman in her own line, Mrs Bradley reflected. Must have amassed a considerable fortune, too.

A rustle of interest betrayed the fact that the prosecuting counsel was coming to what Garde Bing would term the 'meat in the sandwich.' Might as well listen to what the little tub was saying, she decided. Interesting to see how he got his shots home with the jury.

'This woman, then,' the learned counsel asserted heavily, 'well educated, gifted beyond the majority of her sex, planned a dark and awful deed.'

Mrs Bradley nodded imperceptibly. This was undoubtedly a master. He had the correct cinematograph style of diction! It suited his audience. 'Dark and awful deed' was good!

'In spite of the fat,' she said to herself, 'I recognize in this man a psychologist and a brother. Carry on, friend!'

With increasing amusement she listened to a

masterly libelling of her own character, which reached its climax when the learned counsel accused her before the jury of plotting to remove Eleanor Bing from this world so that she might usurp her place as mistress of Chaynings. Eleanor, the loving daughter, having been removed from the scene of operations, the coast was clear for Mrs Bradley to become Alastair's wife.

'At this point,' said the next day's newspapers, in heavy type, 'the prisoner astonished the whole court by laughing loudly and with obvious enjoyment.'

Ferdinand Lestrange took advantage of the stir caused by his mother's unseemly laughter to whisper to his junior:

'Clever woman! That's had its effect on the jury!'

The first witness for the prosecution was called and sworn. It was Carstairs. He was asked to describe the finding of Eleanor's body in the bathroom.

'Had you any suspicion of foul play?' he was asked next.

'Well, yes, of course,' answered Carstairs, raising his eyebrows at what seemed to him a pointless question.

There was a flutter of interest. The audience had become rather bored with the fat little counsel for the prosecution, but this thin, hatchet-faced man promised better.

'Oh? You did suspect foul play? Will you please tell the court why?'

'Well, Miss Bing always seemed to me a strong, healthy young woman. I could not imagine her fainting and so getting drowned in the bath, so I took it that she had been murdered—that is, that somebody had drowned her,' replied Carstairs, without hesitation.

'Had you any reason for thinking so?'

'Yes. She was lying in a bath full of water,' said Carstairs innocently.

It had annoyed him to find he had been called as a witness for the Crown, but he intended to give the prosecution as little help as he could within the strict terms of his oath.

The titters were not very easily repressed, and the counsel glanced towards the judge. His lordship, however, made no comment, and the questioning proceeded.

'I understand that, of course, I mean, why should you suppose anyone in the house had met with foul play?'

'We had had one person drowned in the bath during the same week, and another would have been violently killed as she lay in bed, but for the substitution——'

'Yes, yes! We will come to that later. Keep to the point, if you please!'

'What can one think of a man who bullies his own witnesses?' thought Mrs Bradley, with her sardonic grin. 'Poor Mr Carstairs! He is afraid he'll say something to my disadvantage in a minute. I expect he will, too!'

'I was answering your question,' observed Carstairs mildly. 'I thought you asked me——'

'This is no place for thinking,' said the prosecuting

counsel. At this point in the proceedings a person at the back of the court who cried 'Hear! Hear!' was ejected, and the counsel continued his examination of Carstairs in peace, but elicited nothing further except some precise information as to the position of Eleanor's body when Carstairs, with others, had forced their way into the bathroom.

He was cross-questioned by the defending counsel at this point, and the court learned that it was Alastair Bing who had feared foul play when his daughter did not appear at breakfast on another occasion, the reference being, of course, to Bertie Philipson's attempt to drown her.

'Alastair Bing? That is the father of the dead woman, is it not?' purred Ferdinand in his silky voice.

The witness agreed that this was so.

'The man whom it is suggested the prisoner wished to marry?'

Carstairs again agreed.

'Where is he now?'

The question came with such startling force that the court sat up with a jerk.

'On his way to Tibet. He may have arrived there by now, for all I know,' replied Carstairs, perceiving the drift of this interrogation.

'He is not in court?'

Once again the whip-crack question.

'No,' answered Carstairs.

At this point the prosecuting counsel raised formal objection to these questions, but his lordship allowed the cross-examination to proceed.

'Why did he leave England?'

Carstairs and Garde had made up their minds that if this question were asked they would answer it by pleading complete ignorance, and letting the defence make what they could out of Alastair's absence.

Carstairs, therefore, briefly announced that he did not know, but—with a sudden inspiration—that he believed there had been some unfortunate affair with one of the maidservants.

The leading counsel for the defence nodded his distinguished head.

'I see,' he drawled, eyeing the jury keenly to note whether they were sufficiently alert to note his point in asking these questions. 'Exactly the kind of man, in fact, that one would expect to find the prisoner risking her neck for!'

A roar from the crowded court told that the shot had gone home.

Ferdinand Lestrange sat down, and the next witness was called, in the person of Bertie Philipson. He was merely asked to substantiate what Carstairs had told the court about the finding of the body.

The third witness for the prosecution was the doctor who had re-examined the body to discover the cause of death. From him was extracted a fair amount of information respecting the nature of the drug hyoscin, the means of obtaining it, the amount usually dispensed to a patient, the amount necessary to cause death, the method of giving the drug to a patient, and the probable method of administration in this particular case.

The court learned from this witness that hyoscin was extracted from a plant called henbane, that it was used as a calmative drug for the insane, for cases of extreme nervous disability, for patients suffering from delirium, and was usually dispensed to medical men only, and not sold to the public. Doctors obtained it in the form of crystals which could be dissolved in alcohol, then diluted with water, and then administered to the patient hypodermically— that is, by injection under the skin. It was quite possible, however, said the witness, for the drug to be taken in liquid form through the mouth. In this particular case, there could be no reasonable doubt that such had been the means of administering the poison.

His evidence was supported by that of another doctor, who was called as the next witness.

Evidence was then forthcoming as to the possibility of the prisoner's having been able to obtain the drug. It was proved that she was a psycho-analyst.

'What is a psycho-analyst?' asked the judge, at this juncture.

'I understand, my lord, that it is a disciple of Herr Sigmund Freud, an Austrian specialist in nervous and mental diseases,' replied the prosecuting counsel.

'Wrong, child, wrong!' murmured the prisoner, under her breath.

It was proved that she had visited mental hospitals in this country and in America (where the drug is used more commonly than in England), and that it might have been possible for her to obtain a sufficient quantity for her purpose. This purpose, according to the prosecuting counsel, was to accomplish the death of Eleanor Bing, and become the mistress of Chaynings.

'The motive is the weak part of it,' said Carstairs to Bertie Philipson. 'If they could think of a more reasonable motive——'

The Crown was unable to prove that any word of love or even of ordinary courtesy had passed between Mrs Bradley and Alastair Bing. They had never been found alone together—in fact, as one ingenuous village maiden observed *(without* prompting from the Crown, needless to say!), 'they fair 'ated the sight of each other! If one of 'em come into my shop, the other 'ud go out of it!'

This witness was dismissed rather hastily, Ferdinand Lestrange smiling cynically and not even bothering to cross-examine.

The matter of the coffee was now thoroughly attacked. Carstairs, who stood listening to the other witnesses, drew a deep breath. He felt shaky on the question of that coffee. 'Tasteless in coffee or tea!' The words kept repeating themselves in his brain.

The jury were visibly affected by the fact that the accused had administered coffee to the deceased, and, when the court adjourned, more than three quarters of the people present felt convinced that Mrs Bradley would be found guilty.

'She looks like a murderer,' said one woman to her neighbour, as they pushed their way out. 'See 'ow contemptuous she smiled. She's a deep one, you mark my words! 'Ardened to it, you can tell that. I reckon 'er looks give 'er away all the time.'

'Looks ain't everything, Martha,' came the reply. 'And we got to 'ear the other side, yet, mind.'

When the court re-assembled, there remained but two witnesses for the prosecution still to be heard. The first of these was Mrs Bradley's maid, who was closely questioned about the events of the night preceding Eleanor Bing's death. Her replies, rendered in that broken English which is one of the charms of French servants, did her mistress more good than harm, however. A suggestion that there had been quarrels between Mrs Bradley and the murdered woman she repudiated with Gallic fervour and intensity.

'*Mais non, monsieur! Non, non, non!* Madame, she speak but always the kindness to *la pauvre demoiselle!* She is so sweet! So devoted!'

The court glanced at Mrs Bradley and smiled incredulously.

'You say your mistress asked Miss Pamela Storbin to sleep in her room that night? Why did she do that?'

'But, monsieur!' protested Celestine, gesticulating violently. 'Me, how should I know? I cannot say to Madame, "Why this? Why that?" Me, I should receive the kick—no, the push, as you Engleesh call him! But, no! Nevaire I make the inquiry! Nevaire I have the curiosity! That is not the way to advance oneself!'

The court chuckled appreciatively, Ferdinand

Lestrange smiled ironically, and, having obtained as full an account of the night's happenings as Celestine could give, the prosecution dismissed her and called their last witness.

This was Detective-Inspector Boring. He had caused the prisoner to be arrested, he asserted, on the grounds that she was the last person to have seen the deceased alive, and that she had given the deceased a cup of coffee which probably contained poison.

Ferdinand Lestrange rose to cross-examine this witness.

'How do you know that the prisoner was the last person to see Miss Bing alive?'

'I cannot find anyone who saw Miss Bing alive after Mrs Bradley left her on the night of August 18th.'

'Just so. You cannot find anybody else. Did you *attempt* to find anybody else?'

This question seemed to confuse the witness, and he rendered no intelligible reply.

'Again,' pursued the defending counsel, 'on what fact do you base the statement that the cup of coffee which the prisoner gave the deceased was poisoned?'

'By her own confession that she administered the coffee, and by the evidence of eye-witnesses who saw her do so,' replied Boring.

'Exactly,' purred Ferdinand. 'That accounts for the coffee, but does not account for the poison.'

'Except for a harmless sleeping-draught, also administered by the prisoner, I could not discover anything else which could have contained the poison in a tasteless form.'

'Come, come,' countered the inquisitor almost playfully. 'You don't mean to tell me that if, as you plainly imagine, the cup of coffee contained the poison which killed Miss Bing, the murderer would not realize the significance of allowing all those witnesses to watch her as she administered it?'

'I thought she might be bluffing,' said the inspector, glaring resentfully at his adversary.

'I see.' Counsel's dry acceptance of this explanation provoked chuckles from the court. Without giving the unfortunate witness time to recover, he continued:

'Why did you not read the warrant for her arrest to the prisoner?'

'I was under the impression that it had been read to her as a matter of course.' The detective flushed darkly as he made this reply, and muttered something about 'local fatheads.'

Counsel smiled.

'It is a technical point, of course,' he remarked pleasantly.

The witness then stood down, quite discredited in the eyes of the jury, as Ferdinand intended he should be.

Counsel for the prosecution, who had had some idea of re-calling Bertie Philipson, suddenly recollected that the young man himself had no alibi for the night of August 15th, if the unseemly occurrences of that night should be dragged into the light of day by Ferdinand Lestrange, and so wisely decided that the case for the Crown might be stronger without his evidence than with it.

Ferdinand Lestrange glanced at his mother, and wondered how much he could get her to cough up when the trial was over!

The court then adjourned.

Chapter Twenty-One

The Defence

FERDINAND LESTRANGE cleared his throat and addressed himself to his lordship and the gentlemen of the jury with impartial courtesy. His voice was good, his appearance distinguished, and he was determined to do himself credit, his mother's fate being merely a secondary consideration in his eyes.

He did not wish to take up the time of the court, he said, by a lengthy refutation of the statements made by the Crown. It was for the jury to decide, when they had heard all the evidence on both sides, whether the prisoner was guilty or not guilty of the terrible deed which had been attributed to her. It was not for him to suggest that there might arise grave doubts in the mind of any reasonable man—any man of the world, that was to say—as to whether the woman they saw before them— wealthy, famous, extraordinarily clever, and, he would remind them, a true benefactor of the human race in that, while others were physicians of the body, she, gentlemen, might be termed a physician of the mind—that strange and marvellous attribute, gentlemen, without which men would be as the beasts that perish—as to whether such a woman could stoop to the sin of Cain, to the horrible crime of murder. For murder *is* a horrible crime, gentlemen—a terrible, an almost incredible crime—and if they thought that the woman before them had committed such a crime they must not shirk their responsibilities, as men and citizens.

But—the learned counsel paused, and fixed the jury with a hypnotic eye—*were* they so convinced? Had the Crown proved its case? For, remember, gentlemen, that the burden of proof rests upon the prosecution. If the prosecution cannot prove the guilt of any person brought into this court for trial—more, gentlemen, if there is the *slightest shadow of doubt* involved—the accused goes free.

He paused again, to allow this principle of English justice to sink into their minds.

'Now I propose,' he continued, 'to call witnesses who will show you that there were no less than five other people staying in that house (on the night when the poison was administered) who were in exactly the same position there as the woman who is standing her trial at this moment. They had equal motive—or lack of motive—to commit the crime, and—here, gentlemen, is a point I ought to stress—*they had equal opportunity of doing so*. But we are not trying them, gentlemen! No! They will be called upon to give their evidence, as, in a moment, the prisoner will be called upon to give hers; but their evidence heard, they will be free men and women, gentlemen, whereas the unfortunate prisoner will return to the dock where she now stands!'

Abruptly, it seemed to the listeners, he stopped, almost like a runner who halts in the middle of the race, and called his first witness.

Dorothy Bing, *née* Clark, stepped to the witness-box and was sworn. Ferdinand addressed this obviously nervous witness with suave courtesy.

'You are Mrs Garde Bing?'

'Yes.' The reply was nothing more than a whisper.

'You were living at Chaynings when this unfortunate affair took place?'

'When Miss Bing was—when she died?' faltered Dorothy.

'Speak up, please, Mrs Bing. Yes, that is the time to which I refer.'

'Yes, I was staying in the house.'

'You were married then?'

'Yes. I—I had very recently married.'

'Quite so. And everybody congratulated you both and wished you happiness, I dare say?'

'They were—yes, they were all very kind.'

'Of course they were. All of them, Mrs Bing. Everybody?'

'Yes—well—perhaps——'

'Ah! We are in doubt! We would like to think about it for a minute. Among all those very kind people, Mrs Bing, there was one, was there not, who was—let us say, not quite so kind?'

'I'm afraid I don't understand you.'

'Let me make myself clear. Will you tell the court what was Miss Eleanor Bing's attitude towards your marriage?'

'She was—very cross when we became engaged,' faltered Dorothy, 'but——'

Ferdinand shot a triumphant glance around the court.

'Ah!' he exclaimed, without allowing her time to conclude her sentence. 'And what did you think about that?'

'I—I—well, I thought it was rather unkind of her. I—we—I mean, it wasn't as though she was very fond of Garde—of my husband!'

'So you quarrelled about it?'

'No. We—it was more horrid than that. You—I don't think a man could quite understand——'

Loud laughter from the court interrupted this sentence, and greatly added to the nervousness of the witness. Order was restored, and Ferdinand continued smoothly:

'Perhaps not! I suggest, though, that on one occasion Miss Bing told you she hated you?'

'Yes.' Very low came this admission.

'And that on another occasion she flung a clock belonging to you heavily upon the floor in a fit of passion?'

'Yes. She might have dropped it by accident, though. I don't think she meant to throw it down and smash it.'

'Mrs Bing'—Ferdinand's beautiful voice became husky with well-simulated admiration—'you are that wonderful and tender thing—a good woman. You have a power of forgiveness that I wish could be extended to us all. For this woman, whose passion you are trying to conceal from us, did worse than break your property. She made an attempt upon your very life!'

The witness grew deadly white and swayed dizzily on her feet, but remorselessly the counsel pressed his point home.

'Can you deny it, Mrs Bing? Did she not creep into your room in the early hours of the morning——'

But the witness could bear no more.

'Oh, don't! Please don't!' she cried. 'She did do that! But please don't talk about it!'

The next witness was Garde, who looked exceptionally big and tall in his plus-fours. He grinned engagingly at Ferdinand and stood at ease, waiting to be questioned.

'How did you get on with your sister, Mr Bing?' The counsel shot a keen glance at him.

'Not at all!'

If Dorothy's low voice had been difficult to hear, this young man's trumpet-call was even more discomforting. It had a kind of prairie note about it which made smaller people feel ineffective and effete. It rang through the over-heated court like a clarion.

Ferdinand glanced at the jury out of the corner of his eye. They appeared to observe the damaging nature of this admission, so he carried on briskly.

'Do I understand that you actively disliked your sister, Mr Bing?'

(With a witness as sure of himself as this one, it was possible to introduce a note of pained surprise into the voice, reflected Ferdinand. It did not do to let the jury think that you were coercing your witnesses, and this young ox of a fellow was apparently non-suggestible.)

'Disliked her?' Garde's voice was almost a snort. 'Hated her would be nearer the mark!'

'When you say "hated her," Mr Bing'— counsel's voice was almost deprecating now—'you mean——?'

'I mean exactly what I say!' Garde's open-air tones boomed out again. 'I knew she meant to do in—that is, to kill Dorothy—that's my wife—and any chap here will know what I felt like. I could tell you——'

Counsel held up a silencing hand.

'I am sure you could, Mr Bing,' he agreed gravely, and, amid the laughter of those in court, Garde stood down. There were many present who felt that Mrs Bradley's counsel had only just prevented him from confessing to the murder itself.

The prisoner next went into the witness-box. The exquisite courtesy of Ferdinand to the accused made its impression on the jury, although they themselves were unaware of the fact.

'I am not going to defend myself,' said Mrs Bradley, as much at her ease as though she were addressing a mothers' meeting on the subject of birth control, in the arguments for which she was extraordinarily well-versed. 'I am just going to tell you what happened that night—the eighteenth of August, wasn't it?—yes, the eighteenth.'

Hereupon she gave a concise statement of the events of the night—a story which everybody in court knew by heart by this time, and the prosecuting counsel rose to cross-examine.

'How do you answer the statement of the police that the dirty coffee cup had contained poison?' he asked.

Mrs Bradley considered him gravely for a moment, and then replied:

'*Honi soit qui mal y pense, monsieur!*' (Evil be to him who evil thinks).

The court howled delightedly, and there was some commotion at the back caused by a person in the preliminary stages of intoxication who expressed a desire to shake Mrs Bradley by the hand. When order was restored, the learned counsel was heard to demand that Mrs Bradley should answer the question. She smiled serenely.

'Account for the statement? Oh, I can't!' she replied. 'Why should I? I cannot undertake to read the minds of the police, and I'm glad of it.'

She was then put through a searching cross-examination as to her knowledge of mental healing and her acquaintance with American institutions where the drug hyoscin was used, and was compelled to make several damaging admissions.

'The witness,' said the papers next day, 'then returned to her former position in the dock, and sat quietly through the rest of the proceedings.'

These proceedings consisted partly of the formal evidence of two doctors, who agreed with the pronouncement of the other medical witnesses that the poison recovered from the body was hyoscin in a sufficient quantity to cause death, but, examined by the defence, admitted that there was no more reason for supposing murder than for supposing that the drug had been self-administered. Cross-examined by the prosecution, the second of these medical witnesses agreed that hyoscin was not the easiest drug to obtain in a quantity sufficient to cause death, but, re-examined by the defence, he admitted that the painless action of the drug would be a great incentive for suicides to obtain it in preference to other, painfully acting poisons. He admitted, under examination, that hyoscin was used in ophthalmic clinics.

The next witness was an oculist, who stated that Eleanor Bing had suffered from eye-weakness, and had habitually worn spectacles.

With the stage-sense of the born actor, Ferdinand Lestrange had kept his most impressive piece of evidence until last. He astonished the whole court by calling Ellison Rallery, the Home Office analyst, into the witness-box.

In reply to Ferdinand's suave questions, the expert informed the court of the medicine-glass discovered by Carstairs and sent to him for analysis of its contents. Feeling ran high, and the air was electric with excitement as he testified that the residue in the medicine-glass was that of a solution of hyoscin-hydrobromide. Even greater excitement followed the statement of the next witness, Boring's stolid sergeant, who was compelled to admit that finger-prints on the glass corresponded exactly with those he had previously taken from the dead woman herself.

'Of course it doesn't prove anything, really,' thought Carstairs, 'but it may make just all the difference to the jury's verdict.'

This completed the evidence for the defence, and Ferdinand Lestrange rose leisurely to make his closing speech.

He based his remarks, he said, on two main premises. First, it must have struck the jury, as intelligent men, that there had been no more real evidence brought against the prisoner than could have been brought against nearly everyone else who was living at Chaynings on the night of Eleanor Bing's death. What proof had the jury received that Mrs Bradley had committed a crime? He ventured to say that they had received no proof at all. A wineglass had been mentioned. Well, the expert's report on the analysis of the contents of that wineglass was entirely in the prisoner's favour. The prisoner had voluntarily confessed that she administered a cup of coffee to the deceased. It was the theory of the prosecution that the coffee had contained poison. Had they brought forward any proof of what he was compelled to consider a mischievous assumption unsupported by the smallest particle of fact? Against that, they had just been given strong presumptive evidence that the deceased had poisoned herself. If that medicine-glass had been discovered sooner, and the residue of its contents had been analysed sooner, he dared to suggest, gentlemen, that the prisoner would never have been arrested. He would not labour the point. It was sufficiently clear that the police had acted with more haste than discretion.

That brought him to another point, gentlemen. Where, he would like to ask the prosecution, was the man who should have been one of their most important witnesses? He referred, of course, to the dead woman's father, Mr Alastair Bing. Where was he? Why had he absented himself from the trial? It was not for the defence to suggest that Bing had reason for believing that his daughter had not been murdered at all, but had died by her own hand. It was certainly not for the defence to suggest a still more terrible possibility, but there it was! This man, this father, was in Tibet! He was not present at the trial!

This point, gentlemen, brought up another. In the opinion of the defence, the theory of suicide had never been properly investigated. There had been the unfortunate death of the deceased's friend, Miss Mountjoy. It was possible that such an occurrence had induced deep depression of spirit in Eleanor Bing. There was a suggestion that the deceased had killed this friend. He suggested that in a fit of remorse, following such a deed, the deceased might well have made away with herself. It was known to the court that the deceased had made a violent attempt on the life of one of the witnesses they had listened to that day, Mrs Garde Bing. Surely that fact alone must predispose the court to regard the woman Eleanor Bing as, to say the least, abnormal and mentally ill-balanced! But—here the learned counsel paused that the full purport of his next words might be understood—the jury were not in this court to hear him theorize about suicide. They were there to find the prisoner guilty or not guilty of murder. And in considering this question they must ask themselves what evidence they had heard which would cause them to agree upon their verdict. Had they been shown any reason—any adequate reason, that was to say—why the prisoner should have murdered Eleanor Bing? Had she any more motive for doing so than, say, the witness whose life had been attempted by the deceased? Or more motive than the husband of that witness, who had confessed before them all how great was his dislike for this dead sister? Had they, in fact, heard anything at all which caused them to feel certain that the prisoner was a murderess? He would willingly leave twelve such intelligent men to answer these questions, and to find a true verdict.

The formal recalling of the prisoner, and the closing speech for the prosecution followed in due course, but were not accorded the same amount of close attention as that given by the crowded court to the closing speech for the defence.

Mrs Bradley, too, was beginning to find the proceedings a little wearisome, although she automatically followed the fat little counsel's points in his closing speech. He was certainly making the best of a bad job, she decided, for the analyst's

report on the contents of the fateful medicine-
glass had certainly 'knocked the guts out of the
prosecution,' as a young reporter told Carstairs
subsequently.

The judge summed up in the usual admirable
manner of the bench, and addressed the jury gravely
and courteously. He defined murder as 'causing the
death of another intentionally and by your wilful
act,' cautioned them, and finally dismissed them
to consider their verdict.

They were absent for twenty-two minutes by
Carstairs' watch. Dorothy and Garde stood beside
him, and Bertie Philipson, unusually nervous and
fidgety, was at Garde's side. They talked but little,
and every three minutes, or less, Carstairs dragged
out his watch and consulted it anxiously.

At last the twelve men filed in again.

The verdict was received with unrestrained
cheering.

Dorothy wept without shame on Carstairs'
shoulder, and Garde and Bertie thumped each other
on the back with idiotic heartiness.

The discharged prisoner seemed the least
concerned of any person present.

Chapter Twenty-Two

Points of View

'THANK goodness that's over!'

Garde started up the car as he spoke, and his face was set in the habitual scowl he wore when driving in traffic.

Dorothy laughed.

'Anybody would think you had had your doubts about the verdict,' she teased him.

'Don't know about doubts,' her husband grunted. ('Oh, go *on*, you fool!' he apostrophized an elderly lady who seemed uncertain whether to cross the road in front of him or wait in the middle until he had driven by.) 'I should think anybody might be forgiven—(Damn that fool of a Robert! He's going to hold us up! No, he isn't! Good egg!)—for being a trifle windy when they've got a friend in the dock.'

'Oh, yes.' Dorothy drew the rug a little farther over her knees, for the autumn weather was chilly. 'She was in the dock, of course, and that is very dreadful, but, still, there wasn't a shadow of evidence against her, was there?'

'I don't know.' Garde's eyes were fixed on the road ahead, and this gave his conversation a detached air, as though he were a broadcasting announcer or a dictaphone. 'After all, when a woman is guilty of murder, there must be *some* evidence of it somewhere, if people take the trouble to ferret it out, you know.'

'Guilty!' Dorothy echoed the word in accents of sheer horror.

Garde laughed aloud.

'You poor innocent!' he said. '(Damn these gears!) Who the hell do you think did it, then, if she didn't?'

'But—but——' wailed Dorothy. 'Oh, I can't believe it! She didn't do it! How could she? Besides—the verdict!'

'Well, what about the verdict, sweet chuck?' Garde blew his horn with savage gusto.

'They said she was innocent! They—they acquitted her! The jury said Not Guilty!' Dorothy's voice was defiant.

'And very nice too! I like the old girl, and I should be damned sorry if I thought she was going to dangle for putting old Eleanor's light out,' returned Garde, 'for, between you and me, my sister was as mad as a hatter, darling. You know that, don't you?'

'Mad?' Dorothy faltered.

'Yes, mad,' reiterated Garde curtly. 'I'll go a little further, and inform you that, if Mrs Bradley hadn't so kindly lifted the job off my hands, I was seriously thinking about laying Sis out myself.'

Dorothy gasped.

'But why didn't they say she was guilty if—if she was?' she faltered. ('Oh, look out for that little pig, Garde!')

'Well, it had to be proved,' said Garde, missing the pig by inches. 'And I doubt if it ever will be. The prosecution hadn't a leg to stand on, poor devils. Especially with that Lestrange lad against them. Clever bloke, that one. And about as honest as a Dago dog!'

He turned the car in at the lodge gate of Chaynings, and drew up in front of the house.

'After all,' he added, as they walked into the great hall a moment or two later, 'it was jolly sporting of Mrs Bradley. That's my opinion, child. She took a big risk for other people's sakes.'

But Dorothy shuddered.

'Of course, Mother,' said Ferdinand Lestrange, holding his glass to the light and pensively admiring the rich colour of the wine, 'if I'd been prosecuting——!'

Mrs Bradley laughed good-humouredly. In the candle light she looked more like some ghoulish bird of prey than ever, in spite of the jewels which gleamed at her throat, and the flashing rings upon her claw-like hands.

'Of course, you did do it?' her son continued, setting down his glass and turning an inquiring gaze upon her.

'Oh, yes,' his mother admitted, in her curiously arresting voice, 'of course I did it. One day I will tell you how.'

'Tell me why,' suggested the young advocate, with a connoisseur's interest.

'Tell you why? It is difficult to do that. I had no personal feeling in the matter, of course. It was what one might term a logical elimination of unnecessary, and, in fact, dangerous matter.'

Ferdinand nodded slowly.

'I begin to realize whence I derive my own extraordinary abilities,' he observed modestly.

Mrs Bradley cackled delightedly. 'Yes,' she continued. 'I did not, in the everyday, newspaper, pot-house sense of the word murder Eleanor Bing. I merely erased her, as it were, from an otherwise fair page of the Bing family chronicle. It all simplified itself to this:

'If I did not kill Eleanor, she would kill Dorothy, the girl Garde Bing has married.

'Or, more possibly:

'If I did not kill Eleanor, Garde himself might do so.

'Or, more terribly:

'If I did not kill Eleanor, Eleanor would kill Dorothy, and then Garde would kill Eleanor, and then the law would kill Garde.'

'Or, more irritatingly:

'If someone didn't kill Eleanor, she would kill that quite inoffensive child Pamela.'

'The law didn't kill *you*,' her son pointed out dryly.

'I am rather an intelligent woman, darling,' his fond mother reminded him, 'and poor Garde and poor Bertie are rather unintelligent young men.'

Her son smiled sedately. The candle lit up his gleaming shirt-front, and shone on the thick, glossy smoothness of his hair.

Mrs Bradley sat still, smiling wisely into her glass, like an amused and mocking death's-head at a strangely casual feast. Her son rose, glass in hand. Without a word, he lifted it high and bowed to her.

Mrs Bradley cackled with pleasure.

'Thank you, my dear,' she said. 'It is nice to have one's motives appreciated!'

Detective-Inspector Boring glared resentfully at his sleeping wife. As though aware of his annoyance, she opened one eye and gave the slight moan which, with her, was significant of a return to conscious life. She opened the other eye, and became aware of an unshaven and distinctly irritable face about twelve inches distant from her own.

'Hullo, Herbert! Surely it isn't time to get up?' she moaned.

'It's after seven,' barked Mr Boring, in the ill-tempered tone of one who has been awake for hours.

'Is it? Still, it's Sunday. No need to stir for a while yet,' remarked the unfeeling and undutiful woman.

She turned over with a heave and a roll, drew

the bedclothes up to her chin, and immediately
relapsed into slumber.

Detective-Inspector Boring looked and felt
aggrieved.

'Here's me, with my whole future jeopardized,
and that's all you care,' he apostrophized the back
of his wife's neck audibly.

His wife stirred and grunted.

'Yes, that's right,' groaned the unfortunate police
officer. 'Go to sleep! Never mind *my* troubles! Never
mind if your unfortunate husband has to send in his
resignation because a lot of ——, ——, one-eyed,
flap-eared police yokels and a dozen ——, ——,
fat-headed, rubber-necked —— jurymen couldn't
tell a murderess when they'd got one stuck in the
dock right under their —— —— noses!'

'Herbert, dear,' remonstrated his wife, now wide
awake, 'do hush! Remember both windows are
open!'

Detective-Inspector Boring then described the
open windows in no measured terms; in fact, with
such appalling minuteness of detail that his partner
arose, put on her dressing-gown, and went off to
make the early morning cup of tea, observing that
even a wife was not compelled by law to stay and
listen to such language.

'After all, poor old lady,' she observed, 'you
wouldn't like to think she was going to be hanged,
even if she did do it. And she couldn't have done
it, or the jury would have said so.'

'Couldn't have done it!' yelled Mr Boring, flinging
himself about in the bed until it creaked and howled

in unavailing protest. 'Couldn't have done it, did you say?' He laughed with an ironical bitterness which, in the whole course of a chequered career, even he had never previously equalled.

'I *know* she did it!' he shouted at his wife's retreating footsteps. 'And how do I know? Because I —— —— *do* know! That's how!'

'But it couldn't be proved,' his wife called back over her shoulder, 'could it?'

'Proved?' howled her incensed spouse. 'Proved, did you say? Well, prove to me black isn't white! Go on! Let's hear you prove that!'

'Don't be silly, dearie,' said his wife fondly from the foot of the staircase.

Detective-Inspector Boring writhed in anguished bitterness.

'Of course, I am very much relieved at the verdict,' said Carstairs to Bertie Philipson, as the two sat in the grandstand at Twickenham one fine Saturday afternoon in November.

'Rather,' agreed Bertie absently. 'Wonder why they always start the second half a minute or two late on this ground? Or is it my imagination?'

'It wants another three minutes yet,' said Carstairs. 'She was lucky to get off, don't you think?'

'Oh, I don't know,' said Bertie. 'Wonder who did kill old Eleanor, though, after all. Or do you think it was suicide?'

'Suicide my hat!' replied Carstairs, laughing. 'No, it was murder, right enough, and Mrs Bradley did it!'

'Oh, come now!' said Bertie, all his apathy turning to interest. 'What about the verdict?'

'Would have been "Not proven" from a Scottish jury, I fancy,' said Carstairs dryly.

'Spin us the yarn,' said Bertie. 'What do you think happened that night?'

'After Eleanor and the carving-knife had parted company,' said Carstairs, 'and Mrs Bradley had managed to get Eleanor into bed, I think Mrs Bradley went back to her own room and felt horribly worried.'

'Wind up in case Eleanor should have a go at somebody else?' suggested Bertie.

'Exactly. In this state of mind I think she went to her secret store of hyoscin and poured the fatal dose of poison into the thermos flask, from which, as she confessed at the trial, she had already drunk half a cupful of coffee. With the poisoned draught at hand, she felt prepared for emergency. The sleeping-draught she had offered to Eleanor was refused by the poor young woman, or so I think. Possibly she scarcely relished the taste of the bromide solution administered to her by Mrs Bradley on the night of Dorothy's lucky escape. She always hated any form of medicine. I think it was this refusal on the part of Eleanor which caused Mrs Bradley to poison the coffee. Had Eleanor taken the sleeping-draught, the chances were that she would not have shown her murderous tendencies again that night, but, as things were, with Eleanor wide awake and filled with jealous hatred of young Pamela Storbin, and probably with serious resentment towards yourself——'

Bertie nodded gloomily.

'Mrs Bradley thought anything might happen. Yes, I can see how she would have felt,' he said.

'Yes. Here come the teams,' said Carstairs.

'Oh, go on,' said Bertie. 'Let's have the yarn.'

'Well, when we saw Mrs Bradley give Eleanor the cup of coffee, we were watching a murder take place,' said Carstairs simply.

'Then you think, if the police had found the coffee cup, as they found the wineglass which had contained the sleeping-draught——' suggested Bertie, leaving the other to complete the sentence.

'I think there would have been a rope for Mrs Bradley,' said Carstairs. 'As a matter of fact, that is the one bit of the crime which is a real puzzle to me. I cannot understand how Mrs Bradley could have been so frightfully careless as to leave that cup about. It isn't like her to have run such a clumsy risk as that. An artistic risk—like getting the body to the bathroom—yes, she would enjoy taking a chance like that—but the cup no. The cup won't fit into place.'

'Yes, why did she take the body to the bathroom?' asked Bertie. 'And, by the way, I should think she had her work cut out to manage it. Eleanor was every bit of nine stone, and Mrs Bradley is a small, thin woman.'

'With immense nursing experience, remember. Nurses get used to handling big helpless men, don't they? And, besides, she had muscles of iron. As to why she put the body there, I think it was just her freakish sense of humour. Eleanor's victim,

Mountjoy, was found dead in the bathroom, and Mrs Bradley decided that Eleanor should be found dead there also. She may have had some idea of confusing the investigators, too, or of misleading people as to the time of death. She ought to have pushed the head under water, though. It was a mistake to leave the hair dry and yet arrange the body face-uppermost.'

'And did you think all this out before the trial?' asked Bertie. 'Oh, look! He's scored! Good man! Just let's see if he'll convert it! Oh, well taken, sir! Very pretty!'

He turned to Carstairs with a smile.

'Sorry, sir. Will you please go on?'

'With pleasure. No, I did not think along these lines before the trial. It is true that I saw the facts looked bad for Mrs Bradley. For one thing, you see, there is no doubt that she could have obtained the hyoscin. She is a distinguished psycho-analyst, as we know, and she has been in America visiting mental institutions. I happen to know—although the defence took care to keep this fact very dark—that while in America she acted as assistant to a distinguished alienist in order to have an opportunity of treating some of his cases psycho-analytically. Now, under these circumstances, what was there to prevent her from obtaining what we will term a murderous quantity of this drug? It is a calmative drug, used fairly freely in our mental asylums and quite extensively in America. The alienist she worked with possessed a store—probably of several grains—and a quarter to half a grain of the stuff, remember, is a fatal dose.

'Very well, then. She could have obtained the poison. Mind, I don't mean to imply for an instant that she obtained it for a criminal purpose. That is not my conception at all. She was supplied with a small quantity for professional purposes, I imagine, and simply saw no occasion for returning it. Then, when she realized how dangerous Eleanor was, the remembrance of this poison came to her. It was a quick and merciful form of death, as unerring and as free from cruelty as a properly constructed lethal chamber. What had she to do? Why, dissolve a microscopic amount of the crystals in alcohol— probably they were so dissolved already—and either dilute the liquid so formed with water, or drop a little of it into coffee or tea. It is tasteless in either.'

'You said Eleanor didn't drink the bromide sleeping-draught,' remarked Bertie, 'yet the glass was empty. What did Mrs Bradley do with the draught?'

'Drank it herself, I expect,' answered Carstairs, with his eyes on the players. 'It was quite harmless, you see, and the empty glass played quite a part in helping to make the issue of the trial doubtful.'

'I wonder whether she reckoned on Mabel leaving it for the police to find,' grinned Bertie.

'I shouldn't be a bit surprised,' chuckled Carstairs. 'But that makes it all the more extraordinary that she ran such a foolish risk in leaving the coffee cup lying about.'

'Knew the maid would be certain to collect up a common kitchen cup,' said Bertie.

'Maybe. But it was a risk,' argued Carstairs. 'And a risk I should have thought she would have avoided,' he added, wrinkling his brow. 'Of course, it was a piece of rare good luck, my finding that medicine-glass.'

'Yes, but surely that was strong evidence in favour of supposing that Eleanor committed suicide,' said Bertie. 'What did poor old Boring think about it?'

'He thought what I thought, and said as much,' replied Carstairs, smiling.

'And what was that?'

'The medicine-glass was a red-herring,' replied Carstairs. 'Directly I had found it, so carefully placed where the police had already looked and were not likely to look again for some little time, and yet so easy to detect and so beautifully simple and convincing once anybody did look, I smelt a rat. Still, I was keen to save Mrs Bradley, and it was for the police, not me, to detect the odour of the rodent. To their credit, be it said, they did! But circumstances—and the complete absence of Mrs Bradley's finger-prints—were too much for them. From that time onwards, especially during the progress of the trial, I put two and two together——'

'And made five,' giggled Bertie. 'I'm sorry to butt in, but, you see, jolly interesting as your reconstruction is, it leaves out the one big point on which the prosecution really tripped themselves up. Where is the hyoscin? I mean, dash it, the bottle, or whatever contained the stuff, has just vanished into thin air. It hasn't been traced to anybody. Because of that fact alone they couldn't prove Mrs Bradley did it. Good thing too! I think that if that old woman did do Eleanor in, then she deserves to be regarded as a benefactor of the human race!'

'I am afraid the law would not take the same charitable view of her conduct,' said Carstairs dryly. 'However, as I am going round to her hotel this evening to felicitate her on the happy result of the trial, I will tell her what you say.'

The whistle blew for time, and the two men parted at the gate of the football ground.

True to his word, Carstairs called at the hotel where Mrs Bradley was staying for a few days before she started on her American tour, and solemnly congratulated her on her escape from the clutches of the law.

They sat silent for several minutes after he had concluded his rather formal felicitations, and then Mrs Bradley suddenly and startlingly hooted with laughter.

'Poor Inspector Boring!' she said, in answer to Carstairs' surprised smile. 'That man worked really hard, and very intelligently. He deserved to win his case if ever a policeman did. I admired that man's quality. He had a solid, unimaginative, exhaustive way of going about things which I can never sufficiently commend.'

'You mean?' said Carstairs, biting back the remark that was on the tip of his tongue.

Mrs Bradley smiled her reptilian smile. Carstairs had seen boa-constrictors at the Zoological Gardens with the same expression on their wide, thin mouths, and he shuddered involuntarily at the recollection of it.

'You may ask your question, my friend,' she said, with her uncanny knack of reading his thoughts.

Carstairs, who, through familiarity with it, had become inured to this phenomenon, shrugged his shoulders very slightly, and then laughed.

'On your own head be it, then!' he said.

'How very unchivalrous of you!' mocked Mrs Bradley. 'But never mind. Fire away!'

'Well,' said Carstairs, with pardonable hesitation, 'I was rather curious to know how you managed to hide the hyoscin bottle. I mean, that was the crux of the matter at the trial, wasn't it? Although the prosecution tried to gloss over the fact that the poison could not be traced to anybody, I noticed that the defence made rather a point of it.'

'Yes, that, and the apparent absence of motive on my part,' said Mrs Bradley, 'formed very formidable obstacles to the prosecution; not to mention the clever way in which you found the dirty medicine-glass.'

'But if they could have traced the hyoscin to you?' Carstairs gently insisted.

'Ah, but that, my friend, was what they could never do,' said Mrs Bradley, with her eldritch screech of laughter. 'You see, I hadn't it in my possession after I was arrested, and neither had I hidden it anywhere.'

'Then I don't see——' began Carstairs, beginning to wonder whether all his theories were wrong, and whether the shrivelled little human macaw in front of him was entirely innocent of the crime after all.

'I'll tell you who has the hyoscin,' said Mrs Bradley, lowering her vibrant voice to a conspiratorial whisper. 'It will surprise you. Yes, you will receive a shock, my dear friend. It is yourself, and yourself only, who have hidden the hyoscin bottle so well! But you must return it to me now. I shall commit no more murders with it, I promise you, but I must have it, for it is useful to me in my work as an alienist.'

'But I don't understand! Surely you are amusing yourself at my expense!' cried Carstairs. 'Do you, or do you not, admit that you poisoned Eleanor Bing?'

'Since I cannot be tried twice for the same offence,' said Mrs Bradley equably, 'I will confess to you that I did poison Eleanor Bing deliberately, and as the law quaintly expresses it, by my wilful act. The poison, as, no doubt, you have determined for yourself, I administered in the coffee which I gave to Eleanor instead of the sleeping-draught. I waited until I knew she was dead, then I hid her body in the wardrobe, got into her bed, and answered the girl Cobb (who is verging on mental deficiency) when she called Eleanor next morning. The dangerous part of the business lay in getting the body to the bathroom, and in returning to Eleanor's room without being seen. However, luckily for me,

Eleanor was a remarkably early riser, and there was little chance of meeting any of you at that hour of the morning. As for the hyoscin, you know better than I where it is. What did you do with the little dark-green bottle of lavender water I asked you to return to Dorothy Bing?'

'The—the lavender water?' cried Carstairs, his eyes nearly starting out of his head. 'Why—why—oh, so *that's* what it was! Dorothy had her own bottle, of course, and returned me yours. I expect it is still in the pocket of that same suit, which, by the way, I haven't worn since.'

'Well,' remarked Mrs Bradley calmly, 'I think you had better find out whether Dorothy returned you the right bottle. Hyoscin-hydrobromide isn't very safe stuff to leave in the hands of the general public. My bottle had a tiny label on the bottom, so it can be distinguished easily enough.'

'Then it is yours I have,' said Carstairs. 'I imagined it was the maker's label, and did not trouble to decipher it.'

'Just as well,' said Mrs Bradley. 'That little formula means the same thing all over Europe, I presume.'

'But,' said Carstairs, chuckling in spite of himself, 'why was I chosen for the honourable role of accessory after the fact?'

'Well, you see, the inspector loved you so!' said Mrs Bradley, cackling with glee. 'Don't you remember telling me how much both he and the Chief Constable doted on you? I recollect your exact words. You said if every one of us was murdered and you were the only one left alive to tell the tale, the police wouldn't have the heart to arrest you. So I thought they would hardly imagine that you were hiding the cat in the bag so nicely for me. But I had one very hard piece of luck, Mr Carstairs. I am sure I shall have your sympathy when I tell you what it was. I took a great deal of trouble to wash out that coffee cup and flask in the bathroom after I laid out poor dear Eleanor in the bath, and I ran a dreadful risk by stealing downstairs to obtain the dregs of the coffee which Bing's servants always seem to leave in the coffee-pot. If only the good Boring could have come to the house a little sooner, he would have had the joy of sending the dirty coffee cup to be analysed, and he would have discovered that it contained—coffee! When I found that my intelligent anticipation of his movements had been ruined by the zealous Mabel (thank heaven she had the sense to leave the wineglass alone), I was obliged to lay another trail. I put a weak solution of the hyoscin into Eleanor's medicine-glass, then, with the aid of my penknife, I slid a fish-slice underneath the bottom. Thus I managed to carry the glass without touching it with my fingers, and so imposing my own prints upon those made by Eleanor, when she drank the sal-volatile after having been nearly drowned by darling Bertie that morning. I locked up the medicine-glass in Eleanor's own medicine cupboard, and hoped for the best.'

'What the devil is a fish-slice?' asked Carstairs.

Mrs Bradley rang the bell for her maid.

'Bring me a fish-slice, Celestine,' she said. Then she turned again to Carstairs.

'What would you have used, then?' she asked, cackling harshly.

'Oh, I don't know,' he replied, half-humorously falling in with her mood. 'A bricklayer's trowel, I suppose.'

'Yes, quite good. But, whereas bricklayers' trowels are hard to come by, the humble fish-slice resides in every well-conducted home,' said Mrs Bradley, hooting with mirth.

MORE VINTAGE MURDER MYSTERIES

EDMUND CRISPIN

Buried for Pleasure
The Case of the Gilded Fly
Holy Disorders
Love Lies Bleeding
The Moving Toyshop
Swan Song

A. A. MILNE

The Red House Mystery

GLADYS MITCHELL

Speedy Death
The Mystery of a Butcher's Shop
The Longer Bodies
The Saltmarsh Murders
Death and the Opera
The Devil at Saxon Wall
Dead Men's Morris
Come Away, Death
St Peter's Finger
Brazen Tongue
Hangman's Curfew
When Last I Died
Laurels Are Poison
Here Comes a Chopper
Death and the Maiden
Tom Brown's Body
Groaning Spinney
The Devil's Elbow
The Echoing Strangers
Watson's Choice
The Twenty-Third Man
Spotted Hemlock
My Bones Will Keep
Three Quick and Five Dead
Dance to Your Daddy
A Hearse on May-Day
Late, Late in the Evening
Fault in the Structure
Nest of Vipers

MARGERY ALLINGHAM

Mystery Mile
Police at the Funeral
Sweet Danger
Flowers for the Judge
The Case of the Late Pig
The Fashion in Shrouds
Traitor's Purse
Coroner's Pidgin
More Work for the Undertaker
The Tiger in the Smoke
The Beckoning Lady
Hide My Eyes
The China Governess
The Mind Readers
Cargo of Eagles

E. F. BENSON

The Blotting Book
The Luck of the Vails

NICHOLAS BLAKE

A Question of Proof
Thou Shell of Death
There's Trouble Brewing
The Beast Must Die
The Smiler With the Knife
Malice in Wonderland
The Case of the Abominable Snowman
Minute for Murder
Head of a Traveller
The Dreadful Hollow
The Whisper in the Gloom
End of Chapter
The Widow's Cruise
The Worm of Death
The Sad Variety
The Morning After Death

www.vintage-books.co.uk